Caddo Bend

Book 1: Introducing Dr. Maggie McKinley

Mary Dan Eades

This book is a work of fiction. While certain place names and historical current events of the time are real, all characters and events in this work, other than those clearly in the public domain, are fictitious, and any resemblance to situations or actual persons, living or dead, is purely coincidental. Caddo Bend exists only in the world of fiction.

ISBN: 979-8-9857878-1-8 paperback; 979-8-9857878-0-1 e-book

To Rose, whose ideas help build this tale way back in 2002
and to my Sistas who helped shape it.

Table of Contents

PROLOGUE
1100 AD

An early morning mist rose off the dark and glistening river as the first rays of sun glowed pink along the eastern sky. A Caddo shaman, draped in tangles of bone beads, eagles' claws, and crystal amulets and cloaked in animal skins against the chill, stood at the water's edge, holding a pottery vessel in his hands. Behind him, atop a towering earthen mound, a circle of tribesmen gathered in silence, woven baskets piled with dirt balanced on their shoulders, stacks of poles and rushes beside them, prepared to fill the hole they'd dug. All around the base of the mound, the Caddo villagers stood quietly to pay homage.

The shaman knelt beside the water and immersed the vessel to fill it, then stood, arms extended, to make an offering to the rising sun. He chanted softly as he turned to honor the spirits of the four directions, east, south, west, north, and back to the east.

Walking with slow dignity, befitting the occasion, he made his way to the top of the high mound where his tribesmen waited. He poured the water into the hole they had made, offering the empty vessel again to the four directions. Then, reverently, he knelt and placed the vessel gently into the earth beside the body of the young son of the Caddi, their chief.

CHAPTER 1
Frenchman's Mound - 2010 AD

Headlights bounced off the walls of a sparsely furnished child's bedroom, as Ruth Prescott tucked the soft quilt around the shoulders of her sleeping daughter. She sensed the quiet footfalls on the front porch before she heard the light rap on the door and had already crossed the bedroom and pulled the child's door slightly closed behind her.

Ruth cracked the front door, then opened it wider to face the visitor, a man, silhouetted on the dark porch by the light of the low full moon behind him. The porch light had burned out, but she didn't need the light to know who'd come to call.

"I told you before, you got no business here," Ruth said quietly.

"Evening, Mrs. Prescott," he replied, "is Waylon home?"

"No. And you aren't welcome to wait." she said and started to close the door.

Her words were hardly out when her husband, Waylon, lumbered up behind her, taking a long pull from a flat half-pint of whiskey. He wiped his mouth with a calloused hand and returned the flask to the hip pocket of his drooping jeans.

"Ruth, what kinda nonsense are you feedin' this fella? That ain' no way to treat company," his slurred speech indicated it wasn't his first drink of the evening. Or likely his last.

Waylon brushed past her, a bit unsteadily, and pushed through the screen door to join his guest on the porch, stumbling slightly on the threshold. The sharp twang of the stretched spring broke the stillness of the summer night. Ruth made to follow him outside, but he put out a hand to stop her.

"Go on back in, now, and leave us be. We got business."

He let the screen go and Ruth instinctively caught it to stop it from slamming. She stood, hesitating a moment as if she might defy him, then slowly guided the screen soundlessly back into place and closed the front door. She turned the lock and returned to check on their daughter, Rose Ellen.

Leaning against the doorjamb in the dimly lit hallway outside the small bedroom, Ruth watched the shadows play across the child's faded quilt as moonlight filtered through the leafy branches of the big oak outside her window. The window was open to let in the night air, and in the quiet she could hear the men talking outside.

"Jesus! You're tanked already," the visitor said. "How in God's name do you expect to find anything in that mound drunk in the dark? How much have you had?"

"Hell, I hadn't hardly got started yet. Don't you worry about me."

Ruth flinched as the truck doors slammed and the engine rumbled to life. At the sharp sounds, Rose Ellen stirred, sending Ruth hurrying to the bed to snug the quilt more closely around her, murmuring softly and gently smoothing back strands of her honey brown hair. After a few quiet moments, she kissed the child's forehead, tiptoed out, and drew the door softly closed behind her.

In the front room, she quietly unlocked and lifted the lid of an old cedar chest, instantly enveloped in the pungent wood smell that opening it had released along with the memories it held. She pulled out a gilt-framed photograph lying on top, a wedding portrait of her younger self and Waylon, handsome in his full military dress, chest filled with ribbons and medals. So long ago. So much had happened since that happy day. So much had changed. She touched the glass, her fingers lingering on her husband as he had been, before laying the photograph aside.

Returning to the trunk, she rummaged deeper and lifted out a heavy cloth-wrapped bundle, laying it on the floor and hesitating a moment before pulling the oil-stained material from around the contents. She ran her hand over the smooth wooden stock of her father's double-barreled shotgun, then picked the gun up and cracked the breech. Cradling it in the crook of her arm, she stood and walked to the gunrack on the nearby wall where Waylon kept the ammo and opened the drawer.

She grabbed a couple of shells and dropped them into the barrels. *Snick. Snick.*

Laying the gun down, she slipped a light sweater over her thin cotton dress; it was often chilly by the water, even in summer. Then, she picked up the gun and, with a last glance at Rose Ellen's closed door, she left to follow the men.

The sharp slap of the kitchen door screen stirred the child from sleep.

***

The pickup's low beams scarcely lit the way ahead as the visitor's truck bounced along, plowing through the bitterweed growing lush between the double ruts of the dirt road; the broken stalks filled the night air with the unmistakable scent of rural Southern summer, musky and pungent.

"You sure nobody else has been digging out here?" the driver asked.

"Some've tried. Nobody in a long while, though," Waylon replied. "Old man Morrison was real protective of it when he was still around. Family's always watched over it."

The rough road bent sharply right, and the hulking shape of a vine-choked earthen mound loomed before them in the truck's twin beams.

"There she is. Frenchman's Mound." Waylon pointed, unnecessarily, at the shape now dominating their view.

"Holy shit! Be hard to miss that. Gotta be thirty, forty feet high."

"Drive on across that gully on the culvert right over there," Waylon said. "Get us a little closer."

Almost before the truck stopped, Waylon shoved open the door and clambered out. "Kill the motor -- don't want to attract any O-fficial interest, you take my meanin'. Leave the high beams on and grab the tools," he said, over his shoulder. "I'll go find the spot."

In the light of the truck's headlamps, Waylon stood and turned somewhat unsteadily on the uneven, rock-strewn ground in front of the mound, silently scanning the perimeter of the clearing over and again as if to get his bearings.

Beyond the mound, the murmur of the river was the only sound. Then, gradually, out of the quiet, the thrumming of the tree frogs resumed, along with the occasional deep, harsh *braaaaps* of bullfrogs calling to one another along its reedy banks.

At last, Waylon paced off the distance between the north end of the mound and a towering old loblolly pine that grew in the dense thicket of younger pines where the clearing met the brushy wood. Then he paced a similar distance around the base of the mound and up the sloping side, finally stopping.

"Gimme that piece of rebar." Waylon took the iron rod and pushed it into the mound in first one spot and then another and another. Finally, he looked up, smiling. "Here," he declared. "Right here."

***

Ruth picked her way around the edge of the kitchen garden behind the farmhouse, past the hen houses, and onto the path that led down to the river road. The going was easy in the bright light of the rising moon, but she'd have had no trouble even without. She knew every inch of this ground backwards and forwards, moonlight or not. Every rise and gully was deeply etched in her mind, a part of her. The farm had been in her family—the Morrison's—for generations; she'd been born in that farmhouse, as had her daddy and his before that. She and her cousins had grown up romping all over its acres of woodland and pasture and up and down the country lane that led down to the Caddo River.

Once on that familiar road, the raw, broken stalks of bitterweed confirmed, if she'd needed confirmation, that Waylon and his 'company' had recently passed this way, headed down to the river. That direction could only mean one thing, and it wasn't frog gigging. They were headed to the big Caddo mound that lay on its banks.

She, like all locals, understood that the mounds were ancient burial or ceremonial sites, sacred ground to the Caddo Indian tribes that had lived here for centuries before. Everybody around here knew this one as Frenchman's Mound, so named from a skirmish that history books said took place nearby between the usually peaceable Caddo, who owned it, and a French expedition, who desired the land around it.

As kids, she and her cousins and friends had been raised to respect it and all the mounds, to never disturb them or the eternal rest of the dead they held. But, although they gave the mounds a wide berth, they'd scoured the furrows of newly plowed fields all around, looking for and occasionally turning up points, flint arrowheads, relics that bore testament to those earlier inhabitants. The craftsmanship on some of them was incredibly fine, like the perfect little bird point she'd found once, with edges honed wafer thin and a tip still sharp as a needle. She had kept it and dozens more in a polished wooden box her grandfather had made.

As she drew nearer the mound, the scraping of shovels in the rocky soil broke the stillness of the summer night. She quietly slipped from the road into the thick low pine and brush that rimmed the clearing near where the mound rose and her husband and his pot-hunting friend were busily digging. From her position, Ruth could see the men clearly through the fringe of pine boughs. She watched them, silent and intent, straining so hard to hear their conversation over the harsh scraping that she missed the light snap of a dry limb behind her.

"Whoa! Hold up." Waylon's friend said as he dropped to his knees and began to scoop dirt more carefully with a trowel and then with his hands. He lifted a small object from the hole and, as he gently brushed loose dirt from it, whistled softly.

"Well, I'll be goddammed. Drunk as your sorry ass is, you found them."

The man continued his careful digging and one after another gently lifted out several more objects. He held one up in the moonlight, turning it around in his hands, admiring the distinctive figure of an armadillo that decorated the open mouth of the pot.

"Damn," he exhaled, shaking his head. "Fine as you said. Finer maybe."

"Told ya, didn't I?" Waylon said. "I was right over there," he went on, indicating the thick brush near the loblolly, prompting Ruth to lean a little farther into the dark recesses of the surrounding low-hanging branches, "ten, twelve years ago, when old man Morrison made them other pothunters rebury 'em." Reaching into his hip pocket for the flask, Waylon offered it to his friend, who declined with a shake of his head, then he took a swig himself. "I knew you thought I was lyin'."

"I'll admit I was skeptical."

"How you likin' me now?" Waylon slapped his friend on the back. "What you think they'll bring?

"Depends, whether we sell here or the East Coast." Holding up the armadillo effigy pot, he said, "Collector I know in Little Rock would probably pay ten grand for this one alone, and..."

Both men started at a sudden rustling in the brush and the sharp snap of a dry limb. Ruth stepped out of the shadow and around the pickup into the light of the headlamps, the shotgun cradled in the bend of her arm.

Waylon relaxed a bit when he saw his wife and not the sheriff. "What in hell do you think you're doin'? Put that thing down."

"Glad to, soon as you put those back where you got 'em," Ruth said. "This is Morrison land, not Prescott's. I've told you more than once that mound and those pots you just dug out of it aren't yours to take." She took a step forward and gestured with the barrel toward Waylon's pal. "And for sure, not yours, mister."

The man set down the pot he was holding, stood slowly, and raised both palms. "No need to get all bent. This isn't what it looks like. Everything we're doing here is ultimately going to benefit you and your family." He took a step toward Ruth.

She retreated a step and said, "I might not have gone to war like Waylon or a fancy university like you, but I'm not a fool. I know what y'all are up to and I'm through turnin' a blind eye." She snapped the gun's breech in place with a sharp metallic click, leveling the barrels at him.

He stopped where he was and spoke calmly, "Just put the gun down and go back to the house," he said.

"Come on, babe. Do what he says." Waylon added. "This ain' no big deal."

"Me and this gun go nowhere 'til those pots are back where they belong, and your pot-thievin' friend is off this property." She motioned with the barrel of the gun, "Go on now. Y'all put 'em back." When they made no move to comply, she moved nearer to the men. "Waylon can tell you I wouldn't have missed from back there – bein' he knows I've been shootin' practically since I was a toddler – but mister I can promise you I won't miss from here. Get busy."

"Okay, okay. You're right." The man backed up and slowly squatted, picking up a pot and lowering it into the hole. He troweled some dirt in to cover it and leaned over to get another, but the pile was just beyond his reach. He crabbed around the hole, until he was just a few feet from the gun barrel. Crouching, with his back to Ruth and the gun, he reached for another pot, sending it tumbling down the slope, drawing Ruth's attention. His hand found the handle of the shovel and in one swift motion, he spun around and swung the shovel in a wide arc that caught Ruth squarely across the side of the head, knocking her to the ground.

The shotgun blast echoed in the night air and when its reverberation ceased, the sound of the quiet was almost as deafening. In the shock of the moment, neither man heard the muffled gasp or saw the small night-gown-clad figure hidden behind the fringe of low pine boughs at the edge of the clearing.

Ruth's body lay crumpled and still on the bare rocky earth, her neck at an unnatural angle, blood already matting her hair and flowing in a dark rivulet from her ear down her cheek. A burgundy stain bloomed at the neck of her cotton dress.

Waylon ran to her and fell to the ground, gathering her limp form to him, shaking her, wailing, "Oh, Jesus, Jesus. What have you done? Ruth! Ruth! Oh, Jesus. We gotta get help."

The man knelt beside him and put his fingers to Ruth's neck searching up and down for a pulse. He covered his face with his hand and muttered, "Shit."

"Do somethin', dammit!" Waylon pleaded.

"What do you want me to do, Waylon?"

"Help her."

"How? She's gone."

"Whatta you mean gone? She ain' gone. She's...she's...Ruth! Come on. This ain' funny, babe." Waylon cradled her, rocking back and forth, tenderly smoothing a strand of hair away from her soft, pale face.

"It was an accident. You know I didn't mean to hurt her; I was just trying to knock the gun out of her hand," the man stood and backed away a bit.

"We gotta call somebody. We gotta get her some help," Waylon's eyes, red-rimmed from both whiskey and bristling tears, pleaded with the man.

"Goddammit, what don't you understand? There's no help to get." He turned and walked toward the mound then spoke over his shoulder, bluntly, "She's dead."

"That can't be right. We gotta call Sheriff Perkins or somebody."

The man stopped and turned to face Waylon again. "And just what do you propose we tell them?"

"The truth! It was an accident."

"Oh, that's a great idea. We'll call the sheriff and … what? You'll say: 'Me and my buddy here were robbing this Indian grave—that neither of us had any legal right to, by the way—so we could sell these nice artifacts on the black market to some rich collector in New York City, when we accidentally killed Ruth.' Is that what you're planning to say to the sheriff?"

"What you mean *we* killed her?" Waylon's temper blazed, but he stayed put, holding Ruth's body closer. "I didn't have anything to do with it. You killed her all by your goddam self!" He returned his gaze again to Ruth's ashen face and began to quietly whimper.

"Oh, really? And you weren't right here committing a felony with me when it happened? Accessory to murder during the commission of a felony is a capital offense in this state, bud."

Waylon's head dropped, and his shoulders sagged and began to slowly shake.

"And besides, even if the sheriff did come, who do you suppose he'd believe? Me or your drunk, drugged up, sorry ass? Everybody in this town knows you've been either stoned or drunk since you got discharged."

He let the silence fall between them long enough for the drone of the tree frogs, abruptly stilled by the commotion, to resume. Then he softly continued, "The only thing that we are going to do, since we're now in this together, is bury this body. Come on. Help me get her up on my shoulders."

The man squatted beside Waylon and extracted Ruth's body from his grasp. Waylon, still and stunned, as if he were somehow unable to comprehend this awful, new reality, didn't move but just sat there blankly staring. Though Ruth was a slight woman, the man struggled to wrangle her dead weight, unaided, onto his shoulders and stand.

"Ground over on the river side'll be easier digging," he called back over his shoulder. "Bring the shovels and a lantern. We need to get this done."

When the scraping of shovels had finally assumed a steady rhythm on the far side of the mound, Rose Ellen emerged from the safety of the pine fringe. Running tiptoe, she gingerly skirted the disturbed ground where her mother had fallen and turned away from the few glistening black drops that caught the moonlight in the rocky clearing. At the base of the mound, she picked up the pot that had tumbled down and clutched it to her thin chest. Without a backward look, she noiselessly scampered to the pines, to the dusty road, to home.

CHAPTER 2
Manhattan: Two Years Later

The taxi pulled to the curb and stopped in front of the entry awning of 15 Central Park West, where a liveried doorman stepped from its shadow to open the door, extending his hand to the passenger within.

"Good evening, Dr. McKinley," he said, as the slender woman in an elegant black dress stepped onto the curb and absently tucked an escaping strand of blonde hair back into the neat chignon at the nape of her neck. "And welcome."

"Thank you, David," she smiled warmly, "it is a lovely evening, isn't it?"

"That it is," he replied, walking ahead to open the lobby door for her. "Beautiful night for a party." The sharp *click clacks* of her heels echoed on the marble lobby floor, as he followed her inside and used his key to call for the elevator. "Plenty of people up top already."

The doors opened almost immediately, and she stepped inside. "I'm sure there are. I got held up a little at the hospital, but better late than never, right?"

"That's right. And Doc, I've got a feeling tonight they won't really start things without you," he said, turning his key to send the private car to the Winslow's 18th floor penthouse.

She flashed crossed fingers and a smile as the doors glided shut.

They opened again directly into a graciously appointed reception gallery already filled with guests, a few of whom she acknowledged with a smile and small wave. She handed her pashmina and clutch to a uniformed young woman and headed toward the buzz of conversation emanating from the living room and terrace. The view from there was magical, especially after dark, when its walls of glass overlooking Central

Park offered a million-dollar view of the twinkling Manhattan skyline by night. *More like a 50-million-dollar view in today's real estate market,* she thought.

The penthouse took up almost two full floors of a park-facing building that had once been the pre-war Hotel Mayflower; developers had demolished the old landmark and built in its place a high rise of ultra-high-end luxury residences a number of years ago. This one belonged to her boyfriend's parents—Herbert Winslow, the international steel magnate and his wife Claire—though they rarely used it anymore. They spent most of their time, at least in the years since Herb's semi-retirement, cruising the world in their multi-room private condo on a residential luxury ship as peripatetic globetrotters – this week Mallorca, next month Naples. Or, when the spirit moved them, on a jet back to *terra firma* to ensconce themselves at the family estate in Rhode Island.

Jeffrey, their only child, held down the fort in Manhattan nowadays. He'd lived there throughout most of his surgical residency and fellowship, though to be fair, the bulk of his time then was spent uptown at the hospital or in the call room. Now, as a rising star of the trauma surgery staff at Columbia, the penthouse was his home.

She took in again the expensively curated and very modern décor of the room, a current style she dubbed *prison chic*: all sharp, clean lines, and a palette in black, white, and fifty shades of gray, with the occasional bright touch of color in artwork, pillow, or throw. In this case, a color plucked by some decorator, no doubt at great expense, out of the large, original Gustav Klimt that hung over the fireplace. The style was not particularly her cup of tea, but she had to admit it was still quite beautiful. And it was most definitely not your typical medical resident/young staff doctor digs. Certainly, a far cry from the tiny uptown 4th floor walk-up she'd shared for over three years with a pediatric ICU nurse. But then medicine for Jeff was more a hobby than a career, even if he clearly loved the heart pumping excitement of trauma surgery. And, admittedly, he was dedicated to his art and remarkably good at it.

She made her way through the living room, nodding hello and exchanging a few words with several acquaintances as she passed, and then into the dining room beyond it, where a runway-length buffet table fairly groaned with platters of catered delicacies. She plucked a salmon blini from a tray and stuffed the morsel whole into her mouth; she felt it a most unlady-like maneuver, but she'd had no time to eat since breakfast. At last, she arrived at the tended bar at the far side of the room, where a few clutches of people were chatting.

"A prosecco, please," she gave the bartender a smile.

"Mags!" She turned, flute in hand, to see Jeff coming in from the terrace. "There you are! What kept you?"

A head taller than most of the crowd, he was easy to spot. And easy on the eyes. His tousled, sun-streaked hair, athletic build, and the rosy golden tan that went with them were just a set up for a smile so disarming that it made her heart skip a momentary beat. The effect was not so different now than when she'd first seen him three years ago, laughing across a scrub sink on day one of an 8-week surgery rotation in the first year of her Family Medicine residency. And those dashing good looks were on full display tonight in an open-collared, crisply starched, blue-and-white striped shirt and navy spun-cashmere jacket, complete with silk pocket square; he looked every inch the international playboy he could probably have become, but thus far hadn't.

He bent to brush her forehead with a quick kiss, enveloping her in a subtle but heady combination of good whiskey and Paco Rabanne.

"Hey. Sorry I'm so late," she said. "One of my critical patients went south just as I was about to leave, so I stayed to help the oncoming team. And then I had to run by the apartment and change into something more presentably 'after five' than a labcoat."

"My magnificent Maggie, diligent to the last, but late to her own party." There was that smile again. "You know your leaving's gonna punch a hole in the Family Medicine program big enough to drive a tank through, right?"

"I'm sure they'll muddle through." She took a sip from her glass.

"Well, perhaps just barely, but I'm equally sure they'd love to bring you on staff permanently. You know they would. Thompkins told me as much."

The cluster of people around the bar swelled as more and more of the crowd on the expansive terrace migrated inside, pressing them all closer together.

"We could turn this into a celebrating-your-decision-to-stay party instead of a send-off," he whispered into her hair. "That would get my vote."

"You know I can't, Jeff. I have to be -"

Before she could finish, a man with a body shaped a bit like a fireplug in a jacket as wide as it was long slipped off his tasseled loafers and—with much more agility than his size and apparent degree of inebriation would indicate was possible—hoisted himself up onto an upholstered bench near the bar. He began vigorously tapping his half-empty glass with a spoon until the buzz of the room quieted.

"Ladies and gentlemen, fellow indentured servants of the Columbia Medical system, esteemed staff, gracious host, and ... the rest of you, whatever you are." A ripple of laughter arose. "For any who don't know, I'm Rob Griffin, and I'd like to thank you all for coming tonight to honor our friend and colleague, Maggie McKinley, who I've been assured has finally managed to join the party, if somewhat belatedly." He scanned the crowd until he saw her tucked into the circle of Jeff's arms. "Ah, yes, there she is," he indicated with a lift of his brow and head tilt in her direction. All eyes turned to Maggie, who gave a weak smile and finger waggle in acknowledgement.

"Sadly, we must bid adieu to our dear friend, who, rumor has it, has shunned a plum spot on the Medicine staff at Columbia," he put a hand beside his mouth with a wink and stage whispered: "I know this, because I was their second choice. So, thank you, Maggie!" He lifted his glass to a scattering of laughter. "Instead, she'll be leaving civilization next week to take the torch of Hippocrates to the uncharted wilds of deepest, darkest Arkansas."

From the terrace door, a man shouted over the crowd, "Where's that, Robby?" An eruption of laughter followed.

Rob shrugged. "Down south, someplace." He held up a palm in surrender. "I confess it was not my US Geography grade that got me into med school, but I seem to recall it's somewhere in the middle, like above New Orleans and below Cincinnati. Right, Maggie?"

"You've got it in the right general third of the country, Rob."

"Yes!" He gave a fist pump like he'd just holed a 30-footer for birdie. "But that's not what's important. What's important is that my glass is almost empty, and this is supposed to be a toast. Bartender, a top off with some of good Dr. Winslow's very rare Middleton, *s'il vous plaît*," he said, bending precariously to put his glass within the bartender's reach. He then raised his replenished drink and proclaimed, "Please, raise your glasses to Maggie; may she somehow prosper in cultural exile and return unscathed."

"To Maggie!" the crowd echoed with glasses raised. Those nearby wished her well, some called out that they would miss her, others told her not to stay away too long, but before anyone could really corner her, Jeff took her elbow and guided her back out onto the terrace and around to a more private corner.

Standing behind her, he wrapped his arms around her shoulders and pulled her close; they gazed out at the view in companionable silence for a few moments before he spoke. "Can you really shelve our relationship for two entire years?"

"Jeff, please. We've been all through this. I have to go; you know I do. I made the commitment when I accepted the Rural Practice Loan money for school. A year for a year."

"I could pay it off."

This was a running conversation, and one Maggie didn't want to have again right now. She closed her eyes and breathed in deeply before she spoke; the line of her mouth stiffening slightly. "Money's not the answer to every problem, Jeff. The program doesn't want the money. They need doctors where there aren't any. And even if that weren't the case, it's about keeping promises when you make them."

"But why some Godforsaken backwater for Christ's sake? A million miles from here."

She turned in his arms and tipped her face up to challenge his eyes with her own. "Some people call that 'Godforsaken backwater' home. I seem to recall a US President, for one." She paused. "My mother, for another."

Jeff winced and nodded in chastened agreement.

Maggie pushed slightly away from him and continued. "People living in cardboard boxes on Park Avenue probably think this place is pretty Godforsaken."

"Fair enough. But there are rural pockets closer to the City you could have considered. They need doctors, too."

"You act like Arkansas's the end of the Earth, Jeff. It's not like I'm sailing off for the new world or joining a wagon train west and you might never see me again."

He glanced over Maggie's head as a tall, slender woman with a cloud of chestnut hair quietly approached them from around the corner of the terrace. She pinned Jeff with a sultry stare before laying a hand on each of Maggie's shoulders from behind.

"Here you are. I wondered where you two had gotten off to," the woman said.

"Judith." Jeff cleared his throat, "I thought you said you had to leave earlier."

"Oh, I couldn't without saying goodbye to our darling Maggie," she replied a little too sweetly for the openly inviting look she flashed at Jeff.

Maggie turned to face her. "Judith, it's so nice of you to have stayed. I'm honored." At least that's what came out of her mouth. Her honest thoughts about Jeff's ex-girlfriend were another matter entirely, one where she envisioned herself tossing the woman over the balcony and watching as she fell the eighteen floors to the sidewalk below.

Judith bent to air kiss Maggie on both cheeks before moving around to stand a bit closer to Jeff. The stilettos she wore made her only a few inches shorter than he was. "I wouldn't have missed this party for the world. I want to be sure you know just how much we're all going to miss you. I think it's wonderful what you're doing. So selfless and noble."

"That's very kind," she said, thinking *What you want to be sure of is my departure.*

"And it's just a couple of years, right? God knows it can't be worse than your residency. And don't you worry about this one," she said, beaming a toothy smile and laying her hand on Jeff's shoulder. "We'll do our best to take good care of him while you're away."

Oh, I'll bet you will was the thought that went through Maggie's mind. What came out her mouth was, "Honestly, I wouldn't expect anything less, Judith." She returned Judith's smile somewhat stiffly and casually threaded her arm through Jeff's, drawing him away. "And I do apologize that we can't stay and chat longer; there are so many people I still need to speak to tonight. If you'll excuse us."

Hours later, the last guests had finally left, and Jeff and Maggie were alone in the penthouse. Well, alone except for Esmeralda, his housekeeper, who lived in the service quarters off the kitchen downstairs, and the catering crew, who were still busy with the after-party clean up. Occasional muted sounds of their activities seeped up the staircase to the master suite.

Maggie kicked off her heels in the sitting room just off the master and sank gratefully into the enveloping comfort of a down sofa and the soft jazz playing from somewhere unseen. This sofa was, hands down, her favorite piece of furniture in his home; but then comfort always trumped fashion for her. Not that it wasn't both. Absently rubbing her aching feet, she watched the lights of the City shimmer in the night skyline visible from the expansive windows.

Jeff poured them each a cognac and joined her. He handed her the snifter and eased onto the sofa beside her, draping a casual arm around her bare shoulders and propping his feet up on the coffee table.

"Quite a turn out, yeah?"

"It was, yes. And lovely to see so many old friends before I go." She rested her head against his shoulder and took a sip. "Thank you for doing it."

"My pleasure," he said and turned to kiss the top of her head and settle his cheek lightly against her hair. "But if we're being honest, I was maybe also nurturing a faint hope that seeing them all together might make you realize that you belong here. Might make you change your mind and stay closer to home. To me."

"I can't bail out at this point. You know I can't." She turned her face to his. "The clinic at Caddo Bend is expecting me next week. They've been making do without a fulltime doc for years."

"Well, couldn't they keep making-" he began, but she put a finger to his lips.

"Shhh. It's two years, not forever."

"Well, it's going to feel like it."

"We'll talk; we'll text; we'll FaceTime. And the planes fly both directions," she said. "You can write me love letters. General Delivery, Caddo Bend, Arkansas. They even have a zip code. I can keep them tied up with a satin ribbon."

"Not the same as having you beside me." He kissed the tip of her nose. "So, while I still do have you … beside me… I'd like to invite you to consider slipping out of that incredibly flattering black strapless number and joining me next door." He stood and took the snifter from her hands, setting it aside and pulling her to her feet. He wrapped his arms around her slender waist, drawing her to him.

Her fingers slowly worked open the buttons of his shirt and her hands slipped beneath the still-crisp fabric to caress the muscular smoothness of his chest and back. She laid her head against his bare skin and breathed in the musky blend of his cologne and the starched cotton and let her hands rove across his back and down. She looked up into his eyes as she deftly worked open his belt buckle and unbuttoned the waist, loosening his fly; she could feel his desire, straining through the fabric.

He bent his head and let his lips gently meet hers, tender nibbling kisses at first, then echoing her response, with deeper urgency. His hands cupped her face, roved lightly across her bare shoulders, and moved lower, sending shivers down her back, until his fingers found and eased down the zipper of her dress, sending it collapsing into a puddle of black taffeta around her bare feet. Only her black thong and strapless bra remained. She reached behind her back and popped the catch of her bra, dropping it onto the floor.

He let out a soft appreciative groan and gently pulled her toward the bedroom, and between planting soft kisses on her neck and shoulders he muttered against her hair, "I'm praying you've got everything packed up, because if all I've got left for a while is the next three days, my plan is not to let you out of my sight."

At the foot of his bed, he shucked his shirt and kicked out of his trousers and, picking her up effortlessly in his arms, fell backward onto the foot of his bed with her lithe body on top of his.

She breathed in the musky scent of him and enjoyed a pleasant sensation that bordered on giddiness. Reveling in his muscular warmth, she eagerly allowed herself to be swept up into the unbridled bliss of a last few days with him.

Maggie awoke the next morning and stretched lazily, reaching her arm out for Jeff, finding nothing but an expanse of high thread count cotton and crumpled down pillows. *Had there been an emergency?* She hadn't heard his phone or pager, though they hadn't actually fallen asleep until the extremely wee hours, and perhaps she'd slept through it.

Thoughts of their love making, over and over again during those wee hours, sent a tingling sensation of pleasure pulsing through her. Let no one say they weren't good together in bed. But would they be good together in life? This was the issue that she always circled back to. Two plus two in bed didn't necessarily equal a lifetime of compatibility. His upbringing had been so different from hers. His was a world of money, power, and connection. Of limos and private jets and racing yachts, hell, residential yachts, for that matter. Hers was nothing remotely similar; she had no family.

Was she ready for that kind of privileged life? Charity balls and jet set travel? Did she even want it? It was exciting, she'd grant that. And God knows he, himself, was exciting, and gorgeous, and she loved being with him. But all she'd ever dreamed of, all she'd ever worked for was to become a doctor. Could she, as Jeff had so easily done, come to look at the practice of medicine as a hobby?

Jeff's voice drifted in from the stairs, "Rise and shine, buttercup! Here's your Americano." He walked in, shirtless in just his clinging boxer briefs, which left very little to her imagination, carrying a tray with their coffees.

He sat it down on the bed beside her and handed her a cup, bending to kiss her sweetly on the lips as he did. She didn't have a stitch on and started to get up to grab a robe, but he put up a hand. "Uhn uhn," he cautioned, tossing her his shirt from last night that lay crumpled on the floor beside the bed. "I told you, I'm not letting you out of my sight. And I meant it. Now enjoy your coffee. The clock's ticking."

CHAPTER 3
On the Road

Maggie had gotten an early start, pulling out of the City just before 6 am. She desperately wanted to get on the road and out of Manhattan's traffic gravity well before the morning rush hour hit. She'd gotten up very early to pack her small car – a little RAV4 SUV and the first car she'd ever owned – with all the belongings she was taking to Caddo Bend. She didn't own any furniture, which made it easier. Books, clothes, photographs; her newly acquired weights and the pieces of her rack rig took up most of the room. But because the car was parked on the street in front of their building, she'd been unable to pack it the night before or else there'd have been nothing left in it when she came down this morning.

Late last night she'd said goodbye to her roommate, Bethany Peterson, who had the 11-7 shift at the ICU. An extra set of hands ferrying all her belongings down to the car would have been welcome, but she was glad she didn't have to deal with Beth while packing it all this morning. It wasn't that she exactly disliked Beth, but she couldn't say she really liked her much either. She'd been a dependable roommate as far as getting the rent and shared bills paid on time, and she didn't trash the place or bring seedy characters in, but outside of both working at the medical center, they had very little in common. And Beth had a snarky demeanor that got on Maggie's nerves. Right now, she didn't need that; she was a little nervous already.

This whole driving thing was new to her. Having spent all her teens either at boarding school or living on campus at college and since then in the city of Manhattan, she'd never had any need to drive. She'd never even had a driver's license. To correct that deficiency, she'd spent the last couple of months studying, passing the tests, and was now the proud possessor of not just a legal ID, which she'd always had, but a license to drive. And a car to do it in. All well and good, but she was still a novice driver, and New York City rush hour was not the place to fledge your wings.

The first leg of her planned route would take her from Manhattan through Pennsylvania and down into West Virginia. Final destination: White Sulphur Springs. There she would meet up at The Greenbrier Resort with her college roommate and long-time best friend, Charlotte Schaflien, nee Ainsley, who in a curious bit of happenstance hailed from Charlotte, NC. Maggie had dubbed her *Charlotte from Charlotte* the moment she'd introduced herself in their shared dorm room the first day of college, and the nickname had stuck. She and Maggie had become inseparable buds and roomed together all four years at Washington & Lee, the small, ultra-competitive private university they'd attended in Lexington, Virginia.

They were like mirror images, a yen and yang. Charlotte's exuberance to Maggie's more reserved and thoughtful demeanor. Maggie, with her striking combination of blonde hair, golden skin, and eyes so deep brown they almost seemed black under a fringe of thick black lashes that went on until tomorrow and Charlotte, the quintessential Southern belle, with large, sage green eyes, a mass of dark curls that fell past her shoulders, and a flawless pale complexion. Scarlett O'Hara in Lululemon.

Maggie had been laser focused on sciences from the jump. Charlotte, on the other hand, had come there, like her father before her, to play golf for the Generals, after turning down a full ride golf scholarship offer at the University of North Carolina. She had dabbled first in history, then psychology, and had settled, in the end, on business. After graduation, Charlotte had landed a job as a financial analyst back in her eponymous hometown, but within a year had met and subsequently married the professional golfer, Ford Schaflien, and gone mommy track. About five years ago, when Charlotte and Ford had welcomed twins, analyzing finances beyond her own checkbook had become a thing of the past.

Maggie had been maid of honor at their wedding—in a coterie of eight attendants on each side of the aisle—and the lavish reception that followed at the incomparable Duke Mansion in Charlotte. Maggie had never attended any private event remotely as huge. Five hundred people seated for a five-course meal, multiple live bands for dancing, and enough flowers to decorate every float at the Rose parade. And a half dozen or more young, handsome, up-and-coming pro golfers, buddies of Ford's, who had vied the whole weekend for Maggie's attention with marginal success, though she'd had to admit, it was flattering and a load of fun.

Charlotte was by far the closest of a small handful of Maggie's school friends and the only one that she'd kept in regular contact with—her sista from anotha motha, as Charlotte put it in her charming Southern drawl. Between her raising kids and the intensity of residency on Maggie's part almost three years had gone by since they'd last gotten together in person. It would be just a one-day reunion, but Maggie had eagerly looked forward to it since the day they'd talked a couple of weeks ago about making it happen.

The empty road stretched out ahead of her and Maggie thought back to all the good times the two of them had in those four idyllic years at W&L. The many holidays and the long weeks in the summers she'd spent with the Ainsleys at their stately Belle Epoque mansion in Charlotte. One July 4 weekend stood out in particular: they'd scored front row tickets to a Rod Stewart concert at the Verizon Amphitheater there. She'd seen a few truly memorable performances over the years, but this had been one of the all-time best concerts she'd ever seen.

Even now, she could call up the image of him strutting his stuff in his skintight black pants and a loose-sleeved white shirt open to his waist, shaking his trademark spiky hair. She and Charlotte had agreed that however old he was, he was still hot, hot, hot. Toward the end of his set, when that iconic mandolin intro began, the arena had gone berserk. The fans could name that tune in two notes. Rod had squatted down close to the edge of the stage during the intro, right in front of where they stood entranced in the front row, and looked down smiling at the crowd. Then he had pointed, she was sure right at her, when his raspy, sexy voice proclaimed *Wake up Maggie, I think I got somethin' to say to you…* It was like he was singing to her, straight to her. She'd become a fan for life! And come away with a nickname of her own.

She thumbed up Rod's *Essentials* on her iTunes and cranked the volume. The sound of that unmistakable jangling mandolin riff filled the car, and Maggie was soon singing loudly along with him, paying zero attention to the road signs cautioning her to reduce her speed. *It's late September, and I really should be back at school…I know I keep you amused, but I feel I'm being used. Oh, Maggie I couldn't have tried any mo-oh-ore!*

Blue lights flashed in her rearview mirror, and she looked at the speedometer, which read 80 mph. *Shit! What's the speed limit here?* She tapped the brakes and slowed down, but the trooper stayed behind her and now bleeped his siren and flashed his headlights. *Double shit! Damn you, Rod!* She turned down the volume.

Maggie signaled her intent to pull over and slowed, finally coming to a stop on the shoulder, well off the highway. She rolled down her window, took her wallet out of her purse, and got her brand spanking new license out. She'd worked with enough cops in ERs to know the drill: hands visible, nothing in them but the license, if it's dark turn the interior light on, but it was day. She could see him sitting behind the wheel, talking on the radio. *Checking to see if it's a stolen car. The temporary dealer's license was still in force, wasn't it?* She'd decided to wait to license it until she got to Arkansas. Finally, he climbed out, and she watched him approaching in her side mirror.

"Morning, ma'am," he said. He was tall and fit and looked to be around her age, 30ish maybe. Seemed friendly enough. She noted his name plate: Adams.

"Good morning, sir," she said giving him her best mega-watt smile. *Is it sir? Officer? Trooper?* She didn't want to say the wrong thing and insult him. "I realize I might have been going a little fast."

"Yes, ma'am. Speed limit coming into town here is 55 miles per hour."

"Oh, I'm sorry. I didn't see a sign."

"Well, I clocked you at 81, and there's no stretch of this road where 81 is the posted limit," he said. "May I see your license?"

Maggie handed the license to him, and he took it and returned to his car.

She picked up her phone, held it in her lap, and texted Charlotte: *b lil late xpln when icu.* Then she laid it back down on the seat and put both her hands again on the steering wheel.

When he came back, he said, "Ms. McKinley, where are you headed so fast?"

"I'm going to Arkansas. From New York," she added, as if that mattered.

"Long trip," he said, eyeing all the boxes and suitcases. "You moving there?"

"Yes. I'm taking over a clinic in Caddo Bend," she added.

"You're a nurse or a doctor?"

"A doctor, yes, sir."

He smiled and handed her back her license. "My wife's a nurse. It's my personal policy to never give a speeding ticket to a doctor or a nurse. I'd just ask that you try to slow it down when the signs tell you to. And drive safely."

Maggie couldn't believe her good fortune. "Thank you. I promise I'll keep a better eye on my speed."

"Yes, ma'am," he touched his fingers to the brim of his campaign hat. "You have a nice day, doctor."

An hour or so later Maggie pulled up in front of the white-columned portico of The Greenbrier, where she'd stop for the night. She thought the central façade of the building bore a passing resemblance to the White House, but if anything, the wings were larger. Imposing and regal, its lush plantings were manicured to the last blade of grass by a veritable army of gardeners bent even now to their work.

They'd decided on The Greenbrier because it was generally on Maggie's cross-country route and an easy little commuter flight from Charlotte. Plus, it was a drop-dead gorgeous place to stay. It would definitely be a Holiday Inn Express or Motel-6 tomorrow night to make up for this splurge, but from the looks of the place, it would be darn well worth it.

Ford had generously agreed to watch the kids for the night to give the ladies an uninterrupted chance to catch up. Tomorrow Maggie would head south toward Nashville, and Ford and the twins would drive the four hours up to meet mom for a couple of days of R&R and family golf at the resort. As to the ladies, their plan was to hit the spa this afternoon for a good massage and maybe a facial, enjoy drinks and dinner in the posh dining room tonight, stay up late chatting and laughing over a bottle or so of decent wine, and then sleep in. And Maggie couldn't wait.

A smiling valet opened her door, "Welcome to The Greenbrier, ma'am. Are you checking in?"

"Yes, thanks," she said. Every nook and cranny of the small SUV was crammed with her belongings, barely leaving room for her in the driver's seat.

"Traveling through, ma'am?" he said taking in the packed interior with a cool, practiced nonchalance that still somehow made her feel a bit like one of the Clampetts from the old television comedy *The Beverly Hillbillies* she'd watched in reruns as a child. She turned off the engine, climbed out, and handed him the keys. Then opened the back door and lifted out the small rolling overnight bag she'd positioned there for easy access.

"We'll get that for you, ma'am," he said, snapping his fingers to signal for a bellman.

"No, it's fine," she said. "I'll just be here for the night. This is all I need."

"Enjoy your stay, then" he said, stepping back and subtly waving off the approaching bellman.

As she headed up the entry walkway, Maggie saw a petite woman wearing a polka dot sundress, Jackie-O sunglasses, and a broad-brimmed straw hat waving madly from the portico, and she waved back. *Charlotte from Charlotte.*

"Maggie May!" Charlotte squealed her nickname as she wrapped her arms completely around Maggie, rocking from side to side and enveloping her, both physically and sensorially, in the cloud of Tea Rose perfume that was her signature scent. "I'm so happy to see you and hug you!"

"Sorry I'm a little late. I got stopped for speeding." Maggie whispered under her breath as she extracted herself from the bear hug.

"Come inside; I've got us a table on the bar patio and a bottle of prosecco chilled and waiting. You can tell me all about it. Was the trooper cute?"

Maggie just smiled and shook her head. *Charlotte's gonna Charlotte.* "Let me check in, and I'll meet you there," Maggie said.

"No way, missy," Charlotte said linking her arm through Maggie's, "You got way too much to catch me up on; we can't afford to waste a second. We'll just talk as we walk."

Once Maggie was checked in and they'd stowed her bag in her room, they headed down to the patio bar and that nicely cooled libation that awaited.

Charlotte poured them each a flute of the wine and raised her glass, "To the Sistas," she said.

"Cheers, Sista," Maggie said, clicking her glass.

"Soooo… tell me," Charlotte leaned closer across the table, expectantly.

"What?" Maggie asked, but with a sly smile that said she knew full well 'what'.

"Don't tease! I want the whole skinny on you and Jeff," Charlotte said.

"What's to tell?" She sipped some prosecco and nibbled at a cucumber and mayo tea sandwich. "Jeff threw me a nice going away party, and we spent the next three days saying goodbye for a while."

"And?"

"And we had a really good time." Maggie pursed her lips, trying to suppress a laugh as best she could.

Charlotte looked utterly exasperated and glowered at her.

"OK, OK," Maggie said, "it was memorable."

"Memorable?" The look on her face was almost comical.

"Fabulous, actually," Maggie admitted. "So fabulous that it really made it hard to leave him."

"Well, why did you, girl?"

"Honestly, you're as bad as he is. I have a commitment in Caddo Bend," Maggie said, emphasizing each word. Then twisting the stem of the glass and spinning it slowly on the tabletop, she added, "I didn't really have a choice."

"But where does that leave you two?" Charlotte reached across the table and grabbed Maggie's left hand. "I don't see any sign of long-term commitment in this department."

"No. I don't think we're quite there yet. I mean, I do love him, I think. And he says he loves me, too, but..." she trailed off.

"But what? He's rich. He's gorgeous. Right?"

"Yeah."

"He's fun. He loves you. So... what?"

"I don't know. I just want to be sure he's my forever guy."

"Maggie May, you're doing that thing you do."

"What thing?" Maggie said.

"The fear thing. Being afraid to trust, to just let go and love and risk losing. And I get it. But your fear is keeping you from thinking straight. Let me run it again for you," she ticked off on her fingers. "Rich, gorgeous, fun, loves you. What have I missed?"

"Great in bed?"

"Exactly! What is holding you up?"

Maggie sipped from her flute and paused, pondering the 'why' of something that she wasn't entirely sure of herself. "I think we need to see how this cross-country thing works out over these next two years. If we're strong, we'll still be strong no matter the time, no matter the miles. Right?"

"Uh huh," Charlotte reached for the bottle. "What you need is more prosecco."

"And a good massage," Maggie added. "Let's take this with us and hit the spa."

They'd spent the rest of the afternoon in the spa, relaxing. Charlotte went for the seaweed wrap, which Maggie complained stank to high heaven. Maggie, having sat crammed in a car for the last 8 hours, had opted for a deep tissue release and a salt glow. The first left her limp as a ragdoll, and the second made her skin feel as smooth as a baby's butt. *All in all, a great way to pass an afternoon*, she thought. Later they'd enjoyed a scrumptious meal, and after that, lots more wine, laughter, and wicked conversation until the wee hours.

She was pleased and a little surprised to be getting on the road again by a few minutes past one, even after sleeping in and enjoying a leisurely breakfast with Charlotte. But she'd been more than delighted that Ford and the kids happened to pull into the resort just as she was loading up to leave and saying goodbye to Charlotte, meaning she got to see them too, and that made her happy. They were such a beautiful family. The love radiated off them in waves, and it was easy to see that Ford was Charlotte's forever guy. Had been easy to see from the very beginning, which led her to the inevitable thought: *is Jeff mine?*

The twins were getting so big. Ainsley was starting to turn into a mini-me of his handsome, athletic dad. He was half a head taller than Caroline already and dressed to the nines in seersucker golf shorts and a polo shirt with the logo of some exclusive golf club or other on the chest. A regular little lady killer already. Caroline's dark hair was the image of her mother's and pulled into a long braid secured with a big blue bow that matched her knit cardigan and the tiny repeating flower motif in her golf skort and the trim on her blouse.

"Your hair looks beautiful," Maggie said to the girl.

"Daddy did it!" she squealed and wrapped her arms around her father's thigh.

Maggie gave him an appreciative lift of her brow. "How did..."

"YouTube video," he said with a modest shrug. "It's harder than it looks, but we got it done, didn't we angel?" Caroline nodded and looked up adoringly at her dad, who wrapped his hand in a casually protective way around her shoulder.

As the bellman was removing their bags from the car, Maggie had noticed that even Ainsley and Caroline had their own pint-sized golf clubs.

"Start 'em young; raise 'em right!" Ford had said when she'd remarked on it.

They stood and chatted longer than she'd intended, and by about 1:30 she gave each of them final hugs and kisses and the promise that they'd get together again, soon. She should still have plenty of time to make it from The Greenbrier to Nashville—her next planned stop, about seven hours away—before nine tonight if all went smoothly.

When she'd been on the road a few hours, she called Jeff but got his voice mail. She left a quick message just letting him know she'd gotten back on the road and where she was planning to stop and saying to call her if he got a break. And that she missed him. She really did miss him, and the long hours alone in the car did nothing to relieve her loneliness.

Neither did Adele, who was at present tearing her heart out with a plaintive vow that she'd find someone like you. *Sometimes it lasts in love, but sometimes it hurts instead.* She didn't need that sentiment right now, or she'd be bawling her way down the interstate, so she thumbed her iTunes playlist to find something more upbeat and happier. And soon, Freddie Mercury's incomparable voice filled the car warning the world against stopping him, and her spirits soared right along with him.

She turned up the volume and sang along. *I'm a racing car passing by like Lady Godiva. I'm gonna go, go, go there's no stopping me!* Then the face of Trooper Adams swam into her mind; she looked down at the speedometer, which currently registered 82, and immediately slowed to 70. *Gotta watch that lead foot!* She turned Freddie down to a little less exuberant volume. The next trooper might not be personally averse to giving her a speeding ticket, and she had another 4 or 5 hours to Nashville.

After a decent night's sleep, the next morning Maggie was again speeding along I-40, the grey ribbon of highway splitting the deep green of the overgrown forest that framed the view on either side. She had gotten back on the road out of Nashville before 7 o'clock after grabbing a quick breakfast of eggs, bacon, fruit, and coffee from the complimentary buffet at the Holiday Inn Express she'd found conveniently located right off the freeway. Even with last night's motel austerity, though, averaged with the final tab at The Greenbrier, she was still over budget, but *YOLO.*

Her cell phone rang, cutting off Jack Johnson's *Banana Pancakes* in mid verse and announcing 'incoming call from JEFF' on the dash display. She thumbed the control on the steering wheel to answer.

"Hi, there, stranger," she said. She hadn't heard from him last night and had left another voice message from the hotel before she crawled into bed. *Probably operating late.* Such was the life of a trauma surgeon.

"Hey, sweets. You there yet?"

"Still working on it. I'm somewhere in Tennessee. Where are you?"

"Just finished a case. I was up most of the night with it. Had a little break between and couldn't get you off my mind." He dropped his voice to a whisper, "Or the days and nights before you left; I've played them over in my head about a dozen times."

She felt herself blush slightly with the memory. "Uh huh, me too." Then changing the subject, "God, it's so green here; just unbelievably green. You'd think you're in Ireland or something, though I've never actually been to Ireland. It's definitely on my Bucket List. In my mind, it's miles and miles of rolling green fields, and that's what I've been driving through."

"So where are you exactly in this sea of green?"

"I'm almost to Memphis, according to Waze, and that's the end of Tennessee, which, let me tell you if you are driving through it, is re-e-a-a-ly lo-o-o-ng." She drew the words out.

"Now aren't you glad I talked you into that app?" he said.

"Yes, I admit I am," she smiled, "But it failed miserably to find me a shortcut through Tennessee. I feel like I've been crossing it for a month."

"Which rings true, since on this end that's exactly how long it feels like you've been gone."

"And yet, it's been two days."

"Not possible. Clearly much longer," he teased.

She smiled, imagining him in his scrubs in the doctor's lounge between cases, that disarming smile, the always delicious smell of him. "Anyway, once I get through Memphis, I'll cross the Mississippi River and finally be in Arkansas. And then from there it's, let's see, a couple of hours or a little more to Little Rock and then maybe another hour and a half beyond that."

"You know it's still not too late to change your mind. You could turn around at Memphis and come home."

"And drive all the way back through Tennessee? Are you nuts? Not an option."

His pager sounded and he said, "OK. That's my next case. You'll call me, right, as soon as you get to Whistle Flats."

"Caddo Bend."

"Whatever. Just call me."

"Will do," she promised.

"Love me?"

"Yeah," she said, "you me, too?"

His emergency pager blared again. "Yep. Gotta go. Call me."

CHAPTER 4
Break Down

Maggie's car sat on the shoulder of a two-lane farm road; its brand new left rear tire flat. Standing beside the car, she examined first the tire, then her cell phone display.

"No service," she said aloud. "What the hell good is a cell phone with no service? I can answer that: None. Zero. No good at all!"

She pitched the phone through the window into her purse in frustration, shoved the sleeves of her light hoodie up over her elbows, and got to work. She opened the rear hatch and off-loaded enough of her belongings to get to the roadside emergency pack and jack stored beneath the floorboard, cursing her lack of foresight for not leaving it out and more accessible. *Who thought a brand new tire would go flat?* She was wrestling the spare off the rear hatch mount when an old Willys Jeepster ragtop pulled up behind her car and stopped on the shoulder.

At the wheel sat a man, who, but for the oddly out-of-place Boston Red Sox baseball cap he wore, looked a little like a farmer in a plaid flannel shirt he left open over a white t-shirt. He climbed out and stood leaning on his open door a respectful distance away, not approaching.

"Could you use a hand with that tire, ma'am?" His voice was resonant and warm.

"No, thanks. I can manage," she said, with more confidence than she felt. Jeff had suggested she read the manual about the car, which she'd done, and the guy at the car dealership had shown her where the jack was and how to put it together. But she'd never performed this operation before herself and didn't relish doing it the first time with an audience, wishing fervently the guy would just get in his car and move along.

She assembled the jack, and the man stayed put, watching her. She placed the jack as securely as she could, considering the ground in front of the flat was uneven, and jacked the car up. *So far so good.* Once the tire was off the ground, she started to unscrew the lugs, when the jack slipped and clattered down.

Without a word, the man walked up, knelt by the rear of her car, picked up the jack and deftly reassembled it.

"I can do this, really," she protested.

"Yes, ma'am, I'm sure you can. Probably better than I can. But, you see, my mama didn't raise me to leave a lady stranded on the roadside. So, if it's all the same to you, I'd appreciate it if you'd let me do this for you."

Maggie opened her mouth to argue but stopped short. The man gave her a smile that was warm and wide, lighting up his face. A chiseled and very handsome face, she noted. Lamely returning the smile, she folded her arms across her chest and moved aside to give him room.

Tire changed, he rose and brushed the dirt from the knees of his jeans, then he brushed his right hand on his pantleg and proffered it to Maggie. More the hand of an artist than a farmer, she noticed, strong but refined.

"JD Langston."

She took his hand and shook it. "Maggie McKinley. Thank you, Mr. Langston. I appreciate your help, but it really wasn't necessary."

He continued to hold her hand lightly and looked directly into her eyes. "It's JD. And you're welcome," he said, with a slight incline of his head.

When he smiled, his dimples made him look almost boyish, though she noticed a few silver strands in the dark hair that peeked out at his temples from beneath the cap and in the light stubble of his beard. *Late 30s? Early 40s maybe?* Mostly what she noticed was that she couldn't stop staring at his eyes, soft gray, intelligent and kind. And utterly mesmerizing.

"But if you're the McKinley who's the new doc coming to town," he said, keeping his gaze on her face as he picked up her other hand and lifted both between them, "then these hands were made to heal, not change tires."

Maggie felt herself swallow hard in the moment that hung between them before she recovered herself and played it off. Laughing lightly, she pulled her hands away and held them up for display, turning them front to back to front.

"Guilty as charged; I am, indeed, that McKinley. But trust me, these hands have had to do a lot worse than change a tire."

"Fair enough," he said with a smile, then busied himself packing up the jack and stowing it in the car. "You need to weight this thing down to keep it on the road?" he said, eyeing the set of workout weights in the back of her SUV and giving her a quizzical side-eye.

"You can never be too careful," she said with a laugh.

Then together they made quick work of repacking her off-loaded belongings in the back, and JD bolted the flat onto the tire mount.

"That spare ought to get you to town," he said. "Eddie Ray's station's just up ahead a little way. You can get your tire fixed there."

She double checked that the hatch was locked. "Thanks, again," she said.

He smiled and touched the brim of his ballcap. "My pleasure, Doc. Welcome to town."

Maggie eased the SUV to a stop at the front of a small, white clapboard building topped with a sign identifying it as Eddie Ray's One Stop & Service. That sign was flanked by a pair of ancient, rusted Standard Oil signs with lettering so faint it was barely still legible. They'd been there since the '50s when Eddie's grandfather had built and run the station, and Eddie refused to remove them. Out by the road, high on a pole, was an Exxon sign of more recent vintage and between it and the building, a pair of gasoline and diesel pumps. On the low wooden porch that ran across the front, beside an old-style red Coca-Cola drink cooler box, a group of locals, clad in dusty jeans, t-shirts, and work boots, sat on a bench, chatting, half-drunk bottles of soft drinks in their hands.

Maggie climbed out of her car and strode toward them. "Hi."

The men quit their conversation and acknowledged her with mute nods of the head.

"I've got a flat tire I need to have repaired. Is there someone here who can do that?"

The men pointed in silent unison toward the screen door entrance, an appraising look passing among them. The one nearest the door leaned over to pull it open for her, causing the spring to screech in protest before the door slapped shut behind her, giving her a start.

Inside were shelves packed with motor oil, insect repellant, and Citronella candles, alongside displays of chips, candy, jerky sticks, and snack cakes. On the walls hung fan belts, fishing poles, ball caps, a display of crank bait lures, and tools of every sort. And a Hotty Body Auto Parts calendar, curling at its edges. This month's pin-up, Maggie noted, was a voluptuous red head in Daisy Duke cut offs and a cleavage-baring halter, leaning over seductively to swab the hood of a candy apple red Corvette with a soapy sponge. *Classy.*

There appeared to be no one there, so she called out, "Hello?"

"Down here. Hang on just a sec," came the voice from behind the counter, its owner hidden by a rotary display rack he was squatted down behind and refilling with more of the cellophane-wrapped cards of plastic worms, fishhooks, bobbers, and pocket packs of aspirin and ibuprofen that dangled from its hooks.

For the headaches you get when they're not biting, she noticed the small sign above the pain relievers said.

A galvanized gallon bucket of small bottles of Skeeter Stopper spray and another of mosquito bite No-Itch gel sat beside the ancient cash register on the counter.

The proprietor, Eddie Ray, according to the embroidered name patch on his shirt, emerged from behind the display. "How do, ma'am. What can we do for ya'?" He was a heavy-set, red-faced man with thinning strawberry blonde hair, receding markedly, and blue eyes so pale they almost disappeared. Maggie pegged him in his mid to late 30s.

"Hi!" She smiled warmly at him. "I have a flat tire I need to have repaired."

"Yes, ma'am, we'll, uh," he said, staring and stammering a bit as if he'd really just noticed her, "we'll, uh, be glad to take a look at 'er, and if she can be fixed, we'll sure do 'er. Where's she at? In your trunk?"

"On the back of the silver SUV outside."

Eddie Ray raced around the counter to open the door for Maggie just as JD opened the screen from the other side, a small bottle of Coca Cola in his hand.

"Eddie, that Coke machine's not taking the money again. Here's a dollar – I'll just lay it on the counter." He came face to face with Maggie as she walked up behind Eddie Ray. "Well, hey. Looks like you made it in."

"I did. And thanks again, Mr. Langston for your help."

He pointed his index finger playfully at her, with a hint of a smile, "It's JD."

"Right. Sorry," she pointed back at him. "JD."

Eddie Ray squeezed past JD, heading for Maggie's car. "Take good care of her, OK, Eddie? We need to keep her around."

Maggie followed Eddie Ray out, and JD joined her on the porch. He took a long swig of his Coke, then spoke to the three men still sitting on the bench by the door, "Boys, have y'all met Caddo Bend's new doc?" He waved his Coke bottle first in her direction and then theirs and said,

"Dr. McKinley, this is Boyce, Travis, and Leon, in that order." The men all nodded and smiled a bit sheepishly. "And I guess you've already met Eddie," he said, as Eddie Ray rolled the tire back up to the front.

Eddie let go of the tire and stood. "Nope. Not formally anyways." He extended a tire-blackened hand in her direction, looked at it, thought better, and pulled it back, opting instead for a polite bob of his head. "Eddie Ray Lawson, ma'am. Pleased to make your acquaintance."

"Very nice to meet you, too. All of you," Maggie said turning to include the boys on the bench.

Picking up the tire once more, Eddie said "Lemme take 'er over to the bay and see what we got. You can come back and pick 'er up this evenin'. Or tomorrow."

"Thank you, Mr. Lawson."

"Eddie Ray, please."

"OK. Thank you... Eddie Ray."

"Yes, ma'am," he called over his shoulder as he and the offending tire disappeared around the side of the building. She thought it odd, but in a way charming, to be called 'ma'am' by grown men as old or older than she was. *You don't hear that in New York.*

"Well, in the meantime, I guess I'll try to find the McSwain Boarding House," Maggie said, walking to her car, "that's where I'm staying for now." She opened the door.

JD, walking toward his own car, called across it to her and pointed, "Just head on this way about half a mile or so and you'll come to a cross-roads. Turn left there and the road will take you over a railroad crossing and then over the Caddo on the low water bridge. Just keep on that road and you'll run right into town. You can't miss Miz Hendri's place."

"No, I'm at the McSwain Boarding House," she corrected him.

"Sorry," he chuckled. "Mrs. McSwain's first name's Henrietta. Her husband called her Hendri for short. So, everybody around here has always called her Hendri. To us younger folks, it's Miz Hendri," he explained.

"Ah. I'll make a note. And thanks, again," she paused to get it correct, "J.D. I hope I'll see you around town."

"For sure. It's a small town. You'll see us all around," he said and climbed into his car.

Travis leaned over to drop his bottle into the wooden crate of empties beside the cooler box and muttered, "Didn't nobody ever say the new doc was gonna be a woman, did they?" Leon raised his eyebrows and gave a tight shake of his head. Travis turned to Boyce. "You gonna drop your britches to her?"

"Not for no docterin'," he said with a twitch of his brows.

CHAPTER 5
New Horizons

Maggie eased the SUV over the railroad tracks and down the hill toward the placid Caddo River below. The one-lane, concrete bridge across it cleared the water's surface by two feet at most, its sides protected by only a curb no higher than a concrete block. *Thus, a low water bridge*, she thought. She stopped in the middle of the span to roll down the window and peer into the water; the surface was so close she could see fish darting among the smooth stones in the sun-dappled shallows. And it occurred to her again just how far this place she'd chosen was from Manhattan, both in miles and temperament. *And temperature*, she couldn't help noticing.

She'd never been to Arkansas until now and knew little about it, though her mother had been born here and, she'd been told, it was entirely possible she'd been conceived here. So, since her decision to take the position in Caddo Bend, she'd read a little about the history of the area and learned that the small town took its name from the Caddo River into which waters she now gazed and the oxbow bend along which the town sat. The wide, gentle river below her began as trickling cold springs deep in the Ouachita Mountains of Arkansas that coalesced and tumbled steeply down to become a designated wild and scenic river many miles upstream. That wild stream was joined further along its course by other small creek tributaries that widened and deepened it into a scenic river navigable by canoe for most of the year and created a rich and perfect habitat for small mouth bass and sunfish. Farther downstream the Corps of Engineers had dammed the river to create Lake DeGray, from which it spilled out to join into the Ouachita River and meander on its way toward the sea. It was indeed scenic; she could attest to that. *It will be an adventure*, she reassured herself, admitting in the next breath *and maybe a culture shock*. She gunned the motor to climb the hill on the river's far side.

The town, if you could call it that, proved to be little more than a main square around a central green and a half dozen crossing streets on either side that soon gave way to fields and farms all around. She passed a general store and post office, a tiny City Hall and even tinier local bank, and across the green could see a café, the county sheriff's station and a scattering of small shops and offices of one sort or another that rounded out the remainder of the square. A pair of churches bookended the street, at one end a sturdy, stone Southern Baptist Church and at the other a charming, white clapboard one, complete with a picturesque steeple that, according to the sign out front, was non-denominational. It hardly seemed possible the town held enough people for one, let alone two congregations, but this was, after all, the middle of the Bible belt. The McSwain Boarding House, a large, well-kept, two-story Victorian, painted a rich slate blue with warm taupe trim, sat at the far end of the main thoroughfare. She pulled up in front.

Maggie stood, flanked by two large suitcases, on the shady, wide porch. Beside the front door, a wooden placard read "McSwain Boarding House, est. 1932". What had been established in the 30s as offering bed and board for lodgers would nowadays be called a B&B, but the original name had remained – Boarding House – and the tradition of a dinner meal instead of breakfast. As it had for 80 years, the accommodations, now with *en suite* baths, still included a communal-style dinner each day, which was a benefit, since Maggie wasn't much of a cook herself. What she'd seen in the printed brochure she'd been sent – by snail mail, no less – was charming, plus it was the only such establishment right in town. So it was that or a Motel 6 out on the highway located next door to a seedy bar for about the same price and no meal.

She took a deep breath and knocked. A broad, elderly woman, dressed in a cotton floral print dress and white apron, opened the door. She ran a hand over her short and very curly white hair and smoothed her apron before speaking.

"The Missus Doctor." It was a statement, not a question, and said in a heavy German accent, as thick and impenetrable as cold molasses, like the old news clips she'd seen in history class of Secretary of State Henry Kissinger. As a student Maggie hadn't been able to understand a thing he said, but it was pretty to listen to. The woman pushed open the screen to allow Maggie inside. "Welcome. Come in. Come in." *Velcome*, it came out.

Maggie stepped in, extending her hand, "Mrs. McSwain? I'm Maggie McKinley. Very nice to meet you."

"Hendri, please," she said, taking Maggie's hand in both hers and giving it a firm pat. Behind wire-rimmed glasses, her hazel eyes danced with a no-nonsense energy that belied her years.

"I'll just get these in," Maggie said of her suitcases on the porch.

"You leave those right there. Mr. Purifoy will bring your things inside for you."

"No, no that's not necessary. I can manage," she said, reclaiming her hand and lifting both cases at once, moving them into the foyer.

"I insist." Miz Hendri's tone left little to debate as she purposefully took Maggie by the arm and led her to the back of the main hall, clucking, "Plenty time to do that after you've had something to eat. You must be hungry and tired from your long trip."

They entered a large country kitchen, dominated by a big, square wooden farmhouse table and filled with the delicious aromas of coffee and baking. At the counter a tall, broad-shouldered young man, covered in dust from the top of his sandy blonde head to his work boots, quickly stuffed a large bite of something into his mouth.

"Ach, Nicholas. I didn't know you were home already." His cheeks bulged with what he'd crammed in, and as it prevented his immediate response Miz Hendri continued. "I see you have found the cake that I made for the Missus Doctor."

Nick nodded, tried to swallow, and then put his hand over his mouth and spoke around the mouthful, "Miz Hendri, you know your pound cake is the main reason I board here and not over at Mt. Ida." She gave him a teasing admonishing look and waddled over to slice more of the cake and pull plates and mugs from the cupboard.

He put out his hand to Maggie and noticed her looking at the crumbs on it, "Sorry," he said and brushed them off with his other hand before he offered it again. "Nick Freeman."

Maggie took his hand and gave it a firm shake, "Maggie McKinley. Nice to meet you." She couldn't help noticing his blue eyes, not because they sparkled with suppressed mischief, which they did, but more the way their color contrasted so sharply against his tan if now dusty skin.

"Damn, girl, you got a grip!" He shook out his hand and motioned for Maggie to take a seat.

Miz Hendri set a large slice of pound cake and steaming mug of coffee on the table in front of Maggie, along with a crockery cream pitcher and sugar bowl. Nick looked up, expectantly, and as no plate appeared to be coming his way, got up to grab himself a plate and another slice.

"I will go check on your things," she said to Maggie, admonishing Nick over her shoulder as she left, "Don't eat all the cake, Nicholas. You'll ruin your supper."

"What's on the menu tonight?"

"Fried chicken," she said.

"Not possible to ruin my appetite for your chicken and biscuits," he shouted after her and settled back down at the table with his cake. "You have no idea what a treat you're in for tonight," he said to Maggie, his eyes lighting up at the very thought. "Miz Hendri's fried chicken is the stuff of dreams. And her biscuits? I swear, when dough gets into that woman's hands, it just knows what to do."

"I can hardly wait to experience such a culinary delight," she smiled and tipped some cream into her mug, then lapsed into silence.

"So," he said at last, "you're the new rent-a-doc, come to the sticks from the Big City."

"Well, I guess that's one way to put it," she replied, stirring her coffee and taking a sip. "I'm not exactly rented; I'm here to work off a Rural Practice Loan, so I'll be here for the next couple of years"

"Ah. Indentured servant," he chuckled and took a swig of his coffee.

"Yeah, sort of. On loan, I guess." Consuming a second bite of the rich, buttery cake, she laid down her fork and pushed the plate to the side.

"Don't like the cake?"

"No, it's delicious. I just don't eat much sweet stuff."

"Hmm. Virtuous. And health conscious. Admirable, but I warn you, Miz Hendri'll be pissed," he teased.

"Surely, she won't," Maggie said.

"Well maybe not pissed, but I guarantee she'll think you're sick or something."

Maggie pushed the plate in his direction. "Want it?"

"Is that really a question?" He pulled the plate over and forked the slice onto his own plate.

"So, tell me," she said, "what brought you here? Unless my ears are playing tricks on me, your accent says you're not a local, either."

"Good ear. I grew up on the south side of Boston, then came south. Texas. I guess you can sort of call that the South. Did my undergrad in Austin at UT."

"Neither place exactly Small Town, USA. So, to toss it back your way, what brought you to the sticks, as you put it?"

"These particular sticks have what I'm after." Nick suddenly grabbed her by the hand and pulled her up from the table, leaning back in to retrieve her donated slice of cake on the run. "Come on. I'll show you."

He led her to a large, old shed out back of the house and opened the door. Sunlight filtered in dusty shafts between the boards, and once her eyes became accustomed to the dimness she could see the entire space was crowded with wooden crates and shelves laden with dirty pottery.

"Pots," he announced. "Mounds and mounds of beautiful pots and other artifacts. I'm an archeologist, working on my post doc at U of A. And these sticks have some of the finest examples of Native American burial mounds in the country. We're excavating a site now over nearer to Mt. Ida."

They wound their way between the shelves to a large workbench near the back, littered with tools, partial pots, shards, catalog papers, and grid charts.

"The Caddoan culture, right?" she said.

He gave her a quizzical look, "How do you…"

"My mother's father was a field anthropologist. Part of the team that began the original excavation of the Caddo mounds here, back in the late 40s. And my dad, too. Not here in the 40s, of course, but an anthropologist as well. Actually, a paleoanthropologist." she explained.

"Really."

"Mmm," she nodded. It was unlike her to open up like this to someone she hardly knew, but his friendly exuberance was contagious, and she went on. "My mother was actually born here. Well, not *here* exactly, but in a town called Hot Springs, not far from here; my grandparents lived there when my grandfather was working on the dig."

"Know it well. Nearest city to here. Or what passes for a city. And the most congenial spot to get a cold beer on the road between here and Little Rock. So, I guess that makes you almost a native."

"Only in my heart. Arkansan, once removed, I'd say. But I've never actually been here before."

"Where do your parents live now? Where's home?"

"Good question." She picked up a shard and studied it, not saying more for a moment. "My mom and dad were killed in an accident when I was thirteen."

"Oh, I'm sorry," he said. "I didn't mean - "

"It's okay. Long time ago. You go on."

"Any other family? Brothers, sisters? Grandparents? Somebody?"

"Nope. Just me." She focused her gaze on the shard in her hand.

"Damn. That's harsh," he said. "What did you do? Where did you live?"

"Well," she blew out a long breath, really unsure now if she wanted to go on. "You don't really want to hear all this."

"Sure, I do. We sensitive types love to talk over pound cake and pottery" he said as he popped the last bit of the slice into his mouth.

She took another deep breath in and blew it out. *In for a dime, in for a dollar*, she thought and went on. "I was sent to a Catholic girls' boarding school in upstate New York. So, during the schoolyear, I mostly just stayed there. Summers and holidays I spent with friends' families when I could. But no place ever really felt like home after my parents died." She laid the shard down and looked at him.

"So, tell me—and if it's none of my business, say so—how does a thirteen-year-old afford boarding school?"

"Ah. Yeah. Well, the insurance and settlement were put into a trust and that was enough to pay for school and basic expenses, even after the lawyers got their chunk. My legal guardian," she bracketed the words with air quotes, "managed everything. He was a distant cousin of my mother's, a lot older, a confirmed bachelor, and not especially thrilled about the prospect of having a teenage orphan he didn't really know dumped on his doorstep. Even he's gone now."

Inside the house, the telephone began to ring insistently. Nick cocked his head and listened. "Wonder why Miz Hendri's not getting that? Hold that thought; I'll be right back," he said as he ran to the house.

Left alone in the shed, Maggie picked up a magnifying glass to examine the incising on several other of the shards on the table, then a large effigy pot on the ground beside it caught her eye. It had tripod legs. Was it a bird form? She couldn't quite tell, so she bent to lift it up onto the table to get a better look and, as she did so, a small snake boiled out from under it. She screamed and backpedaled into the table, nearly dropping the pot, and scattering shards everywhere in her haste to crawl up onto the nearest crate. She had a deep, almost primal abhorrence of snakes. And worms, too. Really anything that wriggled and writhed without legs. It was blind panic that had no basis in degree of actual threat.

Nick reappeared at the door. "You OK?"

Maggie pointed a trembling finger at the departing reptile. "Sn..sn.. snake," she managed to stammer.

"Pffff," he blew out a laugh. "Come on down, city slicker. He's not gonna hurt you. He's just a little king snake. You stay out of his way; he'll stay out of yours." He extended his hand to help her climb down from her perch. "That was Therma Faye Cooper on the phone. She's the nurse over at the ... uh... well I guess now it's *your* clinic. She called hoping you'd made it in. Somebody just brought in a kid she says—and I quote here—is bleeding like a stuck hog. You ready to work?"

"Absolutely," she said, regaining some of her composure. "I'll go straight over there as soon as I figure out where there is."

"It'll be faster if I drive you. Come on."

CHAPTER 6
Of Clinical Significance

Therma Faye Cooper was a middle-aged woman with a body like an inverted pear, big chested with slender hips and legs. Dressed in shorts and a ragged Bon Jovi t-shirt, with a mass of bottle-blonde hair somewhat contained by a cotton bandana, she stood waiting for them at the open back door of the clinic as the truck raced into the lot. Maggie was out almost before Nick had pulled to a stop.

"Y'all's quick," Therma Faye remarked. Then seizing Maggie's hand, she pulled her through the door and along the hallway, chattering a continuous rapid-fire stream of information. "Come on in, Doc. My name's Therma Faye Cooper and I'm sure I don't look like it in this get up, but I'm your nurse. Wasn't expecting to see you today, so I apologize. I was in here cleaning and stocking and getting everything ready for you when Waylon Prescott come wheeling up with poor little Rose Ellen just gushing blood. He and I tried our best, but we couldn't get it to quit. So, I took a chance and called Miz Hendri's, just hoping."

Nick followed along in their wake, until Therma Faye pointed to the waiting room and without breaking cadence said, "Grab a chair out there if you want to take a load off, Nick. We got a copy of *Field and Stream* that's probably not much over five years old." Stopping outside a closed door, she took a deep breath at last. "Anyway, we're sure glad you're here."

Maggie put a calming hand on Therma Faye's arm. "Me, too. Let's see what we have."

A white enamel treatment cabinet filled one wall of the room. Glass sundry jars full of cotton balls, applicator sticks, and tongue depressors stood ready on its countertop. A young girl of maybe seven or eight sat stiffly on the exam table, holding a blood-soaked towel to her head, the blood matting the long honey brown hair that fell below it and dripping onto the sleeve and shoulder of her pink t-shirt. More bloody towels littered the table and waste can nearby. She startled when the door opened and looked anxiously toward her father. Waylon, unkempt and unshaven, leaned against the wall, working the brim of a baseball cap in his hands.

When he saw Maggie, he reached for Rose Ellen's hand and growled, "Hell, ain't a real doctor. Ain't nothin' but a little girl. Come on, Rosie."

Therma Faye put out a hand to stop him. "Aw, hush up, Waylon. You would insult the first doctor we've had here in five years. And her here to help your baby."

Ignoring him, Maggie approached the table and stood beside Rose Ellen, extending her hand, "Hi, Rose Ellen." And with an acknowledging glance in her father's direction, she added, "Mr. Prescott." Rose Ellen limply shook her hand. "I'm Dr. McKinley, and I'm going to take good care of you."

Waylon looked at her, then quickly away, muttering something unintelligible and settling himself back against the wall.

Rose Ellen kept her wide-eyed stare on Maggie, who continued, "Gosh what a mess we've got here. What in the world happened?"

Rose Ellen blinked, looked down at her hands in her lap, and said nothing.

"Rose Ellen," Maggie asked again, "what happened to your head?"

"She won't talk," Waylon muttered.

Maggie grabbed a penlight off the tray and shined it into each of Rose Ellen's eyes, asking "Has she been unconscious? Drowsy? Has she vomited?"

"Nope. Not as I know of," Waylon said.

"Then why can't she talk?"

"Didn't say can't. Said won't."

"OK, then, why won't she talk?" Maggie asked with some measure of frustration.

"Don't know. Hadn't since her mama left. And that all ain't none of your business. Just fix her up."

Maggie slipped on a pair of exam gloves. "Therma Faye, can you take this?" she said, taking the towel from the girl's hand, and passing it over. "And put some pressure on with a clean one? Rose Ellen," Maggie said, extending three fingers of both her hands, "can you squeeze my fingers really tightly?" The girl complied, squeezing both firmly. "Therma Faye, do you have a percussion hammer?"

"Yes'm," she said, stretching her free arm to retrieve the instrument from where it lay on the counter and handing it to Maggie, who tapped each of the girl's knees, eliciting a jump of each foot and a giggle from Rose Ellen. Maggie tapped each a couple of times more, just to amuse the girl.

"Can *you* tell me what happened, Mr. Prescott?" Maggie said as she continued the exam.

"Nope." He shook his head. "She was out playin' with some kids and just came into the house lookin' like that."

Turning back to Rose Ellen, Maggie said, "Would it be okay if I take a look?"

Rose Ellen shrugged and gave a slight nod. Maggie pulled the towel away and took a look at the wound. "Hmmm. Quite a little pumper there." She placed the towel back over it and gestured to Therma Faye to apply pressure again.

"Did you fall down and hit your head?"

Rose Ellen shook her head no.

"Did somebody hit you in the head with something?"

Rose Ellen bobbed her head once.

"A rock?"

The look of astonishment on Rose Ellen's face was almost comical, and she nodded her head several times, more animated than at any point so far. Then catching her father's glance, she closed up.

Maggie saw the exchange and went on, "You know the same thing happened to me once. A boy threw a rock and hit me in the head. It bled like crazy, just like yours. But when they looked at it, it was a teensy tiny little cut. Didn't take a minute to fix it. Therma Faye, do you think there's a little repair kit here with Rose Ellen's name on it?"

"Yes ma'am. I expect there is. What suture?"

"Do you have 5-0 Prolene?"

Therma Faye peered into the glass door of the cabinet. "Yep."

While Therma Faye began setting up a sterile field with the surgical tools Maggie would need for the repair, Maggie took Rose Ellen over to the sink and used the sprayer to rinse as much of the matted blood out of her long hair as possible, then inspecting the area more closely announced, "There it is. And it is a tiny little thing, but man do they bleed. Therma Faye, can you put some pressure right on this spot here with a gauze pad? And then we'll walk back over and let Rose Ellen lie down on the table. You keep the pressure on, OK?"

Tableside, Maggie swapped the exam gloves for sterile gloves and loaded a syringe with anesthetic from the vial Therma Faye held out to her. "OK, Rose Ellen, you're going to feel a little stick and a sting; that's just the medicine doing its thing. So, I want you to take a big breath in and hold it, and when I say blow it out, you blow it all out slow and steady, and we'll count down from 10. OK, big breath and blow." As Rose Ellen exhaled, Maggie counted down, at the same time quickly injecting the area around the cut with a xylocaine and epinephrine solution to numb the area and constrict the surrounding blood vessels. And moments later she deftly popped in a single suture to tie off the tiny artery in the scalp, the 'little pumper', through which all that blood had come.

Therma Faye dressed the site with triple antibiotic ointment and gathered the debris from the laceration repair into a bundle she shoved into the bio-waste can, and sanitized her hands with a pump out of the bottle of gel beside the sink. Then she plucked an exam glove out of the box, blowing it up like a balloon and tying it off. The puffed-out fingers and thumb of the glove looked like a chicken's beak and comb, and even Rose Ellen smiled.

She said to the girl, "Come on with me up to the front desk, honey, and we'll get us a marker and put a face on your chicken."

Waylon made to follow them out, but Maggie motioned for him to wait. He treated her to an angry glare then dropped his eyes to the floor, shuffling his feet and working the brim of his ball cap again. The smell of stale whiskey seeped from his pores, rolling off him like a fog.

"Mr. Prescott, that laceration is small, and it's going to be fine; keep it dry and clean until we take the stitches out in five or six days. Please let me know right away if it looks red or angry or if there's any drainage or smell."

"All right. No big deal," he muttered. "Just a li'l old cut, like you said." He again started to leave, but Maggie put out a hand to stop him.

"The cut itself is no big deal, but the blow to the head could be, and we don't know exactly what happened. You'll need to watch her closely for the next twenty-four hours for signs of drowsiness, nausea, dizziness, or vomiting. It's probably a good idea to wake her once or twice in the middle of the night tonight. Be sure she wakes up; have her squeeze both of your hands tightly like I did earlier," she demonstrated by holding out three fingers of each hand, a size the girl's small hands could manage to grip, "They should feel the same. Then, let her go back to sleep. And call me right away at the McSwain Boarding House if you're concerned. I'd give you my direct number, but my cell reception seems kind of spotty."

Waylon shrugged, put his cap on, and started for the door. Maggie stopped him yet again.

"And one more thing. About Rose Ellen's aphasia."

Waylon looked puzzled.

"Her inability to speak. I think that's something that needs to be looked into. It -"

He brusquely cut her off, "I told you she can talk; she just don't."

"Don't you think that's unusual? For a child her age to refuse to speak?"

"Lady, are you thick in the head? I told you she hadn't spoken since her mama ran off. You've done your job. Now butt out," he spat out as he stormed from the room.

Maggie stood with Therma Faye in the front office and watched through the waiting room window as Rose Ellen, chicken balloon in hand, climbed into the cab of the old pickup.

"Do you think he'll look after her? Wake her tonight, I mean?"

"I reckon he will," Therma Faye said turning to tackle a stack of cartons of clinic and office supplies still in need of opening. "I know he loves the little thing, and he looks after her pretty well by himself, when he's sober, anyway,"

"Yeah. He smelled like he'd had a few last night."

"Probably more than a few," Therma Faye said, slicing open the seal of another carton with a box cutter.

"Has she ever talked?"

"Oh, yeah. Talked up a storm when she was younger. Her mama'd bring her in to see Doc Pritchard when she was a baby, and she babbled non-stop. And then after Doc died, she'd bring her in when county health would send over a doc to do vaccinations and check-ups and such. Rosie would always sing us a little song for an extra sucker. Such a cute little thing."

"And she just stopped talking?"

"Yep. When Ruth left – that's her mama's name, Ruth – she just up and quit. Just like that. Waylon carried her up to the Children's Hospital in Little Rock, and they ran all kinds of tests on her, but they couldn't find a reason for it. Said just watch her. Bring her back if something changed."

"How long ago was that?"

"Oh, I don't know. Couple years now, I guess?"

"And her mother just left? Without a word to anybody?"

"Yeah. But, just between us girls, it wasn't all that surprising to some of us, really. Life with Waylon these last years could not have been easy. He and Old John Barleycorn been on a first name basis for a good while, if you get my meaning. He hasn't worked regular for a while, and the family was barely scraping by selling eggs and vegetables and such out of their truck patch. Ruth even took work at Molly's Café from time to time. I expect she just got too beat down by it all to keep on trying, saw a way out, and took it."

She opened a carton and inspected the contents – pens, legal pads, envelopes, copy paper – all front office supplies. She set it on the floor beside the front desk counter and selected another. "Jimmy – that's my other half – said he heard Waylon told the sheriff Ruth said goodnight to him and turned in. And I expect he finished a bottle and passed out. Anyway, he said when he woke up, she was gone. Her clothes and a suitcase, too. Just gone."

"But to leave her child?"

"Yeah, I know, that part was odd for sure. She seemed devoted to Rose Ellen. But you know what they say about not judging 'til you've walked a mile in somebody else's boots."

"Yeah, I get it. Hey, do you want me to stay and help you with all this?" Maggie said.

"No, ma'am. Donna's coming in tomorrow morning to get the office finished up, and I don't have too much more to do in the back. We got it."

"Who's Donna?" Maggie asked.

"Oh, right. I forget you don't know everybody around here. You will before long; there's not that many of us," she said with a chuckle. "Donna

Farmer. She's the girl, I should say young woman, I guess, but I've known her since she was a little girl; she's Jimmy's niece. Anyway, she's gonna handle the front office, the bookkeeping, insurance, billing, appointments, filing. All the secretarial stuff. She's trained for it, so don't worry there. Why don't you come by tomorrow and meet her? I'll have everything put away by then, and you and I can do a walk through, make sure we have everything you need."

"OK. That would be great. I'll do that," Maggie said.

Therma Faye opened the slider window to the waiting room. "Doc's done," she said. Nick sat, feet propped up on the coffee table, thumbing through an old magazine. "Criminently, Nick! Get your dirty work boots off the furniture! Did you not have any raisin' at all?"

"Not much, apparently," he said, giving her a sheepish grin and a wink and wiping at the dusty spot his boots had left on the coffee table. "But I'm willing to let you try to raise me, Miss T."

"You hush," she shook her head in mock disapproval, "and y'all get on out of here."

CHAPTER 7
Touchstone

Nick drove Maggie back to the boarding house, and they walked into the kitchen to find Miz Hendri busy at the counter, cleaning vegetables for tonight's meal.

"Ach, you're back," she greeted them, wiping her hands on her kitchen apron. "I didn't know what happened to you two."

"Had a little emergency up at the clinic," Nick said. "Therma Faye called, and I drove the good doctor up there."

"Is it all OK?" Miz Hendri asked.

"Yes. Everything's fine. Just a little girl with a cut," Maggie said.

"Oh, that's good," she said, "Good, I mean, that things are fine." She chuckled, a little flustered, and wiped her hands more thoroughly on a kitchen towel. "Let me take you up to your room and get you settled in."

Maggie followed as Miz Hendri led the way up to the room on the second floor that would be home for the next two years. She noticed that the old woman hobbled somewhat painfully up the stairs, stopping now and again.

"Can I help you?" Maggie said, coming up beside her to lend some support.

"No, no. Just some rheumatism in my hip. It pains more with the weather change. Rain is coming soon, I think," she pronounced.

"Are you taking any medication for it?"

"Couple little orange tablets when I need it, but they hurt my stomach," she said. "Every month or two I ask Mr. Purifoy to drive me over to Hot Springs to take the hot waters there, and that helps more."

"Hot waters?"

"Natural hot mineral springs," she said, resuming her upward hobbling. "Very famous. People come from all over the world to take the waters."

"Really? I had no idea," Maggie said.

"You should make a trip over sometime and try it. Very relaxing. Very healing."

"I'd like that," Maggie said.

At the door, Miz Hendri turned the lock, opened the door, and stepped back. "After you, Missus" she said, handing Maggie the key.

Late afternoon sun spilled in through a pair of mullioned windows, filling the large room with a pleasing light. Her two suitcases were standing beside the bed, just as promised. But she still had many trips-worth of other boxes of her things out in the car that she'd need to bring up, and she was determined she wasn't going to bother Mr. Purifoy to help her. She could use a good workout after three days cramped in the car on the road.

"You should have everything you need but if not, you will please let me know," Miz Hendri said. "Fresh towels and linens once a week, on Thursdays, when Mabel comes to clean. Usually, in the mornings, there is some sweet bread in the kitchen and always coffee if you want. Supper is at 6:30 downstairs in the dining room each weeknight. Sunday dinner is at 1 o'clock, unless Pastor Buchanan runs on too long. Saturdays I take off, and you are on your own then. No cooking in your room," she said, holding up an admonishing finger, "but use the kitchen if you like. I want you should feel at home."

"Thank you," Maggie smiled. "You've made me feel very welcome already."

"You rest a little now. Maybe enjoy a nice soak in the tub. We will see you at 6:30," she said, and hobbled out, drawing the door closed.

The room was cozy and inviting, with soft lilac and cream striped wallpaper. A quilted duvet cover in a floral chintz that picked up those colors and added several more to the mix lay atop the roomy four-poster bed, along with a pair of fluffy pillows in striped shams echoing the paper. Maggie squeezed one of them. *Not too bad,* she thought. She didn't consider herself at all snobbish in almost any regard, but she was an unapologetic pillow snob. She'd brought her beloved pair of down pillows with her, one in each suitcase.

A patterned rug in tones of ivory, sage, and dark blues covered most of the hardwood floor and even slipped under the front legs of the heavily carved, antique dresser and mirror that took up most of the wall opposite the bed. Tucked into the corner to its right was a comfortable-looking rocker with a small side table and a gooseneck floor lamp for reading. A small four-drawer chest and a writing desk flanked the bed serving as side tables, but with welcome added utility.

In the adjoining bathroom, she was delighted to find both a nice shower and a claw-foot tub, deep enough for some serious soaking, with a tray across it, holding a bud vase with a fresh gardenia blossom, a candle, and a clear lidded dish of bath salts. Maggie lifted the lid and held a pinch of the salts to her nose, breathing in the scent, picking up lavender and something else she couldn't quite identify. *Bergamot, maybe? Nice.* She decided she'd definitely follow Miz Hendri's advice for a soak before dinner, but first she wanted to get the car unpacked.

It took her at least ten trips up and down the stairs to finally get the car emptied of everything except her weight set, and, frankly, she felt like she'd done a full CrossFit workout by the time she dropped the last of the boxes in her room. She'd deal with the weights tomorrow. Unlike in the City, she was pretty sure they'd be safe in her car out back.

She hefted the suitcases up onto the bed and opened them, tossing the two pillows to the head. Then she removed several bubble-wrapped photo frames she'd slipped between the pillows and her clothing for protection. Unwrapping the first, she smiled at a photo of her and her parents at Christmas when she was about three: the tree, their stockings by the fireplace, the piles of crumpled wrapping paper discarded on the floor. Her on her father's shoulders, her mother beside them, a protective hand clutching Maggie's leg. It always made her happy to see them all together that way.

And in the second, a family photo taken in Paris, the twin spires of Notre Dame rose majestically behind them, the copper saints marching stately down its roofline. In the foreground the three of them hugged and grinned for the camera. She'd been ten that summer, and they were there because her father had been hired for a summer lecture series in anthropology at the American University.

It had been a magical couple of months of day trips on the train to Giverny and Versailles, Saturday picnics in the Tuileries, the occasional luxury of hot chocolate at Angelina, even a visit to the caves at Lascaux to view the prehistoric cave art, courtesy of his academic position. And lots of time spent in the Louvre, admiring the amazing collection there. She had to admit that some of it had bored her, but even at ten, she could appreciate the awesome coolness of standing in front of the Mona Lisa. Some of her favorite memories of her parents were from that summer. She set these two photos on the chest beside her bed, where she could see them every morning.

The next was a silver-framed photo of her parents, taken at their wedding. She loved this photo of them; they looked so young and sweet and hopeful. And so clearly in love. She smiled, kissed her fingertips, and touched the image before putting it on the dresser and opening the next bubble packet, a small antique double oval frame holding a pair of black and white studio portraits of her mother and her father. She couldn't recall, now, why they'd had them taken. Speaker's photos, maybe, for conference brochures. She put this one on the dresser as well and took the necklace from around her neck and draped it over the frame. It was a slender, perfect quartz needle, wrapped in silver wire at its blunt end, and suspended from a silver chain. It was an Arkansas crystal her grandfather had found.

So perfect and clear, he'd had it made into a necklace for her grandmother. It had then been her mother's, and in the years since her mother's death Maggie was rarely without it.

She had just unwrapped the last bubble packet in that case when there was a rap on her door.

"Come in," she called out.

The door opened, and Nick stuck his head in. "Need any help?"

"Your timing is flawless," she laughed, waving a hand at the array of boxes already in her room. "I'm just getting things put away." She went to the desk and put the photo down beside her laptop. It was a candid shot of Jeff, shirtless, shorts riding low on his slender hips, their sun-bleached fabric contrasting with his deeply tanned, muscular belly. He stood on the deck of a racing yacht, leaning against the railing, his hair ruffled by the wind, beer bottle in hand, laughing in that boyish way that melted her.

Nick came over and picked up the frame. "Brother or love interest?"

"No brothers, remember?"

"Ah, right. Cousin, then?" he said.

"Not a cousin," she replied, pointedly taking the frame from his hand and setting it back in place.

"Oh," he said, exhaling the word. "He back in the big city?"

"Yeah. He is," she said and felt an unmistakable twinge of wistfulness that surprised her.

Her cell phone rang, and it startled them both. It was the first time a call had actually gotten through, since she'd arrived in Caddo Bend. She pulled the phone from the pocket of her hoodie and saw JEFF on the display.

"I've got to take this," she said.

"Sure. I'll leave you to it. See you at dinner."

"Hello, man-of-my-thoughts!" she said, happily.

"I like hearing that," Jeff said. "But you were supposed to call me when you got there." He sounded a little irked. "I've been calling non-stop and getting nowhere."

"I'm sorry. The cell service here completely sucks, not to put too fine a point on it. I can't believe you got through at all! But I'm so glad you did. Let me give you the number here at the house, so you can get me that way if you need to. She picked up the information card on the desk and read out the number, "870-555-6363."

"Got it," he said. "I was just worried when I didn't hear from you. I was about to hop a flight."

She smiled, half wishing he had done it and feeling more than a little homesick. "I'm fine," she said. "In fact, I already saw my first patient. A little girl with a scalp puncture laceration I had to repair. I had, literally," she stopped midsentence and laughed. "I loathe misuse of that word as you know, but in this case, it's accurate. I had *literally* just gotten to the boarding house when the nurse from the clinic called to see if I was here yet. They aren't even quite ready for business, but the patient was bleeding like you know a scalp wound will do. There was blood everywhere by the time Nick and I got there."

"Who's Nick?"

"Oh, he's a post-doc who boards here with Mrs. McSwain. He was nice enough to drive me up there, since I didn't have a clue about where to go."

"How kind of," he began, but she cut him off with a change of subject.

"So, how's your day been?"

"I'm still at the hospital, waiting for some labs on a patient we operated on late last night. Might have to open him back up," he replied.

"What was it?"

"Abdominal gunshot. Convenience store robbery."

"Clerk or perp?" she asked.

"Perp. A card-carrying member of the Uptown Knife and Gun Club," he said, using the ER slang for a repeatedly-offending, violent hoodlum. "Not his first time, I think, but could be his last." His pager blared. "OK, that's my cue. I've got to run, but I'll call you tomorrow, OK? Or you call me."

"Love you; miss you," she said.

"Me you, too. Bye." And he was gone.

The room seemed suddenly lonelier. She sat down at the desk and picked up Jeff's photo, but that disarming smile looking back at her now just increased her sense of separation. And unpacked boxes beckoned. But so did that clawfoot tub. *No contest.*

She went to the bath, lit the candle, scooped some salts into the tub, and turned on the water. She let the tub fill while she emptied her two suitcases of the folded clothes, arranging them neatly in the scented-paper-lined drawers of the big dresser and extracting the hanging clothes she'd carefully folded in with their hangers, so transferring them directly to the closet rod would be easy.

She located the box containing her Bose tabletop speaker — the bottom one under two others in a stack, of course, but what's a few more lifts? — and pulled it out. Jeff had given it to her for her last birthday. Cutting-edge audio technology, with a sound nothing short of fabulous for something so compact, but with a price tag that took her breath; she'd never have bought it for herself. Right now, though, she was glad to have it. Looking around, she found an open outlet beneath the desk and plugged the unit in.

Connecting her phone, she opened her playlist, and selected *Tom Waits Greatest Hits.* His melancholy vibe fit her current mood, and his guitar and raspy vocals soon filled the room. She slipped out of her clothes and into the steaming, scented water, letting it soothe both her aching muscles and her lonely psyche. All she was missing was the glass of good whiskey that she felt listening to Tom Waits' music demanded. She'd have to figure out where to pick up a small bottle of Jameson to keep on hand for moods like this.

Closing her eyes, she sank up to her chin in the fragrant hot water and thought of those last delicious nights with Jeff, the feel of his lips on her bare skin, of him inside her, filling her up, satisfying her urgent hunger, of lying spent and happy in his arms and then waking to begin all over again. *It's going to be a long two years.*

CHAPTER 8
Steel Magnolia

Maggie slept in the next morning, something she had rarely done since college and, she had to admit, it felt pretty good. She'd turned off the small window air conditioner and opened the other window last night to let in the cool evening breeze and, though the morning air still held some of that coolness, it already hinted at a warm day in the making. If she was going to get her work out gear set up, she'd better be about it before the day grew too toasty. She climbed out of bed, shut the window, and turned the a/c on low to keep the room from getting too warm and to dehumidify the air.

As she did almost every morning, she treated herself to a few minutes of yoga. Standing relaxed but ramrod straight, prayer hands at her heart, she took a deep inhale and, reaching high overhead, she began a flow starting from Mountain for a slow 20 count. Then dropping her folded hands again to her heart, she placed one foot against the inner thigh of her other leg and balanced assuming Tree for 20, then stretching one arm up and over her head, she leaned in that direction and held Falling Tree for 20 and came back to Mountain with eyes closed and hands at heart. Then a shift to Tree and Falling Tree on the other side, and again back to Mountain, with hands folded at her heart. With each return, she re-set her intention – today, Acceptance of Change – and cleared her mind.

She bent at the waist into Forward Fold, nose to knees, chest touching her thighs, then wrapped her arms behind her knees and pulled herself even closer, relaxing deeper with each inhale and exhale and enjoying the stretch of her calves and hamstrings and low back; she let her arms hang loose and laid her palms flat on the floor. After she'd comfortably settled into that pose, she walked her hands out to hold Downward-facing Dog, then dropped her hips to hold High Plank for a full minute or so.

Finally, she lowered her body flat to the floor and pushed her torso upward, straightening her arms and arching her neck and back into Cobra, feeling with each inhale and exhale her travel-stiffened vertebrae loosening. Then she pushed back up to Plank, and with a graceful hop, brought both feet forward to meet her hands and stood again, prayer hands at her heart, silently returning to today's intention. The short series didn't take long, but it was enough to work out the kinks and get the day going smoothly. And just enough to calm and clear her mind. That calming she thought was maybe the most important part of her daily morning ritual. That and coffee.

She slipped into some comfortable shorts, a t-shirt, and cross-trainers, brushed her teeth, pulled her long blonde hair up into a twist she secured with a claw clip, and splashed a little cold water on her face. Then she made her way down to the kitchen to grab a cup of that other most important way to start the day. She'd just poured her coffee when she heard someone clomping down the stairs.

"Can't believe you beat me down," Nick said, grabbing a mug and pouring his own cup.

"Are you kidding? I slept in by my usual standard," she laughed. "Besides, I'm still on Eastern time, so my internal clock thinks the day's half gone."

"What's on your agenda today?" he said with his head and shoulders in the refrigerator. He came out with two hardboiled eggs and a couple of plastic-wrapped sandwiches that he put into a small, insulated lunch pack, along with a banana and an apple. He wrapped up another slice of Miz Hendri's pound cake in plastic and tucked it in the sack.

Maggie blew across her coffee and took a sip. "I'm meeting Therma Faye at the clinic later this afternoon to walk through and inventory everything. But this morning I was planning to get my work out gear and rig set up somewhere out back. Miz Hendri said there might be room in the garage where Mr. Purifoy keeps the car. Wherever that is."

"Where is it all now?"

"The rig? Still in my car."

"I've got a few minutes before I need to head over to the site. Want some help?

"Yeah, if you're sure you have time. It would be fantastic if you could just help me unload it all over by the garage," she paused and smiled. "And show me where the garage is."

"I live to serve," he said, with a touch to his forehead. He zipped his lunch pack and put it into his field pack hanging by the door. "Let's do it."

As they walked out the kitchen door, Nick, helpful as ever, pointed out that there were only two buildings in the back lot – his pot shed and the one that was not his shed. So, by process of elimination, Maggie backed her SUV up onto the concrete pad in front of the 'not his shed' structure, and Nick raised the garage door.

"Come on back," he motioned with his hands, "little farther, little farther. Stop!" he held out his palms. Opening the hatch, he whistled at the sight of brightly colored weight plates covering the floor of the cargo space. "How much weight is this?"

"Three hundred sixty-two pounds, counting the bar," she said, climbing into the cargo area and squatting to move the pair of big red weights, marked 55#, closer to the hatch opening, followed by the green 45# pair, the yellow 25# pair, and the black pairs marked 10# and 15#. Last she put the little blue 5# weights, green 2.5# weights, and the tiny red 1# weights on top of the others.

"OK. I'll get these," Nick said, picking up the little weights and making a show of struggling to lift them.

Maggie hopped down and went to look inside the garage. *Plenty of room.* An old Jeep Cherokee took up one side of the double wide space. Its burgundy exterior sparkled as if it were nearly new instead of more than twenty years old, not a scratch or speck of dirt anywhere on it. And along the back wall she saw an orderly workbench with every imaginable tool, neatly hung on a peg board behind it or stowed on shelves overhead. Garden tools hung on wall-mounted storage racks beside the bench. Like the car, the hoes, rakes, picks, brooms, and shovels were so clean they could be new. The area looked like a staged shot from an old Smith and Hawken catalog.

She'd find Mr. Purifoy and ask if he would let her borrow whatever tools she might need for the set up. She knew there was a screwdriver, wrench, and pliers in the car roadside kit, but nothing much beyond that. Whatever was required, she was pretty sure it was there on Mr. Purifoy's orderly bench.

The side wall opposite where the car was parked would be a perfect spot to set up her rack rig and CrossFit gear. The rack didn't have too big a footprint; she'd still have plenty of room to work out and not really be in anyone's way.

She and Nick made quick work of moving the weights into the garage.

"Damn. You lift all this intentionally?" he said as he lugged one of the two 55 pounders in.

"Not all at once," she laughed. "At least not yet. I'm not much more than half that even on my deadlift heavy days." She squatted and lowered the two green plates to the floor of the garage with the others.

Nick intently watched her behind from behind, and she heard him softly exhale "Yeowza." She popped up and turned back around with a questioning look, but he simply gave her a charmingly innocent smile and went to get the last of the weights.

Then they each took an end and moved the heavy telescoping rigging uprights, cross pieces, and brackets into the garage. Finally, all that was left was the smaller pieces of equipment and the box of washers, nuts, and bolts she'd need to assemble it all. Nick looked at his watch.

"I can get the rest of it if you need to go," she said.

"You sure?" he said. "It's just that today I have to meet some of the team from the U that are coming down on a site visit. I'll just about have time to make it if I leave now."

"Go. Go. I've got it," she assured him. "And thanks for the help."

Once everything was in the garage, she went in search of Mr. Purifoy. She heard his musical whistling before she found him trimming the gardenia bushes that grew beside the front porch. She couldn't place the tune exactly, but it was beautiful and complex and the performance seemingly effortless. Like a haunting soundtrack to the tableau that greeted her when she rounded the corner of the house: morning sun drenching the front garden in a glorious light that made the bright white of the gardenia blossoms stand out in stark contrast against the shiny deep green leaves and the softer purple hues of the bigger hydrangeas that grew behind them.

With hand clippers, he was lovingly snipping off the faded blooms and gently shaping the branches to his liking. He was a slight, elderly man, wearing neatly pressed khaki pants and long-sleeved khaki work shirt, likewise crisply pressed and buttoned all the way to the neck, and a wide-brimmed straw hat to keep the sun off. He didn't seem to hear her come up.

"Excuse me," she said, tapping his shoulder. "Mr. Purifoy?"

He turned, and when he saw her, he removed the straw hat, revealing a shock of thick white hair that swept back in waves from his forehead. "Yes, ma'am," he said.

She extended her hand to him. "Hi. I'm Maggie McKinley."

"Yes, ma'am," he replied again, nodding and taking just the fingers of her proffered hand and giving them a gentle, almost courtly squeeze. "Our new doctor. What can I do for you?"

"I don't mean to interrupt your work," she said. "I'm hoping I can borrow some of your tools and maybe just a few minutes of your time to help me assemble a weight-lifting rig I brought with me. Miz Hendri said I could set it up in the garage."

He nodded and smiled, and when he did it crinkled the weathered skin at the corners of his warm brown eyes. "Be my pleasure," he said. "These gardenias aren't going anywhere." He replaced his hat and gestured with his hand. "After you, ma'am."

It took Maggie and Mr. Purifoy—who, she learned, did have a first name, which was Emmanuel—less than an hour to assemble and securely mount the collapsible rig rack she'd bought used and brought from New York. It was a bit of an extravagance, but she didn't have any confidence she'd find a CrossFit box, as their gyms were called, in a town as small as Caddo Bend. And she wanted to keep on with her training.

Once they'd gotten the rack up, he insisted on helping her assemble a weight stand and install the equipment hanger and bench rack so she could keep it up and out of the way when not in use. And to be honest, she was very happy for the help.

They'd chatted amiably while they worked; he was charming and easy to like. In addition to his first name—which she couldn't imagine ever calling him by; he was old enough to be her grandfather—she learned that he'd known Miz Hendri and her late husband, Robert, for 50 years. He'd met Robert in Germany, when they were both stationed there in the Army, and they'd become lifelong friends. When he'd found himself at loose ends after he left the service, Robert had invited him to come to Caddo Bend and live the quiet, country life. He had taken him up on the offer and never left.

He'd married a local girl, June Dillon, settled down on 40-acres of rolling pasture and woods not too far from town, and become a farmer. He and June had raised two daughters there. He told Maggie the girls' lives had taken them far from Caddo Bend, first for college, then marriages that had sent one to Atlanta and the other to the Texas hill country. And that when June had died, about 10 years ago, he'd been left to tend the farm alone; neither the girls nor their husbands had any interest in farming in Caddo Bend.

Years before that, when Robert had died, Mr. Purifoy had taken over the gardening and handyman jobs at the boarding house for Hendri, trying to manage the care of both properties until that had become too much. About six years ago, he'd sold the farm and moved to a small house in town, a few blocks away.

"Do you miss farming," Maggie asked him.

He thought for a moment. "I miss the happiness of living there all those years with June and our girls," he said, then gave her a sidelong glance. "Can't say I miss early morning milking in the winter."

"Do you see your girls often?" She was enchanted that he called them 'his girls'. She guessed he was mid-to-late 70s at least, maybe older; it was hard to tell. He was a fit and well-preserved 70s for sure. His 'girls' must be at least 50 or close to it and probably had kids not too many years younger than she was. Possibly kids who had kids.

"Oh, yes," he said. "They come when they can; work keeps them busy. When the grandkids were younger, they loved to come stay a month or so with their Papa and Granny in the summers to swim in the Caddo and trap crawdads or look for arrow heads. Sometimes we'd take a pallet out on the grass in the evening, catch lightning bugs, find the Big Dipper, look for shooting stars."

"That sounds like heaven," she said, thinking about her own idyllic childhood before her parents' had died, and the lonelier one it had become afterward. She shook off the sad vibe that had inserted itself into the happy moment. "How many grandchildren do you have?"

"Five," he said. "Julia, our oldest daughter, the one in Atlanta, has a girl about to turn 21 and a boy; he's 17. Eliza has three: a son from her first marriage. He's almost 20 now, too. And two daughters, 15 and 13 with her second husband. They run a vineyard and winery in the Hill Country of Texas," he said with some pride.

"A nice big group when they all get together," she said.

"It's a tableful, that's for sure. When I still had the farm, the grand-kids liked to help me milk the cows. They'd pick fresh corn and gather eggs from the hen house and catch fish in the stock pond. Whatever they'd gather in, we'd cook up for our breakfast or supper. It's good for kids to see where food really comes from."

"I couldn't agree more," Maggie said, lifting the weight plates and or-ganizing them in pairs on the rack posts and hanging her jump rope, wrist straps, and weight belt on the racks. "Makes them appreciate it."

"Amen to that," he said.

"And speaking of appreciating," she said, extending her hand, "I really can't thank you enough for all your help."

"Happy to do it, Doctor," he said, taking her hand in his knobby, calloused one. "Nice to do something a little different for a change."

"Then can I ask you to do one other thing different?"

"What's that?"

"Would it be okay if you just call me Maggie? Doctor and ma'am seem so formal for friends."

"Yes, ma'am," he chuckled at his lapse, "Yes, *Maggie*. And you call me Manny."

"Oh, no. I don't think I can do that," she shook her head. "My moth-er would roll over."

"OK, then. You're not much older than my oldest grandkids. How about Papa."

"That I can do," she said with a smile.

After a quick shower, Maggie headed for the clinic for the last walk through before the doors officially opened on Monday morning. When she entered through the back door, she could hear someone singing along to music. "Got my toes in the water, ass in the sand, not a worry in the world, a cold beer in my hand…"

"Got one for me, too?" Maggie said as she walked into the breakroom.

There was a skinny, young woman in sneakers, very short shorts, and a Kenny Chesney Tour tank top dancing and singing in the middle of the room, her cell phone held out arm's length. *Home grown dance video,* Maggie thought. She turned with a look of horror on her face when she heard Maggie's voice and leaped over to the counter turn down the volume on a small CD player.

"It's OK," Maggie said. "I like it."

"Like what?"

"The music. Who is it?"

"Zac Brown Band," she said. "I'm sorry, ma'am, I didn't hear you come in." She stowed her cell phone in her purse and quickly gathered her long brown hair into the scrunchie she'd had on her wrist. "You must be Dr. McKinley."

Maggie extended her hand to her, "And you must be Donna."

"Yes, ma'am. Donna Farmer," she said limply shaking Maggie's hand. "Pleased to meet you."

"Very nice to meet you as well; I'm looking forward to working together. Where's Therma Faye? I was supposed to meet her here this afternoon."

"She's in the lab, or at least she was. Right down the hall." She pointed then added, "Ma'am." *At least she didn't curtsey.*

Therma Faye was coming out of one of the three small exam rooms she'd fully and neatly stocked with supplies when she saw Maggie and made an about face, so that she could run through it all with her. And everything seemed in order there.

Then she and Maggie went to the lab to ensure that they had if not everything she'd asked for at least everything she'd truly need to function come Monday morning.

On the lab counter, there was an old microscope, still in serviceable condition, a centrifuge for spinning blood and urine, and a small, automated machine for doing blood counts. On the far counter was an autoclave for sterilizing small surgical tools, also old, but again serviceable she was assured, and even a small incubator for growing bacterial cultures.

"Were you able to get the rapid tests I asked for? We're so far out of the way here, I think we'll be wise to have a few."

"Yes, ma'am. Some of them," Therma Faye opened the upper cabinet to show her. "We got the pregnancy and strep tests, here. But we're still waiting on the test kits for mono, flu, chlamydia, and drugs. Account rep said they should be here by Wednesday. Or maybe Thursday. We can also call for a pick-up from Lab Services once a day on weekday afternoons for whatever you need to send out. It's a 24-hour turn around. Usually."

The double-locked cabinet for injectables and controlled drugs, such as diazepam, Demerol, morphine, and naloxone, was also in the lab, and they carefully inventoried those vials and recorded them on the logbook with both sets of their initials and the date and relocked the cabinet.

In the treatment room, Maggie checked the oxygen cylinders—full and functional—and the supply of masks and tubing. There was a new sleek 12-channel EKG machine they'd just purchased – the old one, according to Therma Faye, had been about the size of a car engine and had suction cups and rubber straps and looked like it might have come over with the Pilgrims.

They went through the cabinets checking the supply of exam gloves, sterile gloves, suture material, casting material, splints, slings, rolls of gauze, sterile pads, tape of various types and widths, and needles, syringes, IV fluids, and injectable anesthetics. In covered stainless-steel disinfectant solution trays on the counter were plenty of clamps, forceps, and scissors to do pretty much whatever she'd need to do. Maggie was impressed—and pleased—that the clinic was so fully equipped.

Then Therma Faye came to the crash cart, with a portable defibrillator sitting on top and drawers filled with all the newly purchased drugs and equipment you might need if indeed someone 'crashed' on you. When they got to the bottom drawer, Therma Faye stopped.

"OK. You're gonna find this funny, I think, but they've been here for years." She opened the drawer and let Maggie look inside. There was a large packet, wrapped in a thick clear plastic sleeve. She turned her head sideways to read the label. M. A. S. T. it said in large bold black letters, under which the acronym was spelled out: Military Anti-Shock Trousers. And below that the fine print and line drawings describing how to apply them and activate them.

"Wow," Maggie exclaimed. "I don't think I've seen a pair of those in a crash cart ever. They used to be standard, but not in years. And I sure didn't expect to find them here. Why do we have them?"

"Old Doc Pritchard, rest his soul. He bought them years ago. I mean years; he's been gone now over 5 years, so it was a lot longer ago than that," she explained. "He told us 'Girls, I'd rather have em and never need em than need em and not have em.'" She chuckled at the memory. "We figured they'd never been needed before, so maybe if we hung on to them, that'd be like insurance."

"Who am I to argue with logic like that?" Maggie said. "They stay."

CHAPTER 9
Splintered Loyalties

The first weeks in Caddo Bend had seemed to fly by, and Maggie couldn't believe it was Labor Day already. In the intervening month or so since she'd arrived, she'd settled easily into the slower-paced rhythm of life in a small rural town and developed a pleasant work routine, seeing more and more patients, getting to know them in a way she'd never been able to in the frantic urban pace of New York. Today the clinic was officially closed, but Maggie had decided to come in and take advantage of the peace and quiet to get caught up on charts and correspondence.

She'd awakened early this morning to get her workout out of the way before the day heated up. Today's CrossFit workout of the day—the WOD as it was called among the CrossFit devoted—was 3 rounds of 15 chest-to-bar pull ups, 20 burpees, and 15 sumo deadlift high pulls. There would be sweating involved. And here in Caddo Bend, even though the angle of the light had subtly changed signaling that autumn was on the way, the days were still pretty warm. By now, she thought a little wistfully, it would already be getting chilly in New York, and the thought made her nostalgic for her uptown box and the camaraderie of her box family. By 7:15 she'd finished her solitary WOD, showered and changed, and was at the clinic.

She'd just sat down at her desk with a cup of coffee when she heard someone knocking loudly on the front door. When she got up and went to answer it, through the translucent side panes flanking the door, she could see the blurry outline of a man. He knocked again, and she opened the door.

"JD!" He was dressed in jeans and a pale gray t-shirt that clung, she couldn't help noticing, to a very nicely sculpted torso and arms.

"Hey, Doc," he said. "I saw your car in back. Hope it's OK to disturb you this early."

"Of course," Maggie said stepping back from the door. "Come in. It's just me here today – it's Labor Day – but I'm here to help if you need me. What's going on?"

"I rammed a piece of wood up under my fingernail this morning, and I can't get hold of it to get it out."

"Ouch! Come on back, and let me look at it," she said heading to the treatment room. He followed her back. "Have a seat," she said pointing to the exam table.

JD climbed up onto the table, and Maggie pulled the bright overhead exam light down and focused it on his hand. A large splinter of wood was buried under the nail of his right ring finger from tip all the way to the cuticle.

"How'd you manage this?"

"Stupidity," he said with a smirk. "I was cutting up some deadwood for the fireplace with a chain saw this morning, and I tossed a log up onto the stack and it rolled off. I reached out to grab it and didn't quite get it, just raked it with my hand and wound up with this crammed under my nail. Shoulda worn gloves."

She laid a fresh disposable exam towel on the ring stand beside the table and removed a mosquito clamp and a pair of bayonet forceps and splinter forceps from the solution tray and laid them on the towel. Donning a pair of exam gloves, she took his injured hand in hers, noticing again its appealing combination of strength and artistic gracefulness, and focused the bright exam light on it to examine the nail.

"Do you play piano?" she asked.

He laughed out loud. "No. My mama made me take lessons when I was in grade school, but it didn't really stick. Why?"

"Just curious," she said.

Gingerly grasping the end of the splinter with the jaws of the mosquito, Maggie gave a gentle tug and wiggle, eliciting a grimace and sharp intake of breath from JD, but getting nowhere with the splinter. It was stuck fast and was going to take some elbow grease to get out. And local anesthesia.

"OK," she said looking up and meeting his eyes. I'm going to need to do a digital block on your finger." At his questioning look she clarified, "Put your finger to sleep so I can get the splinter out without pain."

"You won't get any argument from me on that," JD said.

"Are you allergic to any medications, numbing agents in particular."

"No, nothing I know of. Except pain," he added with a smile.

Maggie gathered the supplies she'd need, then sat down on the rolling stool in front of him. She donned a fresh pair of gloves and painted both sides of his injured finger with a cotton ball soaked in brown liquid, leaving his finger quite orange.

"That's attractive," he said, looking at his discolored finger.

"And germ free," she smiled up at him. "It'll wear off in a few days." Her movements were deft and efficient as she swabbed the rubber stopper of the anesthetic vial with an alcohol pad, opened a sterile needle and syringe, and drew up the anesthetic. Then she unwrapped another, smaller bore needle, and swapped the needles out.

"Why'd you do that?" he asked.

"30-gauge needle," she held up the tiny needle and the larger one for comparison. "Smaller needle equals less pain, obviously. But I'd do it anyway because the tip gets dulled going through the rubber stopper. Puts a little drag on it."

"Well, it hurts enough as it is," he said. "So, thanks!"

"OK. Little sting now," she said, injecting the solution into each side of his ring finger, about half-way down where the sensory nerves ran from base to tip. Once the nerve block developed the whole finger from there out would be dead to pain for a while. She looked up when she'd finished and found him quietly staring at her, struck again by the intelligence and depth in his grey eyes. *They say the eyes are the windows of the soul. If that's so*, she thought, *there's one wise, old soul in there.* "We'll need to give it a few minutes to work," she said, looking away from his gaze and releasing his hand. "Can I get you a cup of coffee or tea while we're waiting?"

"I'm not sure I've ever had a doctor ask me that," he chuckled. "But yeah, I'd like that. Tea, please."

"I'm not sure what's back there. If there's a choice?"

"Green if you've got it. Black if not."

"Cream, sugar? Lemon?"

"No, just strong."

She returned with his tea and fresh coffee in her own cup and a clipboard under her arm. She handed him his tea and sat again on the stool, putting her cup and the clipboard down beside him on the exam table. Picking up the needle she'd swapped out, she uncapped it and tested the numbness with delicate pinpricks along his finger. "Can you feel this?"

"Nope."

"How about here or here?" He flinched involuntarily on the last prick answering her question without need of words.

"Almost there," she announced.

He took a sip of the tea. "Mmm."

"Green something-or-other. It was a sampler box," she added with a shrug.

"It's perfect. Thanks," he said.

"So, while we have a minute, tell me a little about you." He raised his eyebrows in question. "For the chart, I mean," she clarified. "Full name, birthdate?"

"John David Langston, February 27, 1974." She did the quick math. *Thirty-eight.*

She filled the information in on the patient encounter form on the clipboard and continued, "Allergies, you said none. Take any medications?"

"No."

"Marital status?"

"Single," he said smiling in the most boyish and charming way. "Yours?"

The question surprised her, and she hoped the warm blush she felt crawling up her neck wasn't visible. "Single," she said casually, then after a short pause, "ish."

"Single-*ish*? What's that mean?" he said with an easy laugh.

The blush crawled further up her cheeks, and she was sure it was visible now. She tried desperately to appear professional and unflustered. "I'm not engaged or married, but I do have a steady guy in New York."

"Long way off," he said.

"It is," she agreed.

"He have a name?"

"Yes," she said, a little taken aback and not elaborating further.

"Sorry. None of my business," he said after a moment.

"Jeff," she said after a long pause. "His name is Jeff."

"I didn't mean to pry," he said, then giving her a wink added, "Jeff's a lucky guy." She didn't respond but looked up and held his gaze. After a silent moment he held up his hand and said, "I think this thing's numb."

Maggie picked up the needle again and pricked all around the tip of the finger; JD gave her a negative shake of the head with each prick. "Yes, I believe it is," she said, satisfied pain wasn't in his immediate future. "Ready?"

"I am," he said, looking the other way and closing his eyes.

She worked the tips of the mosquito beneath the nail on either side of the splinter and secured the clamp tightly. Then rocking the splinter back and forth a little to loosen it, she gave a strong, steady pull until it slipped free. She examined the track to be sure no piece of the splinter had been left behind, then irrigated it with the remaining anesthetic solution.

"OK. It's out," she said, holding the offending shard up in the clamp. "Stick your finger in this antibacterial solution for a minute," she said indicating the bowl of brown liquid on the ring stand, "and we'll get it wrapped up."

JD submerged his finger in the brown liquid, as instructed.

"When was your last tetanus shot," she asked.

"Five years ago, I think. About that."

"You're good for about another five then."

Maggie took a roll of tube gauze and loaded it onto an applicator cage. She dried his orange finger with a fresh gauze pad and slipped the applicator over the finger, held the loose end of the gauze with one hand, and then pulling the cage off the finger and leaving the gauze around it, she made a twisting motion to secure it, then back over the finger and up, twisting on each turn, creating a neat tubular bandage around the entire length of his finger that she secured with a piece of silk tape at the base.

"There you go. Keep that dry for the next several days. Then come in and we'll take the dressing off and be sure it looks OK. If it hurts once the anesthetic wears off, take some Tylenol or ibuprofen if you need it. If that doesn't do it, call me."

"Thanks," he said, "for laboring on Labor Day. Tell Donna to send me the bill." He stood and they began to walk to the front door. "And sorry about the questions earlier. I didn't mean to make you uncomfortable, but I think I did."

"No, no. Don't worry about it. It's fine."

At the door, he turned and smiled. "But just so we're even, there's no 'ish' in mine. Just single." He slipped out the door and closed it behind him.

CHAPTER 10
Discoveries

By mid-October, the shimmering heat of summer had given way to the cooler crispness of early autumn. The trees were beginning to color and this morning had even seen a little rime of frost on the windshield. Maggie had to admit, as she scraped the frost away, that she was glad to have the plastic ice scraper that Jeff had insisted she put in the glove box, though she'd laughed about it at the time, sure she'd never need it down south. Mark my words, he'd said. And he'd been right.

Pulling into the large gravel lot behind the clinic, she parked next to a pickup loaded with pumpkins and hay bales. A group of older men, clad in flannel shirts and jackets, collars pulled up against the chilly morning air, stood talking and smoking beside the truck. As Maggie climbed out, the conversation instantly stopped. A deep, rattling, phlegmy cough doubled one of the men over.

"That doesn't sound good," Maggie said to him. "Why don't you come in and let me take a listen?"

He stared back at her and took a long drag on his cigarette. "I reckon I'll be all right," he responded. He cleared his throat and flipped the butt to the ground, grinding it out with the heel of his boot.

"Suit yourself. But we're here if you need us," she said, holding his stare until he looked away, then turning to the clinic door.

Inside the clinic, Therma Faye and Donna sat in the front office sipping coffee. Donna was multitasking with the coffee and the social media feed on her phone. A bell dinged, and Donna put down her phone and opened the glass slider to reveal a large woman on crutches standing at the counter. Behind her, a number of other women, some with fidgeting children, sat on the straight-backed chairs lining the waiting room walls. There were no men among them.

Donna took a clipboard from the woman and said, "Thanks, Mrs. Bentley. Have a seat. We'll get you back shortly. Doc's on her way."

"Doc's here," Maggie said from the doorway, and both women jumped.

"Oh, my gosh, Dr. Mac," Donna said. "You snuck up on us! I almost spilled my coffee."

"Full house?"

"Only five or six waiting to see you," Therma Faye answered. "The rest's transportation and support."

"Ah, that must also explain the gaggle of gents in the non-designated 'smoking area' out back."

Maggie scanned the waiting room as Therma Faye handed her the first of the patient charts, Lyla Green, a young OB patient, now just about seven months along. Maggie flipped through it, then motioned to Donna to close the slider and said quietly, "Is there a sign I don't know about out front that says: 'Women and Children Only'?

Therma Faye and Donna exchanged a glance. "Dr. Mac, they'll come around. It's just been a few weeks," Therma Faye said.

"It's been a few months," Maggie corrected her.

"New things scare some folks," Therma Faye said. "Give 'em a little time."

"I don't know," Donna added, "my daddy said-"

Therma Faye cut off her remark with pursed lips and a bug-eyed glower. "Mrs. Bentley's back about her foot," she said.

"Yeah, I saw her. Has her orthotic come in?"

"Yes'm," Donna piped in a bit too cheerfully. "Velma called and said we had a package over at the post office. I think that's probably it. I'll run over and get it."

"No, I've still got my coat on. I'll run over," Maggie said. "You guys get everybody loaded up and ready for me. Get a urine and blood sugar on Lyla. And a real weight, please. I know she tries to resist climbing on the scale, but don't let her just tell you a number."

"OK." Therma Faye called after her, "Oh, and Dr. Jeff called from New York. Said to have you call him when you got in."

The post office, if it could be called that, was tucked into the back corner of Medlock's General Store behind shelves and tables of dry goods – work pants, jeans, shirts, linens, toys, assorted articles for the household – and hardware and tools of every sort. There was even a large section of non-perishable canned and packaged foods, toiletries and cleaning supplies, and a couple of large refrigerator cabinets for milk, juice, eggs, bacon, and other perishable staples. General was a very good way to describe it.

At a glass-fronted display counter in the middle of the store, the proprietor, Eldon Medlock, a tall, lanky man in overalls, rang up a sale on an old-fashioned cash register. "JD, if your truck's out front, I'll get Scooter to load this sphagnum moss in the back for you."

"Thanks, Eldon. Appreciate that." JD turned to leave just as Maggie came through the door, and he acknowledged her with a nod and a smile.

Maggie made her way to the postal counter in the back, where Velma Bradford, who ran the tiny post office, was busily sorting mail into cubbies behind the clerk's window. She was a small, spritely woman with a mass of salt and pepper hair pulled into a long ponytail that flowed down her back. Stretching in vain on tiptoe to reach the top row, she hooked a small step stool with one foot and pulled it closer, then gingerly stepped up on it, popped the mail in her hand into a slot, and hopped down.

"Hi, Doc," Velma greeted her without ever turning around. *How did she know I was here?* The woman had some kind of sixth sense that Maggie found both a little creepy and totally fascinating.

"Bet you come for that package from Little Rock."

"Sure did."

"It's in the backroom. Let me run get it," Velma said, turning to go, but stopping short as she spotted JD headed for the door. She picked up a small package, waving it over her head. "JD! Don't you get outta here yet. Here's those little pruner things you ordered."

JD walked back to the counter where Velma handed him the package and his mail. He turned the package, unmarked except for the address, over in his hands. "Velma, tell me one more time how it is you always happen to know what's inside my packages."

"That's a postmistresses' secret," she smiled slyly.

JD shook his head, chuckling softly, and as he turned to leave, the mail slipped from his grasp and fluttered to the floor at Maggie's feet. He and Maggie both stooped to retrieve it. As Maggie picked up one of the envelopes, the return address caught her eye:

Harvard University Alumni Association, Cambridge, MA. And addressed to John David Langston, PhD, General Delivery, Caddo Bend, AR.

Maggie handed the letter to JD with a quizzical look; he took it from her and smiled but said nothing.

"How's the finger?" she asked.

He held it up. "Still attached. Thanks again," he added. Then, with a touch to the brim of his ball cap, he turned and left. At the door, he narrowly missed colliding with Rose Ellen, who slipped through the doorway as he exited and scampered back to the postal counter.

"Pruners?" Maggie said to Velma when she returned. "He doesn't strike me as the gardening type."

"Oh, honey," she said, looking over her half-lens readers, "it ain't actual gardenin' really. He does those teeny tiny trees. You know the ones... oh, I can't think what they're called, but they're just like a regular tree, with roots and leaves and all, only they're little bitty," Velma explained, indicating a height of about a foot and a half between her two hands.

"Bonsai?" Maggie offered.

"Yeah, that's it. Bonsai." It came out more like bown-sah in her drawl.

"JD does bonsai?"

"Uh huh. I guess he picked it up in Japan. You know he lived there for a good while with his work."

"And he's a doctor?"

"Oh, no, honey," she said, clutching Maggie's forearm. "Not a real doctor like you that takes care of sick people. I believe his mama — rest her soul, Kathleen was such a sweet woman — I believe she said he was a physics doctor."

"A PhD in physics? From Harvard?"

"Yeah, I think that's it. Anyway, between the service and school and work, he stayed gone most of twenty years, except a visit two or three times a year. When his mama took sick, he came back to be with her. She passed a year or two ago, and we all thought he'd leave, but he's stayed on."

Beside Maggie, Rose Ellen stood on tip toe to look over the counter, catching Velma's attention.

"Y'all didn't get no mail today, sugar." Velma said to Rose Ellen. "Let me get that package for you, Doc."

Rose Ellen looked up shyly at Maggie, who smiled warmly back and leaned down to put herself on the child's eye level. Touching her lightly on the head, she asked "How's that spot we sewed up for you?" The girl bent her head down for Maggie to see her healed scalp laceration. "That looks pretty awesome. You're a good healer. Does it feel okay?" Rose Ellen nodded.

When Maggie had leaned over, the crystal pendant she wore around her neck had swung out from the open collar of her blouse. Rose Ellen reached out to touch it. "It's a crystal, an amulet that was my mom's. I wear it to remind me of her. And to keep me safe."

She was about to say more, when Waylon burst through the door, shouting. "Rosie! Get on out here. We ain' got all day." When he saw Maggie with Rose Ellen, he continued, "Mighta known it'd be your fault. Rosie, get on out to the truck."

Rose Ellen looked up at Maggie. "It's okay, sweetie. Go on," she murmured, as the child turned and ran for the door.

"I thought I told you to butt out."

"Mr. Prescott, I was checking her scar."

"I don't care what you're doin'. Nobody asked you to do nothin'. We don't need your nosey help."

"That's where you're wrong. Rose Ellen is my patient, and I will check on her."

Waylon glowered at her, but said nothing, wheeled, and stormed out the door.

"Don't pay him any mind, honey," Velma said, putting the parcel on the counter. "That's just Waylon. Probably got himself a powerful hangover today."

"I guess. I just worry about that sweet little girl. Is it true that no one has any idea where her mother went or why?"

"Not for sure, not as I know of anyway. Folks figured she'd run off with a trucker that came through. Somebody said they remembered seeing her flirtin' with this guy over at Molly's Café a day or two before. And who could blame her, living with him the way he is now? I know I couldn't." She was lost in her thoughts for a moment, then she continued, "She never seemed to me like the kind who'd just up and leave her baby, but that's all anybody could come up with."

"It's really odd." Maggie said with a bemused shake of her head. "Thanks," she said, picking up the parcel.

"You bet, hon. You take care, now," Velma said.

Parcel in hand, Maggie headed back to the clinic. Outside the store, she spotted a dusty, banged up pickup truck across the street. Nick leaned in the driver's side window, having what looked like a serious conversation with its driver, Waylon Prescott. Nick looked her way as Maggie exited the store, waved, and crossed the street to meet her.

"Well, if it's not my favorite doctor," he said. "Shouldn't you be at your post ministering to the sick and healing the lame?"

"Working on the last part," she said patting the parcel in her arm.

Waylon drove off in a cloud of dust, whipped a U-turn, and barreled back by, a little too close for comfort. Nick grabbed Maggie's arm and jerked her out of the way as the truck whizzed past.

"Damn pickups think they own the roads around here," Nick said.

"Particularly that one. Weren't you just talking to him?"

"Mostly listening. He's got a couple of significant mounds at his place. Keeps asking me about them. Let me walk you back to the clinic," Nick said, throwing his arm casually around her shoulder and guiding her up the street.

"Why?" She moved a little away from him to put herself outside his reach.

"So you don't get run over," he teased.

"No, why is he asking about the mounds?"

He shrugged. "Probably hopes there's something valuable enough in one of them to keep him in gin and cigarettes for a while."

"You mean he'd pilfer the burial cache and sell it?"

"Not without help."

"But who'd help him do something like that?"

"I don't know. Somebody looking to make a buck. Lot of money in it. I've seen your buddy Langston talking to him."

They reached the clinic, and he opened the back door for her to enter. She stopped and turned back to him with a look of concern on her face. "I worry about his daughter. Do you think she's safe?"

"I don't think he'd hurt her, if that's what you mean."

"I'm not sure exactly what I mean," she said, stepping inside.

"See you at dinner?" he asked.

"Yeah," she replied, "I shouldn't be too late getting this group taken care of. Depending on what the afternoon brings."

***

The dining room table at the boarding house was prettily set for four, but so far only Nick and another part-time boarder, a man named Lester Purvis, had taken their seats. Purvis was a sweaty, bespectacled man with shirt buttons that strained to close across his wide belly. He reached across the table for the platter of hot biscuits Miz Hendri had just put down in the center and levered a couple onto his plate with a fork.

"Lester, leave some for the Missus Doctor," Miz Hendri scolded him.

Moments later, Maggie pushed through the swinging door between the kitchen and dining room, drenched to the skin and wiping her arms and hands on a kitchen towel as she entered.

"Obviously, the rain's started up again," she announced.

"Ach! You are soaked to your skin!" Miz Hendri said, heading back into the kitchen. "Let me get you something better to dry with."

Maggie stood, dripping, arms open wide for inspection, which unfortunately revealed her thin knit blouse plastered to chilled skin. Nick and Lester both noticed the unintentional dual display of the normal human response to cold standing erect beneath the wet fabric, and a knowing and appreciative look passed between them.

Nick stood and moved behind Maggie, placing his hands gently on her sodden shoulders and leaning close to her ear to whisper, "Stunning. Totally. And if there's a wet t-shirt contest at the county fair? You'll win it, hands down." He moved slightly away and openly admired the view.

Maggie, embarrassed, glanced down and quickly folded her arms across her chest.

Nick managed to keep a straight face as he said, "Maggie, I don't think you've met Lester Purvis. He's one of those bank examiners you always hear about, but never actually see. He boards here occasionally when he comes through to… uh, examine."

Lester pushed back his chair and stood, extending his hand across the table. "Pleased to make your acquaintance, ma'am."

Maggie took the hand, if a bit awkwardly, as she tried to keep her left arm over her wet chest. "Nice to meet you, Mr. Purvis. How long will you be with us?"

"Oh, about a week this time, maybe longer if this rain keeps up. Water was already coming up onto the low water bridge when I drove in last night."

"Don't I know it," Nick chimed in. "It's been so muddy I haven't been able to excavate at the site in days."

Maggie's teeth began to chatter audibly. "Gentlemen, I feel a bit like a drowned rat. So, if you'll excuse me, I need to get into some dry clothes. Tell Miz Hendri I'll be back," she said and ran up the stairs.

Nick and Lester watched her leave then resettled themselves at the table. Lester leaned over and whispered, "They didn't make doctors that looked like that where I came from."

"Lester!" Miz Hendri clucked as she came through the door with a bath towel. "Such talk. She's a fine doctor, and that deserves your respect. Where is…"

"She ran up to change, Miz Hendri," Nick said. "She'll be right back down."

"Apologies, ma'am," Lester said. A man as fond of food as Lester wouldn't want to get on Miz Hendri's wrong side and miss out on her dinners.

The rain continued to pound on the roof and a deafening crash of thunder shook the house, rattling the windows and making the lights blink. Miz Hendri almost dropped the plate of fried chicken she had just carried into the dining room, bringing Lester quickly to his feet to steady her. "Merciful heaven! Such a storm!" she said. Lester took the platter from her and sat it lovingly on the table.

The desk phone in the hall jangled, and Nick hopped up. "I'll get it, Miz Hendri."

In the dimly lit hallway, the old black rotary dial phone sat on a crocheted cotton doily on a small telephone table in the alcove under the stairs. Like so many other little details of Miz Hendri's establishment, it was out of some other time, not added for effect, but rather preserved. Nick picked up the receiver, "McSwain's Boarding House." The line crackled as it annoyingly did in a storm.

In his luxuriously appointed Manhattan bedroom, Jeff sat propped up, bare chested, against multiple down pillows. Beside him, Judith Rawlins extracted herself from a tangle of gray sheets and blew him a kiss as she scampered to the bathroom. Jeff sat up straighter when the call connected and said, "Hello?"

"Hello?" Nick replied.

"I'm trying to reach Maggie McKinley. Have I got the correct number?"

"Yes, you have, but she'll have to call you back. She's slipping into something a little more comfortable." Nick smiled at his own joke.

"I'm sorry, what?" Jeff said, "This connection's terrible. What was it you said?"

"I said Maggie got caught in the rain," Nick spoke the words louder and slower. "She's upstairs changing her clothes. I'll be glad to go up and get her for you."

"That won't be necessary. Just tell her to call Dr. Winslow at home, please. She has the number," Jeff said and hung up without waiting for a response.

Nick stood for a moment, listening to the pleasantly dead air. "Hello?" he said again, then looked at the receiver, smiled smugly, replaced it in its cradle, and returned to his dinner.

In a bit, Maggie joined them, dry now, and dressed in a warm sweatsuit and a pair of fleece-lined Uggs. As soon as she sat, Miz Hendri put a heaping plate of food, including a couple of buttered biscuits, in front of her.

"Ah, that's much better," Maggie said. "And dinner smells great, Miz Hendri. Thank you." She took the soft chintz napkin from beside her plate and arranged it on her lap. "Did I hear the phone?"

"Telemarketers," Nick answered. "Why is it they always call at dinner?"

Lester pushed back from the table, his plate already cleaned, twice. "Well, if y'all will excuse me, I believe I'll turn in. Be good sleepin' tonight with that rain."

"Goodnight, Lester." Miz Hendri said, as she began to clear his place. "Finished, Nicholas?"

"Yes, ma'am. I'll keep Maggie company while she eats."

"You see she cleans her plate," she clucked, departing with a stack of dishes.

Maggie whispered, "If I ate everything Miz Hendri put in front of me, I'd be as big as…"

"Miz Hendri?" Nick finished for her.

Maggie suppressed a smile and inclined her head in tacit agreement as she tore off another bite of chicken and popped it into her mouth.

"You coming to the fair with me tomorrow night? If the rain quits, that is," Nick asked.

"I don't know," she said, spooning a bit of jam onto one of the biscuits and taking a bite.

"Come on, it'll be fun."

"I'm so behind on my charts, with the clinic closing early for the fair, my plan was to get caught up."

"You have to go! Miz Hendri will never forgive you if you don't vote for her lime ash pickles, and she loses to Mrs. Norman.

Maggie opened her mouth to protest, but Nick put a silencing finger across her lips. "I'll make you a deal. You work on your charts 'til five and I'll pick you up at the clinic. If we hurry, we can get over there before the music cranks up."

He held his finger there a moment longer then slowly took it away, the sensual undercurrent in his action bold and unmistakable. It made her uncomfortable, but she tried to ignore it.

"OK. Deal," she agreed and turned back to her dinner.

Nick then put the finger under her chin and gently turned her face to his. "I think this is traditionally where you invite me up for a drink."

Maggie met his eyes; the usual mischievous gaiety in them had been replaced by a different more serious emotion, and it unsettled her a bit more. With what she hoped passed for a light-hearted laugh she said, "Or where you invite me to look at your etchings?"

He laid his hand over hers. "C'mon," he said as he leaned in to kiss her, almost grazing her lips before she pulled back, shaking her head. "Nick, I can't. No drinks, no etchings."

"The New York connection?"

Maggie nodded her head and pulled her hand from beneath his. In what she hoped seemed a friendly but not inviting gesture she patted his knee. "Yeah," she said, putting down her fork and rising to leave. He stood as well.

"No room for a new kid in town?"

"Plenty of room for new friendships," she said as she moved away from him.

Nick stood as she walked up the stairs. When her door opened and closed, he sat again at the table, sullenly poking at the remains of her chicken with the tip of her knife. "Friendship my ass," he muttered, impaling the chicken breast with the knife and pushing roughly back from the table.

CHAPTER 11
Fair's Fair

The days were growing shorter now and by 5 pm the dusk was already deepening to near dark. Maggie sat, pen in hand, in a circle of light thrown by the lamp on her old wooden desk, working on a stack of patient charts in front of her. The clinic hadn't yet gone digital with medical records, though Therma Faye had told her they'd gotten a bit of Health Department grant money to make the transition. First step, though, was to get improved internet access – which they were waiting on, if the rain would just quit long enough for the work to be finished – and then to upgrade the clinic's computer hardware, some of which was positively ancient. So, for now, at least, charting was done Old School, by hand, with a pen.

Her MacBook Pro looked sleek and modern sitting on her desk, but the current internet speed was so choked down it would hardly even function. A tower of medical journals that had arrived in just the last couple of months teetered atop the file cabinet nearby, threatening to collapse at the slightest bump. She, for one, would be happy to have online journal access again just to eliminate that risk, and sooner rather than later. She kept meaning to box them up and at least move them to the floor, so she wouldn't be accidently buried by a sudden collapse. She laughed to herself at the imagined headline: *Local Doctor Buried in Tragic Journal Tower Collapse.*

The desk phone rang, breaking the quiet.

"Dr. McKinley," she answered.

"Maggie? Is it really you?" Jeff sat at a dictation carrel in the doctor's lounge, in scrubs and white coat.

"Jeff, hi! I'm so sorry I didn't get back to you. The clinic was a madhouse yesterday. The moon must be full."

"I was worried when you didn't call me back again last night."

"Last night?"

"Didn't you get the message I left with your buddy?"

"Buddy?" she looked a bit puzzled until the realization hit. "Actually, no."

"Doesn't matter. You're okay – and God it's good to hear your voice."

"Yeah, yours, too."

Jeff reached into the pocket of his lab coat and pulled out an envelope. "Guess what I'm holding?" She didn't immediately respond, so he continued, "Two box seats for the New Year's Eve Gala at Lincoln Center."

Maggie tapped the pen on the chart in front of her and looked a bit uncomfortable as he continued.

"I thought we could eat dinner first, maybe at Daniel—since I know how much you love his food—and catch the performance, then be back at my place early enough to pop the cork on a bottle of Dom as the clock strikes twelve. And then, I have to tell you, I've been fantasizing about what we might do next, alone, just the two of us."

"Sounds great," she said, but with enough hesitation that Jeff noticed right away.

"But?"

"But… I don't know," she said. "You just wouldn't believe what it's like to be the only doctor in a place like this. It's 24/7. You can't take off at a moment's notice; you just about can't take off at all."

"Tell me I'm not hearing you say you're not coming home for the holidays."

"No. You're just hearing me say I don't know if I can. I'd have to secure a *locum tenens* doc to come in, and you know that during the holidays that's not easy and"

Maggie heard the back door bang open and a loud whistle, followed by Nick's voice, shouting from the back hall, "Maggie! It's show time! Grab your dancing shoes, girl, and let's get out of here." Nick popped his head into the office doorway and saw Maggie on the phone. She glared at him and signaled him to shush. He mouthed a 'who is it?' to her and she mouthed back 'New York'. Nick's eyes grew wide, and he covered his mouth with his hand in a gesture of mock dismay.

"Who's that?" Jeff said sharply.

"It's, uh, Nick."

"Nick? What's he doing there?"

"He's," she winced and stalled a moment. "He's driving me to Mt. Ida to the county fair."

"To the what?"

"The county fair. I promised Mrs. McSwain I'd help judge the pickles. It's sort of like stuffing the ballot box, and she -"

"So, let me make sure I've got this correct," he interrupted. "You have time in your busy schedule for a country bumpkin fair, but you might not be able to make it to the Phil's once a year event at Lincoln Center for New Year's Eve?"

"It's not like that."

"Forget it. Give me a call when you have time," he said. She could hear the ice in his voice, and then there was nothing. He'd ended the call.

Maggie stared at the dead receiver and slowly hung up.

Nick crossed to her desk. "Oops. Bad timing."

"Why didn't you tell me Jeff Winslow called last night?" Her scorching stare pinned him in place.

"I did," he said.

"You most certainly did not. You said it was a telemarketer."

"Well, I knew it was somebody selling something." Nick grabbed her coat and purse off the rack in the corner and pulled her by the arm from behind the desk. "But that was last night, and this is tonight, and we're late for the fair."

Maggie pulled her arm free and stood her ground. "Don't ever do that again."

"Do what, Princess?"

"Lie to me."

"I didn't lie."

"A lie of omission is as bad as a lie of commission as far as I'm concerned," she folded her arms across her chest. "A lie's a lie."

"Aw, don't be mad," he pleaded. "Way too heavy a vibe for a fun night at the fair. Come on. The music and bright lights of Mt. Ida await us." He held the coat out for her; she hesitated a moment before relenting.

"You're just too damned charming for your own good, you know that?" She meant it but couldn't suppress a little smile as he helped her on with her coat. "But I assure you this conversation will be continued."

It hadn't rained all day, but the night sky was so overcast that the moon was a creamy blur and not a star peeped through the thick cloud cover. That didn't matter much, though, with the bright lights of the fairgrounds illuminating everything for a mile around. As they entered the midway, the smell of manure assailed them. "Oh my God. What is that?" Maggie pinched her nostrils shut and panted through her mouth.

"Animal pavilions," Nick pointed to the corrugated-tin-roofed buildings off to their right. "Hog enclosure, I think. We're going this way," he said nodding left and pulling her by the elbow. "Unless the wind shifts, we ought to be away from it."

Couples and families wandered down the midway, children breaking loose from their parents and darting happily in every direction, then circling back to implore the folks for cotton candy, corn dogs, funnel cakes, or money for ride tickets or to play at the arcades. Clusters of teenage girls squealed, as only teenage girls can do, eyeing clusters of teenage boys, themselves trying to look cool and nonchalant. It was middle America at its county fair finest.

The crowd meandered in the general direction of the big main stage tent, its white canvas peaks visible at the far left end of the midway, mercifully well away from the hog pens. That was where the evening's musical entertainment was due to begin at 7 pm. Nick and Maggie merged with the flow of people, strolling past contest tables of beautiful pies and cakes, jams and jellies, and, of course, of pickles. They dutifully stopped at that table to cast both their ballots in favor of Henrietta McSwain's Lime Ash Pickles, which, Maggie had to admit, really were delicious.

Down both sides along the way were a dozen or more carnival games scattered amid food trucks and stalls selling cotton candy, caramel apples, and deep fried everything, from corn dogs to pickles to Snickers to Twinkies. Really, deep fried Twinkies! *Who deep fries a Twinkie?* Nick indulged in a basket of cheesy jalapeno nachos and tried to tempt Maggie to indulge, too, with the last chip. She wrinkled her nose at the proffered morsel.

"C'mon, pretty lady, loosen up. One chip's not gonna croak your heart."

"Neon cheese is not my thing. But I'd kill for one of those gyros, after the concert," she replied with a nod to the big red 'Baba's Ga-Noosh' food truck up the way.

Time was short before the music would start, so they continued down the midway stopping only once more, at the Sharp Shooterz booth, where Nick's prowess with aiming an air rifle garnered him a string of bullseyes and Maggie a long-legged, flop-eared, chartreuse bunny.

"He's adorable," Maggie said as he presented her with the prize. "I love his red button eyes."

Nick moved in front of her, facing her and settling both his arms around her waist. "He doesn't have the corner on beautiful eyes, you know.

Have you looked at those sexy, dark browns that stare back at you in the mirror?"

Maggie found his nearness and the intimate familiarity a bit too much and casually pulled away, taking her eyes from his and glancing down to check her watch. "Gosh, it's almost 7."

"You're right," he said, dismissing the moment and mercurially adopting his usual playful demeanor. "We better shake a leg, or we'll be seeing the show from the back row. Or worse, the front one," he said, putting a hand onto her back and turning her toward the big tent where the bandstand had been set up.

On the stage, several knots of performers tuned their instruments and checked the mics. She noticed most of the best seats were already filled when they entered.

"See if you can find two together – not too close – and I'll get us something to drink," Nick said. "What do you want?"

"Unsweet tea?"

Nick gave her a look. "You know they're not going to have that. Ma'am, you are in the South. Sweet tea is the standard here."

"Coffee?"

He rolled his eyes at her. "Seriously?"

"OK, lemonade, I guess."

"Finally, something fair-worthy," he said, with a mock bow and a wink.

Maggie scanned the rows ahead and located two empty seats on the far side of the tent. Inching her way along between people milling in the aisle and the outside tent wall, she finally reached the open pair. A familiar, loud voice on the other side of the canvas wall drew her attention, and she stopped to listen.

"Well, just exactly when would be a good time?" she heard the man say. "You drug my ass into this, and I ain't seen nothin' yet."

Maggie put her purse and coat and the bunny down to save the seats and moved to peek through a small rip in the tent wall. Outside, Waylon Prescott stood at the edge of the tent in heated conversation with someone standing around the corner out of her view.

"And you're not gonna ever see 'nothin', as you call it, if you don't back off," the one she couldn't see said in a harsh, low whisper.

"I got bills. I got a kid to feed. You owe me," Waylon bristled.

The man extended a wad of bills, which Waylon quickly grabbed from his hand.

Maggie felt a tap on her shoulder and turned to find a small man and a very large woman standing in the aisle.

The man said, "Ma'am, are you saving these seats?"

"Yes. But I thought I saw a several empty toward the front there," Maggie said, scooting into her row and pointing toward the front corner of the tent where she'd seen the open seats. She spotted JD as he pushed through the flap at that front corner with a coil of microphone cord in each hand. He looked up and acknowledged her, raising one coil over his head, and giving a lift of his chin in greeting. She tentatively waved back and took her seat, leaving the one, still empty, beside her. She propped the stuffed bunny in it, crossing its long legs; it almost filled the seat. Nick reappeared moments later, lemonades in hand.

"Really?" he said, eyeing the bunny. Maggie smiled and removed it, so Nick could slide into the seat just as the lights dimmed and the emcee, a tall, lanky man with a huge Stetson walked to the center microphone on stage.

"Evenin' y'all, and welcome to the annual County Fair First Night Pickin'. We got a great show lined up for you folks tonight, so let's skip all the jawin' and get 'er started. Give a hand to the Mountain Valley Boys."

The crowd applauded warmly as the band took the stage and began a spirited medley of blue grass tunes that set everybody to stomping and clapping, clearly enjoying the show.

When the medley ended and the applause died down a bit, one of the 'Boys' leaned up to the mic. "Y'all give a big howdy to our own JD Langston."

"I didn't know JD was in a band," Maggie whispered to Nick.

"Yeah, he's probably in all kinds of things you don't know about," Nick whispered back.

JD appeared on stage, crossed to the mic, and took it from the stand. He acknowledged the audience with a minimal raise of his hand and a wink that seemed, Maggie thought, directed straight at her.

"OK Boys, let's do it."

The band struck up a familiar tune, and JD had scarcely begun to sing, when lightning cracked very close by, followed almost immediately by a loud thunderclap. In an instant, the sky opened, releasing buckets of rain that beat down with deafening heaviness on the canvas tent. The lights blinked off and back on, eliciting a collective gasp from the crowd, and suddenly went completely out, plunging the crowd into darkness and murmuring quiet. A few lighters flicked on and then a flashlight or two, then the lights flickered back on, accompanied by an awful squeal from the PA system.

The emcee took the mic from JD. "Sorry 'bout that folks. We'll have her back steady here in a jiffy," he said. Then a deputy sheriff walked onto the stage from the wings, approached the emcee and handed him a piece of paper, whispering something into his ear, then stepping back.

"Sheriff Perkins just" the emcee began, but the PA emitted another ear-piercing squeal, and he pulled the mic away, pausing to let it subside. Holding the paper up as if it were proof, he went on, "The sheriff just sent word that the weather service says we're in for a real toad strangler tonight. Flash floods possible. Said all y'all not stayin' this side of the Caddo better head on back while you can still get across the low water bridge."

Nick and Maggie joined the press of people leaving the tent. At the exit, over the din of the rain pounding down overhead, he shouted to her, "C'mon."

"Shouldn't we wait for it to slack up?"

"No. Trust me; you don't want to see the Caddo when it's roiling mad. We need to get across ASAP."

"What about my long-legged friend here? He's not much of a runner," she said.

"Take off your coat," he said. She did and Nick took the rabbit, laid it on Maggie's back, wrapped his long legs around her neck, and knotted them in front. "Now tent your coat over your head, and he can go pig-gyback." They pulled their coats over their heads and made the mad and muddy sprint to Nick's truck.

The rain was coming down in sideways sheets as they barreled down the unlit, two-lane highway toward Caddo Bend. Nick flicked the wipers to their highest speed, but they still struggled to clear the windshield.

"I can't see anything," Maggie said, gripping the handhold of the door so tightly her knuckles blanched white.

"Fortunately, you're not driving," Nick replied, but she noticed his serious expression contrasted with the somewhat light-hearted tone of his words.

"Shouldn't you slow down a little?"

"I'm hoping we can get across the river on the low-water bridge," he said, "but if it's already flooded, we'll have to go back around the long way, and it will make for a late night."

Driving in pounding rain put Maggie's teeth on edge. She absolutely hated it. Unbidden her memories rushed in, and she was transported to that awful night fifteen years ago, her father fighting to regain control of the car as it fishtailed and hydroplaned on the rain slick highway. Her mother's screams, the crunching of crumpling metal and shattering glass as the car rolled over and over. Maggie, thrown clear, had been found hours later bloody, but alive, in the mud and weeds above the Susquehanna River in New York.

At this moment all she wanted was to be safe and dry in her bed at Miz Hendri's. And to top it off, she was soaked to the skin and chilled. She started to shiver.

"Cold?" Nick said, reaching over to crank up the heater and direct the air flow from the windshield to the dash vents. A gust of wind hit them, and the truck swerved a bit.

"No," she said sitting straight up and grabbing the dash. "Yes. But let me do it. Just keep your hands on the wheel and your eyes on the road," she said, the strain evident in her voice. "Please," she added, striving for a calmer tone.

When they finally reached the railroad crossing signs, Nick almost missed the turn, but skidded to a stop and backed up on the dark highway, then pointed the truck down the incline to the river. In the headlight beams, the placid river she'd crossed on her arrival was anything but. Churning white, the water rushed through the scuppers on the low concrete sides of the bridge, but so far hadn't completely submerged it.

Nick stopped for a moment and peered upstream, then gunned the motor. "Here we go. Hold on," he said and sped across the bridge, sending a spray of water higher than the truck's roof on either side.

They'd just gotten across and a little way up the far incline when a thunderous rumble filled the night air. Looking in her side mirror, Maggie saw a wall of frothy muddy water and debris rushing past behind them. The bridge completely disappeared from her view, and she shuddered again, but this time, not from the cold.

Maggie awoke the next morning feeling stiff from the white-knuckle tension of the drive back from Mt. Ida and a restless night of disturbing dreams of the kind she hadn't experienced in a long, long while. Glancing out the window, she was relieved to see bright morning sun; at least the rain had stopped. After a few extra minutes of yoga flow, the physical kinks had mostly disappeared, but she still felt a bit unsettled emotionally. She sat down at the desk beside her bed and opened her laptop to check emails. The internet at Miz Hendri's was glacially slow, but she noticed as she watched the maddening wheel whirl that she had several bars on her phone, so she took advantage of the unexpected cellular largesse, dialing Charlotte's number.

"Maggie May! What's the word from Gopher Crotch?"

"Just needed to hear a friendly voice," Maggie said softly.

"Why? What's wrong?" the alarm instantly evident in her voice. "Are you OK?"

"I'm fine," Maggie reassured her. "Now anyway. There was a huge rainstorm last night that we had to drive through." Just hearing Charlotte's voice was a comfort. She was the only person Maggie had ever fully confided in about that awful night she had survived, but her parents had not. And then only because of a near accident they'd had returning from the Ainsley's home in North Carolina back to school in Lexington, VA after fall break of their senior year. Charlotte had braked suddenly, and her BMW had skidded off onto the shoulder in the rain. Usually calm and stoic Maggie had dissolved into a tearful, quivering mess totally out of proportion to the event. They'd sat in the car in the pounding rain on the side of the road with the flashers on for at least half an hour with Charlotte holding her and letting her sob, until Maggie had finally been able to regain enough control to tell her the whole story. At least what she could remember or had subsequently learned of that night.

"Oh, honey. Are you really OK? And I'm not talking physically," Charlotte said.

"Mostly I am. It just brought up a lot of stuff, you know?"

"I do. I wish I was closer so I could give you a real, honest to God hug, but I want you to feel it coming your way through cyberspace right now." There was a commotion in the background. "Hang on a sec," she said turning her attention to the kids. "Ainsley, leave your sister's bacon alone. If you want more, use your words and ask politely. Caroline, stop tattling; it's unseemly. Stand up for yourself. Now, no more whining! Either of you. Understand?"

"Yes, ma'am," two little subdued voices said in unison.

"Sorry about that," Charlotte said, refocusing on the call.

"Aaah, now that does make me feel better. Situation normal at Chez Schaflien it sounds like. Tell them Aunt Maggie loves them to bits."

"Kids, Auntie Maggie says behave yourselves!"

"Char," Maggie admonished her.

"And that she loves you," Charlotte added. "Let me get these two heathens dropped at school, and I'll call back when I can talk without all this chaos."

"OK. I'm heading down to work out in a minute. I'll call you later from the clinic. I have a better connection from there. Usually."

"I'll be here," Charlotte said. "Ciao, bella."

CHAPTER 12
Revelations

The torrential rain on the night of the fair had been mercifully short-lived and seemed not to have caused too much damage, meaning mainly that the Caddo hadn't breached its banks, and there'd been no significant flooding in the surrounding area or the town itself. Everything had pretty much dried out in the days that followed and, after a quick cold snap ushered in by the storm front, the mild Autumn weather had returned delivering clear blue skies over a fuller and richer palette of gold, red, and orange in the hardwoods. Until late last night, that is, when another front barreled through with more rain; fortunately, it was over quickly and thanks to this morning's bright sun, the skies were once again blue and hardly a puddle remained.

It was, Maggie had to admit on her Saturday morning walk to the clinic, quite beautiful, even compared to the autumns she'd grown up with in New York and Virginia. She adored being out in the crisp air and sunshine, so when the forecast looked good, she'd made it her habit to take the Nike express to work on Saturdays, jogging when she had no patients scheduled and walking when she did, so she wouldn't arrive too disheveled.

She decided to cut across the green to Molly's Café on the square to grab a breakfast sandwich to go and found the tiny downtown a beehive of activity even at this early hour. Workmen on ladders were decorating the streetlamps around the square and the gazebo in the central green with stars and stripes bunting and fluttering flags. Velma Bradford was taping a small poster to the café window as Maggie walked up.

"Hey there, Doc," she cheerfully greeted Maggie without turning around.

"Hi, Velma," Maggie said, marveling once more at her strange clairvoyance. "What's all this for?"

"Veteran's Day Tribute," Velma said, stretching to her full length to tape the final corner up. "Sunday after next. Not countin' tomorrow, I mean.

"The 11th," Maggie said. "The 11th hour of the 11th day of the 11th month."

"That's right," Velma said, clearly surprised she would know such a fact. "Folks your age don't usually know much about Veteran's Day."

"My dad recited the poem 'In Flanders' Field' at 11 am every Veteran's Day – or Armistice Day, as he still insisted on calling it. He said he wanted me to never forget that freedom isn't free," Maggie said.

"No, it isn't," Velma said. "My husband was a Marine. He was killed in action in Desert Storm when our son Benji was just 2. To me Veteran's Day is one of the two most important days of the year."

"What's the other?" Maggie asked.

"Memorial Day," Velma responded with a sad smile. Then she seemed to shake off the pall of memory. "The whole town turns out for the Veteran's Tribute. There'll be food, flags, patriotic songs, a little parade down Main and around the square. My church choir's in charge of the music this year. We trade off with the Baptist Church choir every other year." She paused and gave her a look over the glasses. "JD's singing," she said with a knowing wink.

"Really." *Why would she point that out to me?* "Sounds lovely. I'll try to come," Maggie said, heading into the café to grab her breakfast.

"Here," Velma called after her, holding out a poster. "Could you put one up in the clinic for us?"

"Happy to," Maggie said, taking the poster. "See you later."

The clinic was closed every other Saturday, except for emergencies. Today they had scheduled appointments until about noon, but she liked to get there early, so she could enjoy a little morning solitude and a quiet cup of coffee before it got crazy. And, today, her scrambled eggs and diced bacon on a toasted everything bagel.

The new high-speed internet line had finally been run and hooked up yesterday, and she could hardly wait to get the charts digitalized and everything brought up to current HIPPA standards. And she would as soon as the new computer equipment arrived. But one thing at a time.

She made herself a double Americano in the breakroom with the brand new, top-of-the-line Nespresso machine that FedEx had delivered yesterday to the clinic, courtesy of Jeff, as an apology for their harsh conversation about New Year's the night of the fair. The enclosed note said '*Miss you on Saturdays. Love~ J.*'

That first sip brought back sweet memories of so many Saturday mornings over coffee at his place. Usually after a long night of call. He'd text her one word 'Americano?' at about the time she'd be leaving the hospital, and she'd grab the subway to Columbus Circle and text him as she got to the building lobby. By the time she made it up to the penthouse, he'd be waiting with a double Americano, hot off his built-in Jura, and they'd sit and drink a cup or three together. Then she'd nap on his couch while he read the *Weekend Financial Times* and massaged her feet. And then, if Esmerelda was out, they'd often toss those high dollar accent pillows to the floor, ignore the glorious view, and use that down sofa a little more vigorously.

She sipped again and headed to her office, noticing as she entered, that the window was half open. *That's odd*, she thought; *I'm sure I closed it last night. And that screen's still off.* She made a mental note to put it back up before she left. She'd learned the hard way that you don't want to make it so easy on the mosquitos. The freeze had probably gotten most of them for this season, or so Therma Faye had told her, and the soft morning breeze coming in felt nice, so she left it for now. She sat the steaming cup on a stone coaster, thumbed up a favorite Classic Rock playlist from her iTunes library, and unwrapped her breakfast bagel.

Opening her laptop, she quickly downloaded her current emails, courtesy of the new high-speed internet line, and scrolled through them between bites of bagel sandwich. Most were junk mail that she deleted click by click, until one airline promo caught her eye: GET AN AUTUMN DEAL FOR A STEAL, it read. She clicked on the email and a picture of Central Park, ablaze in fall color, popped open on the screen. Just seeing it made her homesick. And sitting there, coffee in hand, she longed to see Jeff, to feel his strong arms around her, to see that amazing smile up close and personal. She wanted to enjoy Saturday morning coffee with him. And all that would likely come after.

And next Saturday, there would be no scheduled patients. She'd have the whole weekend free if she could arrange for someone to field emergency calls. She made a most un-Maggie-like, completely spontaneous decision: she'd fly to New York and surprise Jeff. She clicked the 'BOOK NOW' button on the email and began to search for possibilities, soon finding what she was looking for. It meant she'd have to drive to Hot Springs after work, grab the last flight to Memphis, and then the redeye on to Newark on Friday night. But she could be standing at Jeff's door by 8 o'clock next Saturday morning. That plan would fly. She booked a refundable ticket.

Lost in her chart work and Eagles' harmonies, she didn't hear the soft scrape on the windowsill, but the next time she looked out at the glorious fall sky, there was a dark something sitting there. A little creeped out by it, she cautiously got up and took a closer look.

It was a pottery vessel about the size of a large grapefruit. Despite the dirt that encrusted it, she could still make out some sort of animal figure fashioned onto its opening. Movement outside the window caught her eye, and she looked out to see Rose Ellen partially hidden behind the trunk of a large sycamore tree that grew beside the clinic, watching.

Maggie opened the window fully and called out to her, "Rose Ellen? Did you put this here?"

The girl peeped around the trunk, gave what might have been a nod, though it was so slight it was hard to be sure, and bolted quickly out of Maggie's view.

The potential significance of the gift, if that's what it was, both encouraged and baffled her. *What does it mean? Is this progress?* Maybe she'd finally earned the trust of this damaged child. *Should I pursue it?* Yes, she decided; she'd follow it up. Today. This afternoon after she finished with all the appointments.

That afternoon, Maggie's SUV bumped along the rutted country road, slowing intermittently to check names on mailboxes, until she spotted one marked 'PRESC TT' in peeling stenciled letters. She stopped and took a deep breath, then turned up the narrow dirt driveway toward the farmhouse.

Two mud-splattered vehicles sat in the scrubby brown patches of grass beside the house. Maggie climbed out of her car and stepped up onto the porch. She gave a firm rap on the screen door; no one answered, but a rooster crowed loudly from somewhere behind the house. She opened the screen and knocked again, louder, on the solid front door itself, and called out, "Rose Ellen? Anybody home?" Still nothing.

She took a latex exam glove from her pocket and blew it up to make a chicken balloon, as she'd seen Therma Faye do, tying it off with a deft twist. Then she drew a face on it with a Sharpie and wedged it behind the screen door.

She hopped off the porch and crossed the weedy dirt expanse, heading back to her car, when around the side of the house Waylon appeared, a pistol holstered on his hip.

"What the hell you doin' here?" he growled.

Maggie couldn't suppress a startled jerk but forced herself to slowly turn to face him and walk a few steps closer. "I came to check on my patient. Is she here?"

"Naw." He stared and said nothing more for a moment, then, "She's fine; we don't need nothin' from you."

JD appeared behind him, and Maggie gave him an openly confused look and took a few more steps toward the men.

"JD? What are you…" her question hung unfinished when Waylon drew the gun from its holster. JD put out a hand as if to stop him.

"Don't take another step, lady," Waylon warned.

"I only came to check on Rose Ellen. I'll come back later," she said, backing away to leave, her pulse pounding in her ears.

"Don't move," JD said firmly as Waylon aimed the pistol in her direction.

"Don't," Maggie softly pleaded, taking another step back, and turning to run.

JD lunged out and knocked her aside as the gun exploded with a deafening crack.

Less than a foot from where Maggie had stood, the weeds were spattered with blood from a large, coiled snake, now lying headless and motionless.

"Copperhead," Waylon muttered.

JD bent to help her up. "You all right?" His eyes, scarcely a foot from hers as he gripped her elbow to help her stand, were penetrating, filled with an emotion she couldn't quite identify. *Was it fear? Concern? Anger?*

"Somebody told me that if you leave them alone, they'll leave you alone," she said, brushing dust from her palms and knees and collecting her wits.

"Depends on the snake," JD amended. "Just watch your step."

"Thank you," she said, crossing to her car and climbing in, "…both."

Despite the ringing in her ears and not quite being able to still her shaking hands, she managed to start the car, execute a three-point turn, and even give a passably casual wave as she departed. But she felt anything but cool. She drove down the road and well out of sight of the Prescott farmhouse before pulling over and stopping at another farm's drive. She closed her eyes and took a few deep, cleansing, calming breaths.

She was no fan of snakes, or guns for that matter, and the incident had unsettled her. But seeing JD there with Waylon may have unsettled her more. *What was he doing there?* She turned the thought over and over in her mind. *Could he really be the one helping Waylon pilfer the mounds, as Nick suggested?* She considered herself a pretty good judge of people, and it just didn't fit. Or did it? Surely it wasn't possible, not with those eyes. But then Ted Bundy had beautiful eyes, or so she'd read.

***

On Monday afternoon, Lester Purvis pulled up to the full-service pump out front of Eddie Ray's station and climbed out. Eddie appeared around the side of the building, wiping his hands on a greasy rag.

"Fill 'er up?"

"Yessir. Reg'lar," Lester answered, heading for the Coke box, where Travis, Leon, and Boyce sat loitering after work in their usual spots on the bench beside it, and currently in a heated argument over whether the former Hog's head football coach, who was now coaching for SEC rival Mississippi, would have enough insider information to tip the outcome of this weekend's Arkansas Razorback contest with Ole Miss.

"Hell, he couldn't get it done at Fayetteville," Leon pronounced, "why you think that's any different in Oxford?"

"Don't know as it is," Boyce agreed and thought a moment. "OK. Gimme Hogs minus the 7," he said, handing a five-dollar bill to Leon. "You was right last week on that Kentucky blow out."

Lester walked up to the Coke box, jammed his hands down into the pockets of his too-tight jeans, and came out with a handful of change, selecting what he needed.

"Howdy, boys."

The trio gave him a nod and a 'hey' as he lifted the lid and fed his coins into the slot. They promptly clinked into the coin return. He collected them and tried again with the same result. He pulled on a couple of the bottles, but none would release.

"Something's wrong with this machine."

Travis got off the bench, came over to him, and rasped out in a hoarse whisper, "Which one you want?"

Lester pointed to the grape soda. "Damn, brother. You feel as bad as you sound, you ought to go up there and see that pretty doctor."

Travis shook his head no, then taking careful aim, hit the machine with the side of his fist dead center in the Coca Cola logo and pulled the grape soda free. He handed it to Lester, who popped the top and took a long pull then put the coins back into his pocket.

"Why not? Make a man feel better just to look at something that pretty."

Boyce chuckled. "Ain't him lookin' at her that's got him worried," he said.

"She's gonna be lookin' down your throat, not down your pants, fool," Lester teased. He stretched and checked his watch a time or two, looking up the road, waiting.

Finally, a truck pulled into the far end of the dusty parking area, and Lester drained his soda, dropped his empty in the crate beside the box, and walked over to the driver's window.

"That it?" he said.

"Yeah," the driver opened the cardboard box in his lap, pulled away the bubble wrap, and revealed a Caddoan pot, well packed and carefully nestled in a form-fitting cushion of crumpled newspaper.

Lester whistled softly and reached for the pot, but the driver roughly brushed his hand away, and gently replaced the layers of bubble wrap over the pot, shut the flaps, and taped the box securely with tamper-evident tape.

"Don't open it," he warned. "For God's sake don't let anything happen to it, and don't take anything but cash from him."

"Okay, okay," he agreed, taking the box from the man and stepping back.

"And bubba," the man warned, "this goes right, or it doesn't happen again."

***

In one of the clinic's small exam rooms the next morning, Travis sat nervously on the table. Maggie was examining his throat with a tongue depressor and light when Therma Faye rapped on the door and stuck her head in.

"Dr. Mac, I need you out here for a minute." She left the door open and stood in the hall, bouncing on her toes, and raising her eyebrows, impatiently waiting as Maggie unwrapped a swab and inserted it into Travis's open mouth. Noticing Therma Faye's insistence, she nodded to her, collected the throat sample, pulled the swab away and dropped it into the test tube. She excused herself and joined the nurse in the hall, pulling the door closed behind her.

"Strep test, please" she said handing Therma Faye the swab and tube. "What's up?"

"Sheriff Perkins's on the phone. Says to get you right away," she said in an urgent whisper as they started down the hallway toward Maggie's office.

"Something's happened down at the river," Therma Faye continued, trailing behind Maggie. "It's Roy Owens – you know, the county coroner?"

"I don't believe I've had the pleasure," Maggie said. "What's happened?"

"Sheriff said he fell out, right there in the river. Said he just dropped over." She stopped at the lab to start the test, but leaned back out the doorway and added, "I bet it's his heart."

Maggie picked up the telephone. "Sheriff Perkins? It's Dr. McKinley." She paused, listening, "Uh huh," she paused again. "It'll be quicker if I come there. Keep him quiet and hang on."

Maggie grabbed her keys and handed them to Therma Faye as she walked by the lab counter. "Put the crash suitcase in the back of my car. I'll step in quickly to tell Travis what's up. He's going to need 1.2 of Bicillin in his butt if that strep test is positive. Give him a home care instruction sheet for pharyngitis either way and some Cēpacol Lozenges samples, if we've got some. Tell him to get more. Got all that?"

"Yes, ma'am. Will do," she said setting the lab timer and grabbing the crash kit.

"And tell Donna to try to reschedule whoever's left in the waiting room. I don't know how long I'll be."

On the muddy, brush-choked riverbank, an assortment of gawking citizens and uniformed deputies gathered around a man, lying in the mud beside the water, just outside the perimeter that had already been staked off with yellow crime scene tape. Maggie slipped and slid down the embankment toward the group, lugging the heavy crash kit suitcase.

A slender, youngish male deputy clambered up the bank to assist her, taking the kit. "Here let me take that. That's heavy, ma'am," he said politely, but when he took the suitcase himself his startled expression revealed just how right he'd been.

The police radio from the coroner's old Bronco squawked and chattered as they hurried toward where Roy Owens lay below. She noticed the man's name tag read BRADFORD.

"Deputy Bradford," Maggie said, "can you tell me what happened?"

"Yes, ma'am. It's Ben, by the way. Nice to meet you, finally. Mama talks about you a lot; I feel like I know you."

Maggie smiled. Would she ever get used to everybody seeming to know everybody? "So, what happened?"

"Oh, yeah. Got sidetracked. Sorry," he said, almost blushing. "As to Roy, I don't rightly know what happened. We got a call earlier this morning that two boys – the two young'uns standing over there – found a body on the riverbank. So, me and Dub, since we both live right here in town, and, a course, Roy, come out."

"I meant what happened to Mr. Owens."

"That's what I was telling you. When we got up here it turned out it was just some bones. No body," he made air quotes with the fingers of his free hand, "left to it. Though I can see why it spooked them kids, 'specially this time of year, so close to Halloween and all."

"Roy?" She reminded him.

"Yeah, I'm just comin' to that. Sometimes you'll see a bone or two come out of these mounds after a gully washer like we had last night. And these were kinda half stickin' out, but pretty well still stuck in the wall of the mound. Like when that river flushed through there, it just sheared off part of the wall, and *boom* there they were. So, we're all kinda digging around and pulling at 'em, and it was real slippery and all, and Roy pulled real hard, then he made this funny noise. And then he staggered a few steps and keeled over, face down in the water. We drug him right out."

The group around Roy parted to let Maggie and the deputy get closer. He was a large, barrel-chested man who looked to be in his late 50s, maybe

60s, with thinning hair, plastered to his forehead. He lay on his back, eyes closed, soaked and muddy, and breathing in shallow pants. His lips had taken on a slightly blueish coloring, and his skin was pale as paste.

Maggie knelt beside him and immediately felt for the pulses at his wrist and neck. *Thready, weak and fast.* His skin was a bit cool and damp, but it was a cool day, and he'd been pulled out of the water. She clipped a pulse oximeter onto his finger and listened to his heart and lungs. *Heart rhythm regular, breath sounds clear. That's good.* She opened the case, removed a blood pressure cuff, wrapped it around his upper arm, pumped it up, and took a quick reading: 105/60. *Low, particularly for someone his age and heft. Not so good.* The pulse ox beeped and read out 88. *Not too bad, considering.* She hooked the tubing and mask to the oxygen cylinder, cranked it open, and positioned the mask on his face, wishing she had a way to get an ECG tracing out here without power.

She shook him gently. "Mr. Owens. Roy. It's Maggie McKinley. Roy? Can you hear me?"

His eyes cracked open. "Yeah, doc," he whispered weakly behind the mask. "Ain't you a... sight for sore eyes?"

"Roy, where do you hurt?"

He lay his palm weakly across his chest. "Be obliged," he said haltingly, "if you could... ask this... elephant to ... get up off me."

She shook four baby aspirin and a nitroglycerine tablet from the bottles in the kit and lifted his oxygen mask. "Are you allergic to any medications?"

He shook his head, no.

"Open your mouth, Roy. I need you to chew these up," she said, putting the four aspirin into his mouth. When he had finished, she said, "Now, I'm going to put this one under your tongue to dissolve. Just leave it there, OK?" He nodded. She put the oxygen mask back in place and squeezed his hand. "You're going to be all right. Just hang on."

She connected tubing to a bag of IV fluid and motioned for Deputy Bradford to hold the bag high for her, while she popped an IV into Roy's vein and secured it.

Another deputy scrambled down the hill and hunkered down beside her as she began to slowly push an amp of morphine into the intravenous line.

"Roy, this is going to make that elephant get up, OK?" Then, to the deputy, "Ambulance on the way?" she glanced at his name plate, "Deputy Langley?"

"Dub Langley, yes ma'am. That's just what I came to tell you, Doc. We radioed, but the EMTs can't get here for a while. Rain last night washed a stump big as a tractor out and it's hung up across the low water bridge. They'll have to go all the way around and come over the big bridge.

"How long?"

"Extra hour at least. Can't nothin' get over here quick 'til they get a wrecker crew in."

The faint, but unmistakable, *whump whump* of a helicopter drifted to them. Maggie scanned the sky.

"I'm praying that's MedFlight and not Eyewitness News," she said.

"Well, I'll be," Dub said, looking toward the approaching aircraft, "I guess the EMTs radioed for the chopper from Hot Springs."

"Roy, how're you doing?" Maggie asked.

He pulled the oxygen mask up onto his forehead and reached weakly for her arm, pulling her closer and said haltingly, "I don't know... how all this is gonna ...turn out..." he started.

"You're going to be just fine," she patted his arm.

"No, I mean... the bones. Could be it's... old Indian bones... could be... it's not."

"Don't worry about that now," Maggie reassured him. "Somebody at the coroner's office will sort it out." She replaced his mask, and he took a few breaths before removing it again.

"Doc, they ain't anybody except me," he said all in a rush. "And a secretary...I'd surely... appreciate it... if you'd take care... of things... Just 'til... I get back."

"But I don't..." she began.

"Won't be much," he said. "Dub's certified...Sheriff's boys... know what... to do."

The helicopter landed in the open field close by, and the rescue crew deployed from it. Maggie quickly briefed them on what she knew and what she'd done so far, as the EMTs efficiently transferred Roy to their equipment and loaded him onto the stretcher for the flight to the hospital.

"We'll take care of things here, Roy. I promise," she said, holding Roy's hand as she and Dub walked alongside the stretcher toward the waiting helicopter.

"Dub, you tell...the boys... I said... Doc's in... charge."

"Roger that," the deputy replied, and he and Maggie backed away to get out of the wash of the blades as the aircraft took off.

They walked back down to the river's edge, and at the tape perimeter they donned paper booties and gloves and walked a short way downstream to where Bradford and several volunteers were preparing to lift the bones into an orange body bag. Maggie squatted beside the smallish skeleton and took a closer look. No flesh remained, but here and there scraps of what looked to be muddy fabric of some sort clung to the bones. She could see a few scrubby tufts of dark hair clinging to the skull and the poignant sight of that made her eyes sting with unexpected, unshed tears. *Who were you? What's your story? How did you come to be here?*

"Doc," Dub said, "what you want us to do with these? We gotta secure 'em someplace; we can't get 'em over to Mt. Ida for a while yet. There's a locked room over at the substation here, but it's chock-full right now with waterproof file boxes in case of flooding; I don't think we got room."

"If they're from the mound," she said, "they may wind up going to the Archeological Survey team at the University either up at Fayetteville or over in Little Rock anyway. For now, take them to the clinic; we can lock them in the storage room there. Therma Faye has the key."

"OK. We'll get 'em over there. We're gonna leave one man here to watch over things. A couple of the guys'll come back to go over the ground and collect surface evidence, but after that hard rain I don't expect they'll find much of value."

Deputy Bradford zipped the bag, secured it with a zip tie, and tagged it. He initialed it and had Maggie initial it, and then he and several others hoisted the bag and scrambled up the bank. As their muddy boots grabbed for traction on the slippery slope, they dislodged a clod of mud that rolled down and broke apart against a river rock at the water's edge. Something shiny within it caught Maggie's eye; she sidestepped down the slick embankment to where it lay and plucked it out.

She stooped and rinsed off the mud in the river and held up small ring made of some kind of metal. *Evidence?* In case it was, she realized she'd need something to put it in. She'd noticed there were some plastic zip bags in the crash kit and brown paper sacks to use in cases of hyperventilation, so she walked back upstream to the kit. She slipped the ring inside a small zip bag and put that into one of the paper sacks, marking it with her initials, date, and time. She folded the neck of the sack over itself several times and stuffed it in the pocket of her jacket. She didn't know what the exact protocol was, but that would have to do. She'd give it to Sheriff Perkins.

CHAPTER 13
Cosmic Compost

That evening, Maggie came through the kitchen door just as Miz Hendri removed a black iron skillet of hot cornbread from the oven and set it heavily on the burner grate beside a steaming pot of bean soup. She hung her purse and jacket on the hooks beside the door and poured herself a tall glass of iced tea. After the day she had, she longed for a big glass of wine, but none was around to be had. Beer, wine, and spirits weren't sold to individuals in this county, she'd learned, except by the single serving in licensed restaurants and bars. And she hadn't made the trek two counties over where it could be bought in grocery stores and liquor retailers. But she needed to for nights following days like this one had been.

"Mmmmm. That smells so good," Maggie said. "You know I'd never tried cornbread before I came here. And now, I can't seem to get enough of it."

"My Robert always said you can find something good wherever you go. You must only… "

A knock on the kitchen door interrupted her, and she crossed the room to open it. Rose Ellen peered in through the screen, a couple of carboard flats of eggs in her arms. Seeing her, Miz Hendri wiped her hands on her apron and took several bills from a small jar on the windowsill above the sink.

"*Danke schöen, leibchen*," she said, taking the eggs and handing the girl the cash. Maggie watched as Rose Ellen hurried back to the waiting pickup and climbed in.

"I just can't understand why she doesn't talk," she said.

"Mmm," Miz Hendri murmured, shook her head, and shrugged. "The grief, I suppose."

"I can relate," she said absently, as unbidden images surfaced again of her 13-year-old self soaked and alone on the side of the road after the accident that claimed both her parents had left her orphaned with plenty of grief of her own to deal with. She shook her head to dispel the thoughts. "But still, it's been, what, a couple of years since her mother left? That's just not normal," she persisted. "And beyond that, what mother could leave a sweet child like that? That doesn't add up either. And if so, why?"

"His whiskey," Miz Hendri said matter-of-factly as she turned the cornbread out of the heavy skillet onto a large platter and sliced it.

"Yeah. I worry about that. Is she safe being cared for by a person who drinks so much?"

Miz Hendri shrugged. "I remember when he and Ruth married. I remember that strong, brave, good man. But that was before."

"Before what?"

"Iraq. He was in the service, like my Robert; but for Waylon, the service was his life's work, his career." She bent to remove a bowl of fried potatoes from the warming oven and took them into the dining room.

"What happened?" Maggie asked when Miz Hendri returned to the stove.

The older woman shook her head sadly and shrugged again. "I don't know. Ruth told me a little. It was in 2005, and he was with his unit at… uh… ach, I can't remember the name of the place. Something happened there, something very bad, terrible; something he wouldn't tell even to Ruth; something he couldn't let go of. I don't know more than that. But I do know that whatever it was, he left the service and came back with his soul broken in pieces. I think the best part of him died there."

They heard Nick and Lester coming through the front door, laughing.

"Glad it went well," Nick said. "We can settle up later tonight."

Miz Hendri hefted up the platter of warm cornbread, Maggie grabbed the soup pot, and they joined the men in the dining room for supper.

"Settle up with what?" Maggie asked.

"Football bet," Nick replied. "Lester was foolish enough to take Baylor plus the points against my Longhorns. Sucker!" he said and clapped Lester on the back.

Miz Hendri ladled beans onto split slices of corn bread and passed the filled bowls around. Lester took a bowl, piled his plate with fried potatoes, green onions, and sliced tomatoes, and began to eat.

Around a large mouthful, he said, "Man up to the bank said they found a body this mornin'."

"A body?" Nick's eyebrows shot up. "Where?"

"Down at the river's what I heard," Lester said.

"Bones," Maggie corrected, "not a body." She took a few of the potatoes.

"And poor Roy Owens fell down with a stroke," Miz Hendri added.

"Roy Owens had a stroke?" said Nick.

"No," Maggie corrected again, "probably a heart attack. And we shouldn't be discussing it."

"So, what's the deal with the body?" Nick asked.

"Not sure yet. And it was only bones," she said again. "They were buried either in or beside the big mound by the river. Roy thought maybe a Native American skeleton," Maggie said.

Nick took a bite of cornbread and put a hand in front of his mouth as he spoke "Could be." He swallowed the mouthful before he went on, "Whole county's practically a burial site. Pass me the tomatoes, Lester. And the salt."

Maggie got up and went to the kitchen, bringing back the tea pitcher and the brown paper sack she'd collected at the river.

She poured herself more tea and opened the sack, removing the zip bag. "I found this." She held the plastic bag out in the palm of her hand.

Nick took the bag and started to open it.

"Don't open it. It could be evidence."

He held it up and turned the bag around so he could see it from all angles. "Piece of steel? Maybe a machine part?"

"Or a ring?"

"It's clearly a ring, Mistress of the Obvious," Nick teased.

"You know what I mean," she said, giving him a sideward look. "Jewelry."

"Where'd you find it?"

"In a clod of dirt near the bones," she said.

"Inside the grave bed proper?"

Maggie shook her head and gave a shrug. "Inside? Beside? I don't know. It was in a dirt clod that got kicked loose and rolled down the embankment when they moved the bones."

Nick examined the ring through the clear plastic again, then handed it back to Maggie. "Cosmic compost."

"Huh?"

"The river could have brought it from almost anywhere. Doubt it means much."

Maggie slipped the zip bag back into the brown paper sack and nodded.

"Can't argue with that; you're the excavation expert here. So how come I got stuck babysitting the bones?"

"What do you mean?" Nick said.

"They're parked in my storage room until they're able to transport them to Mt. Ida or Little Rock or Fayetteville or wherever it is they need to go."

"Why you?"

Maggie pushed back from the table, picking up the sack, "Because, unfortunately, Roy appointed me," she said with a tight smile. "And, if all goes well, those bones will be out of my world by Monday. But,

Mr. Caddo Mound expert, they may ultimately end up in yours." She smiled more genuinely now and disappeared through the kitchen door.

***

On Tuesday the waiting room had been full of red noses, watery eyes, and a symphony of coughing, sneezing, and raspy voices. And, Maggie noted with a little sigh of relief, they weren't all daughters, sisters, mothers, and aunts. This chilly, schizoid weather—hot, cold, and wet by turns as the remnants of a Gulf hurricane washed inland—had provided fertile ground for some respiratory bug to bloom. She'd have her hands full with it for a few days while it made the rounds.

She pulled the next chart off the door, and it was more of the same: "Patient c/o cough and sore throat". She was just about to go in, when Therma Faye stopped her. "Dr. Mac, could you maybe see the boy in the trauma room first? He's just five and he's getting kinda worked up."

Maggie returned the chart to the box. "Sure. What's up?"

"Put a Lego up his nose, and it's stuck," she said. "Dad tried to get it out at home. I tried, too, but no luck."

"What's his name?"

"Charlie," Therma Faye said.

Maggie entered the room to find a little tow-headed boy, fidgeting and crying on the end of the table, clutching a beat up, floppy stuffed elephant. His dad, standing beside him, tried with a tissue to wipe away the ribbon of snot that ran down the boy's upper lip, but he squirmed, twisting his head away and wailing even louder.

She approached the boy speaking in gentle tones, "Hey, Charlie. I don't think we've met." Maggie extended her hand to him. "My name's Dr. McKinley, but you can call me Dr. Mac."

Charlie tentatively reached out his hand and eyed her a bit suspicious-ly, but at least curiosity won out, and he'd stopped wailing for the moment. She gently shook his hand and released it.

"Who's your little friend, here?" She pointed at the bedraggled stuffed toy.

"Jojo," he whispered.

"Can you tell me what's bothering you today?" His father began to respond, but Maggie put up a hand and raised a brow to stop him, then waited quietly keeping her gaze on Charlie.

"Lego..." he sniffed and finally mumbled softly. "In here," he said, putting his tiny index finger lightly on the opening of his right nostril.

"Wow! That's amazing. How did it get in there?"

"I put it," he said sheepishly.

"Can I see it?" Maggie said with enthusiasm.

He tipped his head up, and Maggie pulled the penlight from the pocket of her lab coat and shined it into his nostril. She could barely make out a glistening something wedged just beyond the turbinate. "Hmmm. I can't quite see it. Do you think you could lie down and look up at the ceiling? I might be able to see it better."

He lay down on the table and tipped his head all the way back. When she adjusted the strong overhead exam light onto the target, the boy shield-ed his eyes from the bright lamp. "Let's ask JoJo to help out." Maggie said and took his little hand holding the toy and guided it up, draping his flop-py stuffed animal over his eyes.

"There's that's better, isn't it?" Maggie said, receiving a slight nod in answer.

Therma Faye stood at his head, a hand on either side of his face. Not quite touching, but at the ready if needed to stabilize his head.

"Oh, yeah. I can see it now," she said, picking up a bayonet forceps from among the instruments scattered on the ring stand beside the table.

Damn. It was a small, single, clear Lego block, positioned with the closed end facing out. *Of course it is!* Experience had taught her these things were slippery and difficult to grasp. She'd get one chance at this the easy way. Then it would likely be a papoose restraint board and more tears and a fight. She mentally crossed herself.

"What were you building, Charlie?" she asked, talking sweetly and calmly as she brought the forceps closer to his nostril with excruciating and deliberate slowness, until the tips were just inside the opening but not touching him.

"Spiderman," he said and laughed aloud crinkling his nose. And when he did, his nostril flared, and in a single deft move she snagged the offending piece of plastic and brought it out.

Whew. "And *voilà*! There it is!" she said with more relief than she let on, holding it up like a trophy.

Charlie bounced up to a sitting position, wide eyed and grinning.

Maggie sat on the rolling stool and scooted it up close to the table. She wanted to be closer to his eye level or even below it when she spoke. "Now, Charlie, you and I need to make a deal about Legos and other small things."

He looked shyly at her.

"Let's not put them where they don't belong," she said to him. "Let's figure that out, OK?"

"Kay," he said.

"Do they belong in your hands?" she touched both of his with her own.

"Yes, ma'am."

"That's right. And also in their bag or box or what you're building. How about in your ears?"

He puzzled over that for a moment, then answered firmly, "No, not my ears."

"Your mouth?"

"No."

"Your nose?"

"Nooooooo," they said in unison.

"And not in my eyeballs!" Charlie shouted out with a giggle.

"That's right, never in your eyeballs," Maggie smiled. "So, we're agreed on this. No little things in your ears, mouth, nose"

"Or eyeballs!"

"Right." She extended her hand, "Pinkie swear?"

He hooked his small pinkie to hers, "Pinkie swear!"

She dropped the Lego into Therma Faye's gloved hand. "Can we wash this off, please? Charlie might need it; it could be the master Lego that brings Spiderman together. And I think Charlie deserves a really special chicken balloon, too."

"Thanks, Dr. McKinley," Charlie's grateful father said, extending his hand. "Don't know what we'd have done if you weren't here."

Maggie clasped his hand. "You're very welcome, Mr…"

"Davis. Tom, please," he added.

"You're welcome, Tom. Glad we could help."

The waiting room was finally cleared out, and Maggie had just sat down at her desk to give her aching feet a much-needed rest when Donna tapped on the door and stuck her head in.

"Doc, there's somebody on the line about that," she gave a shudder, "thing in the storeroom."

Maggie picked up the receiver, "This is Dr. McKinley."

"Doctor, good afternoon. Wilbur Aaronson, here, from the State Crime Lab. I'm calling about the bones found there last week. I understand you're holding them?"

"Yes, that's right. We have them. I thought they were going to be picked up yesterday, but they're still here."

"That's what I'm calling about. What with Coroner Owens out of commission, we've been asked by Sheriff Perkins of Montgomery County to handle the details of the post-mortem procedures on this individual. And we will need to have a forensic anthropologist examine the remains first, since, as I understand it, they were found in proximity to a supposed Native American burial mound. Statute says we have to determine age of the bones and ethnicity first."

"That's what I assumed might be the case," she said.

"Well, there's been a snag on this end. Dr. Caldwell—that's the forensics doc who's on tap to look at them—has been away on a major case, a mass grave found up in Canada."

"I think I read something about that online. Terrible discovery."

"Yeah, just awful. Lotta kids. Anyway, he says he won't be able to get back down here for about another week. So, if the bones are secure, we're hoping you can hold onto them there for a bit longer before we make the transfer."

"Of course," Maggie replied, "we have them locked up tight. So, whatever you need us to do, we'll do." *Donna's not going to like it, but she'll just have to deal with it.*

CHAPTER 14
Healing Waters

The rest of the week was a lot more of the same, though the number of snotty noses, sore throats, and coughs in the waiting room had dwindled to a trickle by Friday. Maggie had been able to arrange a *locum tenens* doc with a staffing agency in Little Rock to cover calls through Monday night to give her an extra full day with Jeff, but it was costing her more than she'd figured. At least based on what she, herself, had gotten paid when she'd occasionally moonlighted as a resident. By some miracle, her fill-in arrived early, meaning she was able to get out of town by late afternoon and to Hot Springs in plenty of time to grab a bite to eat before arriving at the tiny airport to board her flight to Memphis—a small luxury she hadn't counted on.

The redeye from Memphis to Newark was half full, and she was pleasantly surprised to have scored the whole row to herself on the bulkhead in coach. *So far, the stars seem to be in alignment.* Pulling up both armrests, she wrapped herself in a soft, warm pashmina and tried to get some sleep. She dozed fitfully for about half an hour, but when the flight proved too turbulent for sound sleep, she finally gave up and pulled out a medical journal, hoping that if the pilots found some smoother air, the articles would be just dry enough to lull her to sleep. Sadly, such air eluded them, and sleep eluded Maggie.

Her reward, if there could be said to be one, was an earlier than expected arrival, courtesy of a tailwind and—miracle of all miracles—no plane sitting on their gate when they got there. She stopped just long enough at the ladies' room to give her hair and teeth a quick brush, splash a little water on her face to clear the cobwebs, and throw on some lip gloss, then she grabbed a cab into the City. It pulled up in front of the familiar awning at 15 CPW just before 7:30 am.

The doorman stepped out to open the taxi's door for her; it wasn't José, the weekend regular, but the guy's face was sort of familiar to her. He apparently recognized hers, too, offering a cheerful 'Welcome back, Miss' instead of a perfunctory 'Welcome' as he collected her small rolling bag from the trunk.

"I'm going to Mr. Winslow's on 18," she said as they entered the lobby.

"Are you expected?"

"Not yet. I got in a little early," she said, shading the truth a bit and giving him a smile with all the wattage she could muster after a sleepless night of travel.

He lifted the house phone. "OK. I'll call up."

Just then, José returned to the lobby desk, recognized her immediately and waved his partner off on the call up. "Doctor! It's been a while. So good to see you."

"José," she said, "Hi! It's great to see you, too."

"We didn't know you were coming."

"Last minute idea. I hopped an overnight flight so I could spend the weekend with Dr. Winslow."

"It's early; you want me to call up?"

"I really want to surprise him."

He nodded and gave her a conspiratorial wink as he ushered her to the elevator. "He's gonna be thrilled," he said turning the key and sending the elevator up.

The elevator door opened onto the silent, semi-dark of the empty foyer. It looked like even Esmeralda wasn't up and about yet. *Perfect.* She left her suitcase in the foyer and tip-toed up the staircase to the master suite.

Jeff's bedroom was cool and dark. He'd closed the blackout draperies over the wall of windows. *Must have had a long night of surgery, and he was planning to sleep in. Too bad, honey. Plenty of time to sleep later.* She contemplated for a moment just taking off her clothes and slipping into bed next to him, but it had been a long night and she was really looking forward to that Saturday morning coffee. She'd wake him; they'd have coffee then sleep and whatever else later.

The room was so dark she could barely make out the bed as she felt her way around the wall to the bedside table where she knew the drapery remote control ought to be and, indeed, there it was. She walked around to the foot of the bed and zapped the remote toward the windows, sending the curtains parting on their track and flooding the room with morning sunlight.

"Wake up, sleepyhead," Maggie said sweetly, spinning back around expectantly to see the look on Jeff's face. But as he sprang up from the pillows, the expression on his face was one of stunned shock. Then she noticed was that he wasn't alone.

Judith Rawlins, eyes wide, chestnut hair a tangled mess, gave a muffled shriek from the bed beside him, hurriedly gathering the bedclothes and clutching them to her naked chest.

It took a few seconds for Maggie to process the scene. She almost couldn't believe what she was seeing. Actually, there was no *almost* about it. She flat out couldn't believe it.

"What the fuh..." her voice trailed off, confused, hurt. Tears stung her eyes, but she'd be damned if she was going to let them spill out and blinked them back.

"Mags!" Jeff jumped up and searched frantically among the pile of discarded clothing on the floor around the bed for something to put on. "Maggie, wait!"

She'd already bolted out the door and down the stairs to the foyer, slamming her hand against the elevator call button. The doors opened straight away—thank God the car was still on 18—and she leapt in with her suitcase and hit the 'close door' button. As the doors glided shut, she saw Jeff in his boxer briefs taking the stairs two at a time. Heard him pounding on the closed doors above and calling her name as the car descended.

When the doors opened into the lobby, she was relieved that neither doorman was in evidence. She rushed quickly out the front door and practically ran down the sidewalk all the way to Columbus Circle, where a taxi was disgorging its passengers at the curb. She grabbed the cab and headed back to Newark Liberty.

Her phone buzzed. 'JEFF' showed on the display. She declined the call. It buzzed again. Decline. And again, and again. Decline. Decline. Finally, she turned it off. Alone in the cab, eyes safely hidden behind a pair of sunglasses, she let the stinging tears quietly flow.

At Newark, she was able to change her Monday return flight and was scheduled to depart for Memphis at 10:35. It cost her a $150 change fee, but she didn't care. She felt gutted, like her heart had been ripped from her chest, and right now all she wanted was to put distance between herself and Jeff.

While waiting for hours at the gate in Newark, it occurred to her that she had call coverage all weekend, and she couldn't very well tell the rent-a-doc she didn't need him now. But she didn't have to go home yet, and frankly she didn't really want to.

What she wanted, needed, was to talk to Charlotte from Charlotte, but she'd texted Maggie last night that she and the kids were flying to be with Ford in Florida, where after a magnificent round on Friday, he had the 36-hole lead in this weekend's lucrative Children's Miracle Network tour event. She didn't want to be a Debbie Downer adding her sadness to what should be a joyous and potentially lucrative weekend for the whole

Schaflein clan. So, much though she longed to lean on her sista, no way would she interrupt them now. And that pretty much left her on her own. After weighing her options, she decided that when she landed in Arkansas, instead of driving back to Caddo Bend, she'd just stay in Hot Springs for the weekend.

She turned her phone back on to use the Newark airport's internet to find a room and saw 16 missed calls from Jeff, a dozen texts, and 5 voice messages. She ignored them and googled *Hot Springs, Arkansas,* which presented her with a wealth of interesting information about the town.

According to Wikipedia, it was a US National Park, famous the world over for its natural thermal springs and the historic bathhouses that had sprung up to take advantage of them. Wiki and Miz Hendri agreed on this. But its history was even older: Native Americans, she read, had for centuries considered the Valley of the Vapors, as they called the area, a safe haven where even warring tribes gathered in peace to bathe in the healing waters. *Big point in its favor. I could use a safe haven about now. And healing.*

On the racier, slightly more recent side, the infamous Al Capone had made Hot Springs a frequent haunt. Back in the gangster heyday of the 1920s and 30s, when it was a free-wheeling, high-rolling gambling town and Las Vegas was a pit-stop in the desert, he and his gang visited there often, so the Wiki entry said, staying at the historic Arlington Hotel that dated from 1875 and was still in operation. She decided that a small town that could boast "Al Capone slept here!" and "We bathe the world!" deserved at least a look. Besides, it was her mother's birthplace; she should make the pilgrimage on those grounds alone.

She'd still have to pay the rent-a-doc anyway, so why not treat herself a little, unwind, have some space to think this whole awful Judith catastrophe through undisturbed? No reason she could muster. Convinced some time alone at the elegant old hotel and spa would do her a world of good, she booked a room at the Arlington, determined to enjoy a long weekend of solitude, soak up some history, get a massage, and, per Miz Hendri's recommendation, take the healing waters from the hot mineral springs. A little healing was exactly what the doctor ordered.

On Saturday afternoon, after she'd checked in, she'd walked the scenic Promenade and fed the pigeons, then strolled back to the hotel, poking into shops along the avenue across from the historic Bathhouse Row. That night she'd eaten well, and also badly, if devouring every last molecule of a Grand Marnier soufflé can be said to be bad—and it was anything but bad. Then she'd soaked to her chin in scalding hot mineral water they piped directly into her bathtub. And slept in.

Sunday morning, she had enjoyed room service breakfast followed by a really good massage in the spa and had come back to her room where she intended to finish the small history of Hot Springs she'd picked up yesterday in the gift shop downstairs.

Her phone buzzed, and she glanced at the display. It was a text from Charlotte. And, she noticed, another dozen text messages, phone messages, and missed calls from Jeff that she'd ignored. She'd need a lot more distance from the painful image that was forever seared onto her retinas before she would trust herself to speak to him. If she ever could.

Charlotte's exuberant text read: *Ford in final pairing!!! Tees off at 2:20 eastern. Wish us luck!!!!!*

She'd texted back, *All the luck in the world! Go get em, Ford!*

Maggie picked up her book and tried again to read, but alone in her room all she could think about was Jeff, and before she knew it, she found herself sucked back into a pit of self-pity and sadness and began to cry again. She pulled a tissue from the box beside the bed and blew her nose loudly. *For Pete's sake, pull yourself together!* The thought brought to mind a quote she'd seen yesterday on a package of novelty cocktail napkins for sale at one of the shops she'd browsed downtown: *Pour yourself a drink, put on some lipstick, and pull yourself together! ~Elizabeth Taylor*

She didn't see the point to lipstick on a Sunday afternoon alone in a hotel room, but there were two splits of prosecco in the mini-bar fridge. She opened one and poured it, and took her glass over to the bed, where she propped herself up against the pile of pillows and threw a soft blanket over her legs. A glutton for punishment, she queued up *Adele 21* on her playlist and drank the split. And its mate. And cried some more. *Liz was wrong. Or maybe you had to do the lipstick part.*

She slept in again on Monday morning and when she awoke everything ached. She was a firm believer that motion was lotion, so she warmed up her muscles with two full Moon Salutation yoga cycles in her room and then decided to take a run up Hot Springs Mountain, which the concierge had been kind enough to point out began on Fountain Street right outside the hotel. She secured a late checkout and headed out.

The paved street took her on a long, steady upward climb for about a mile or two through a forest of mixed hardwoods and evergreens interspersed with rocky outcroppings on either side and then through a short woodland trail up to the summit overlook, where she was rewarded with a glorious display of fall color painting the valley below. She sat on a flat-topped, lichen-covered boulder at the overlook for a long while, listening to the wind blow through the pines and watching a pair of hawks circling on the updrafts.

The autumn foliage reminded her of Central Park, and that reminded her of Jeff, and that made her heart hurt again. A car pulled into the overlook and cruised slowly around the circle twice. Two teenagers, a boy and a girl. *Probably looking for a quiet place to neck.* And that made her heart hurt, too, so she left them to their afternoon delight and headed down the series of switchbacks that led back to the hotel. She didn't want to think about the whole situation anymore and purposefully pushed any thoughts of Jeff from her mind.

She showered, dressed, packed up her small bag and left it with the concierge while she grabbed a late lunch in the dining room, which meant getting off a little later than she'd planned, but she was starving from the run.

She also intended to make a stop on the way back at the big Liquor Barn she'd noticed coming into Hot Springs on Friday night. Miz Hendri kept a decanter of so-so sherry on the buffet in the front room, but that was about the extent of liquid adult refreshment in the house, and since she couldn't buy bottles of beer, wine, or spirits in Caddo Bend or anywhere else in the semi-dry county she wanted to grab a few bottles of wine and maybe a bottle of Jameson to keep in her room for those occasional times when she could use a tasty adult libation. The wine selection had proven much more robust and interesting than she would have thought, and she bought a fifth of Jameson and a couple of nice Willamette Valley pinots and several bottles of Napa cabernet on sale and gotten back on the road.

While she still had good cell service, she checked in with the rent-a-doc, Dan Milsap, to let him know she'd be back in less than an hour, and he could head out if he needed to. He assured her that everything had been quiet in her absence, at least on the medical front, and that he was going to grab dinner at the café then head back to Little Rock.

And then she called Charlotte, who answered immediately and without preamble launched into a hole-by-hole replay of the weekend's final golf round that culminated in Ford and another golfer going to a playoff that went for 3 holes. It finally ended when Ford's long birdie putt to tie and push the sudden death on to yet another hole curled around the edge of the cup and lipped out. Not the win they'd hoped for, but even taking second on the big stage would be a mega boost to his career and a huge payday. Maggie was happy to revel in the vicarious joy of her retelling.

"Sista! It was so exciting. I cannot describe how exciting," Charlotte said. "But enough about that. How was *your* weekend?"

"Not great," Maggie said.

"Why not? Did he end up in the operating room all weekend or something?"

"Not exactly. Well, actually, I don't know."

"Now you're losing me," Charlotte said. "Did you not go to New York?"

Maggie's eyes filled up instantly, and her throat tightened. For a moment the words wouldn't come. She dashed her hand across her eyes and swallowed hard.

"Yes, I went." Her voice broke, "And Judith was there."

"At the penthouse?"

"In bed." Maggie could barely croak the words out, "With him." And she burst into sobs.

"In bed in bed? You can't be serious. What did you do?"

"I left."

"Why didn't you call me?"

"I am calling you," she was a little calmer now.

"I mean before."

"You and the kids were on the way to the tournament on an emotional high. I didn't want to put a damper on that. Besides, what could you have done?"

"I could have called him a rat! I could have called him up and given him what for!"

"None of that would have changed anything. And I really needed some time alone. I spent the weekend in a hotel spa in Hot Springs alternating between being a tourist and wallowing in the Garden of Poor Me. I'll be OK. I just have to figure out what's next."

"Have you talked to him?"

"No. He's called and texted fifty times, but I haven't answered. I will at some point."

"Is it something you can forgive? A dumb-ass one-off?"

"I don't know. Honestly, I just don't know. They have a history."

"Well, I'm here tethered to this phone if you need me. Day or night."

"I know. Thank you. Tell Ford I'm proud of him. And kiss the angels. I'll give you a shout in a day or two."

It was late when Maggie turned into the drive at Miz Hendri's. She noticed Nick's truck wasn't in back, but there was strange car parked in her usual spot in the small lot behind the house. *Must be a new guest.* She pulled in beside it and came in through the evening chill to a kitchen that was cozy and welcoming. And smelled pleasantly of baking and warm autumn spices. *Gingerbread? Had to be.* She spotted the source of the delicious aroma cooling on the counter.

She'd missed dinner but had phoned ahead to let Miz Hendri know she'd be late, which, of course, despite her protestations, elicited a promise to keep a plate warm for her in the oven. After overdoing it all weekend and eating a late lunch, Maggie really wasn't hungry now; she just wanted to get upstairs and unpack.

The house was quiet – thank God. Nick wasn't home, and she thought Lester had already moved on to examine the next bank on his circuit. Even if not, he usually ate and went straight up to his room. She didn't relish fielding any questions about her New York getaway, and as luck would have it Miz Hendri seemed to have turned in, too, so she didn't have to.

Maggie took the plate from the oven and lifted the foil – not one pork chop, but two, big thick ones, with generous mounds of turnip greens and squash casserole of some sort, and a big piece of cornbread. Her stomach rebelled at the volume. *Lunch tomorrow… and maybe the next day.* She replaced the foil, slipped the plate into the refrigerator, and headed upstairs.

She'd just tossed her suitcase onto the bed and unzipped it when there was a soft rap on her door. *Uh oh. Did Miz Hendri find the plate in the fridge already?* Formulating a plausible excuse, she opened the door.

Jeff stood there in the dim hallway light. Her heart lurched, and though she was able to suppress an audible gasp, despite her best efforts, tears stung behind her eyes. She blinked them back and swallowed hard.

Taking a ragged breath, she finally found her voice. "Why are you here?"

"You wouldn't return my calls," he said softly. "Can I come in?"

"I'd rather you didn't," she didn't budge from the door.

"Maggie, we need to talk."

"There's really nothing to say. A picture's worth a thousand words, and that's a picture I'll never forget." She started to close the door.

"Please. I don't want to do this in the hallway," he pleaded softly, keeping his hand on the door.

"I don't want to do it at all."

"Please," his eyes implored her. "I've come all this way. Can't you just give me a chance to explain?"

She stepped back from the door. "Make it quick. I'm tired, and I have a full day tomorrow."

He closed the door softly behind him and came to stand closely to her.

Maggie backed away from him. "Say what you have to say and go."

"What you saw meant nothing—less than nothing—to me."

"Well, it sure didn't mean 'nothing' to me!" She folded her arms across her chest and stared silently at him. "I've been gone, what? Two months?"

"Judith and I are just old friends."

"With benefits," she added.

He ignored her remark and continued, "It's a meaningless hook up that goes all the way back to when we were in school at Andover. Friday night she came back with me for a drink after a board meeting at the hospital, and I'm honestly not sure how it happened."

I'll bet she knows precisely how it happened, Maggie thought, but then an awful thing hit her. "So, this went on the whole three years we've been together?" Maggie asked, incredulous.

"No! We'd ended things. This was just a stupid lapse of judgement."

"Stupid, yes, but costly," she said, "because now I know."

"What do you know?" he asked.

"That I can't trust you to be honest with me."

"Mags," he began, but she interrupted him with a raised palm.

"If you wanted to be free to see Judith, you should have had the decency to be up front about it."

"I'm not 'seeing' Judith," he pleaded. "I don't want to 'see' Judith."

"OK, fine. If you want to have sex with Judith, or anyone else for that matter, that's your call. But you owed it to me, to us, to what I thought was our committed relationship to say so honestly." She paused and looked straight into his eyes. "Although I think you know me well enough by now to be pretty sure I would have no desire to dance in a chorus line."

"Mags, please," he said softly, reaching out for her, "it's not like that; you know I love you."

"Don't," she said stiffening and stepping out of his reach. "Your actions scream otherwise. It's going to take some time for me to get beyond this. And I'll at least be honest enough with you to say I'm not entirely sure I can. Now please go. I'm tired."

He started to speak again, but she waved him off, shaking her head 'no' and, he dropped his arms to his sides and left her.

She took the bottle of Jameson from the bag and cracked the cap pouring herself a healthy shot into the water glass beside the bathroom sink. Catching a glimpse of her image in the mirror, she thought *what the hell* and pulled a tube of Chanel Rouge Sari Dore out of the drawer.

Thumbing up her iTunes, she sat down in the rocker in the darkened room with her whiskey, her shattered heart, and Tom Waits. In lipstick.

The next morning, she found an envelope had been slid under the edge of the door of her room. The bold slant of her name written across the front unmistakably and achingly familiar. She hesitated for a moment then opened it, inhaling as she did the slightest hint of Paco Rabanne that still clung to the paper.

"My dearest Maggie,

I can't begin to say how sorry I am for my impossibly stupid lapse. I know it has made it hard for you to believe me or have faith in what I say, but I promise you, you can trust me from now on. I just need you to believe how much I love you and need you and how much I regret hurting you. I made an awful mistake, one that won't ever happen again. I was being honest when I said it truly meant nothing, but I realize that's cold comfort.

I am going back to New York tonight, so you won't have to worry about running into me tomorrow. I want to give you all the time and space you need to – I fervently hope – forgive me. I still have the Gala tickets and our favorite table at Daniel reserved for New Year's Eve, and I'm praying we'll be able to use them to welcome the new year together. Please just think about it. I'll be waiting…patiently…to hear from you when you're ready. -All my love, J"

CHAPTER 15
Veteran's Day

Maggie was relieved that in the days since Jeff's departure, he'd kept his word and hadn't tried again to contact her. Hearing his voice right now would simply be too hard. She'd promised him that she'd sort all this out in her head, and she appreciated his giving her the time to do that, but every time she was alone with her thoughts that image of Judith in tangled sheets forced its way into her mind and tied her stomach up in knots.

Consequently, she'd spent every morning this week with the 'girls', the killer CrossFit workouts named, like hurricanes, after feisty, powerful women—Angie, Barbara, Cindy, Diane, Fran...and more. She'd discovered them in med school, when a classmate had introduced her to the CrossFit gym – or box as the gyms are called – in the neighborhood not too far from her apartment. She'd been hooked right away on the measurable, hard-driving, physical challenge of the exercise philosophy, but even more so on the warm camaraderie she'd found there. She'd become a regular, turning up at the box four or five mornings every week at 5:30 am for the workout of the day—the WOD—or sometimes in the evening after she got off if she couldn't make the morning class.

A hard workout distracted her mind like nothing else, and she'd purposefully worn herself out with her 'girlfriends' all week long to keep from thinking about the Jeff mess. Performing Angie's prescribed regimen of 100 pull ups, pushups, sit ups, and squats as fast as possible, as she'd done yesterday, left little room for other thoughts of any kind. At least during the half hour that she spent warming up to the grueling 20 or so minutes it took her to perform that WOD.

But today was Sunday and, for her, always a CrossFit Rest Day. She'd learned that the rest interval was as important as the work, and she scheduled a couple of rest days in every week. Thus, though it was after eight, she was still snuggled under the duvet, soaking in her thoughts, letting her mind drift. She stretched lazily and climbed out of bed to perform a double Moon Salutation. That and a scalding hot shower gave her the grounding and mind-cleansing effect she sought. She dressed in Sunday-appropriate light wool slacks and a cashmere cowl-neck sweater and open cardigan to walk over to Molly's Café for breakfast before the Veteran's Day Tribute, schedule to begin at 11.

The bunting and flags fluttered in the morning breeze as she crossed the green, walking past the white folding chairs that had been set up in precise rows on the grass in front of the gazebo; she felt like she was stepping into a Norman Rockwell painting. Bright sun, blue skies, puffy white clouds, neat storefronts facing the square. Red, white, and blue bunting everywhere.

When she entered the café, the owner, Molly O'Connor, stood behind the counter pouring coffee and bantering with the diners. She was a woman of about 60, and though the bright copper color of her hair now came from a bottle, her broad, welcoming smile was still quite genuine.

"Good morning to ya', Doctor," she said. "Will it be your usual today?"

"Hi, Molly," Maggie said, taking the last stool at the counter. "No, I think I'll have just a couple of over easy eggs and some bacon this morning and fruit. No toast."

"Cuppa?" Molly said lifting her brows and the pot.

"Yes, please," Maggie answered and pushed the empty crockery mug in front of her forward.

"OK, here you go." Molly poured steaming coffee to the rim. "Eggs'll be right up." She jotted the order on her pad, tore it off, and impaled it on the spike on the ledge of the pass-through to the kitchen behind her. "Order in," she announced loudly and hit the little desk bell.

Sitting at a table in the corner, Charlie Davis, from whose nose she'd extracted the Lego block, and his parents were just finishing their breakfast. When Charlie saw her, he hopped up and ran over to greet her, his stuffed elephant waggling in his hand.

"Dr. Mac," Charlie shouted, "Dr. Mac!"

Maggie turned when she heard her name and saw Charlie barreling her way; she acknowledged Tom's wave with a smile and gave a nod and wave to his wife, Becky, whose growing silhouette announced Charlie would be a big brother before long. She climbed off the stool and squatted to meet Charlie at his eye level.

"Hey, Charlie!"

"Me and JoJo are gonna watch the parade," he said

"I am, too," she said.

"Daddy says there's gonna be two Army jeeps!" He held up his two fingers for emphasis.

"Really? That sounds so cool. I can't wait to see that." She narrowed her eyes a bit and gave him a questioning look. "Do you remember our pinkie swear promise? We never put anything small in our ears, mouth, or nose?"

"Or eyeballs," he giggled and crooked his little finger and held it up. Maggie hooked her pinkie to his. "Pinkie swear!" they said in unison.

From the door, Tom called to him, "Let's go, buddy. Parade's about to start."

"'Kay. Bye, Dr. Mac," he said.

"Bye, Charlie." His enthusiasm at seeing her again warmed her heart and made her glad she'd come.

"Here ya go, Doctor," Molly said, laying the plate in front of her.

"Thanks," Maggie said, cutting up the eggs and sprinkling them generously with salt and pepper and a dash of Tabasco before digging in. *Mmmmm. Perfect.*

Outside, she heard the booming of a bass drum and four shrill whistles. She looked up to see the Caddo Valley High School band marching down Main Street on the far side of the square, followed by a color guard, then a small troop of scouts in uniform, both boys and girls, marching behind in formation and carrying a hand-painted banner that read 'Thank You For Your Service!' A flat-bed trailer pulled by a pair of sturdy mules and bedecked in red, white, and blue crepe paper streamers and tiny fluttering flags held a tableau recreation of the US flag being raised at Iwo Jima. Then came the two olive drab Army Jeeps Charlie had been so eager to see, each driven by an ROTC cadet from the area high school and bearing a pair of elderly veterans in uniform, who waved to the crowd along the street. After that came the town's fire engine, letting loose an occasional wail of the siren to the delight of the kids on the sidewalk, and last of all, with lights flashing, came Sheriff Perkins in the big black and white patrol wagon. The procession made its way slowly around the square in front of the café, finally coming to a halt a few blocks up the street. Not exactly the Macy's parade, she mused, but short, sweet, and utterly marvelous.

A big, barrel-chested man came up beside Maggie to pay for his meal. He was dressed in a bright white shirt, dark suit and tie, his carefully combed, unnaturally brown hair swept back from his forehead. He laid the check and a twenty on the counter beside the register and greeted Maggie. "Well, good morning, Dr. McKinley. I don't believe we've formally met." He proffered his hand, "Coot Raines." Maggie took his hand, finding the experience something like she would imagine shaking a catcher's mitt might feel, not that she'd ever actually done that. She'd heard his name mentioned and knew he was Caddo Bend's mayor. From the size of him, probably also a former star tackle for some football team or other.

"And this is my wife, Billie," he said indicating the petite woman beside him, very proper in a prim, navy shirtwaist dress and a single strand of pearls at her throat, her salt and pepper hair pulled into a tight bun. A winter white cardigan thrown around her shoulders. A jeweled flag pin on its lapel.

"Lovely to meet you, both," Maggie replied.

"I do hope you're planning to join our little celebration this morning," Billie Raines said in a sweet Southern drawl.

"I'm looking forward to it. I thought I'd grab breakfast beforehand."

"Of course," Billie said, "enjoy your meal, and we'll see you over at the Tribute." The couple departed, with Coot stopping at almost every table to shake someone's hand or clap someone on the back or laugh at a joke. *Must be exhausting to be a politician,* she thought.

After breakfast, Maggie wandered across to the green and spotted Miz Hendri and Mr. Purifoy sitting side by side. She made her way through the milling crowd and took an empty seat beside them. "Hi. Mind if I join you?"

"Not at all," she replied, patting Maggie's knee as she slid into the seat. "Sit. Sit."

"Good morning, Maggie," Mr. Purifoy leaned around and said, "and a beautiful one it is, isn't it?"

"Glorious," she said, taking in his neatly pressed uniform and the clutch of ribbons and medals on his chest. "Papa, was that you I saw riding in one of the Army Jeeps?"

"It was. The local VFW occasionally asks me to ride, probably only because I can still fit into the old uniform," he chuckled.

The gazebo stage was now crowded with the seated choir, speakers, and other dignitaries. And Velma, at a spinet piano. She also spotted JD, sitting on the end of the back row of singers. The happy chatter of the audience stilled instantly when at 11 o'clock the bell from the church tower sounded, deep and resonant, then slowly tolled 10 more times. When the last reverberation finally disappeared, Mayor Raines stood and walked to the microphone.

"Ladies and gentlemen, will you please stand for the color guard and Pledge of Allegiance." A quartet of Eagle scouts in uniform appeared from behind the gazebo, one bearing the American flag, another the Arkansas flag, and the last the flag of the Boy Scouts of America, marching to the cadence of a drummer who followed behind them. They made their way to the front, came to a halt, and presented the colors. Hats came off, hands covered hearts, veterans saluted, and everyone stood and joined in when Mayor Raines intoned "I pledge allegiance to the flag of the United States of America…"

Maggie hadn't had occasion to recite the Pledge in many years, possibly since boarding school. She began to repeat the familiar words, but on this beautiful day, with the flags snapping in the breeze against the clear blue skies, her throat clenched, and she felt the saliva gather in the back of her mouth and the tears well in her eyes. She sniffed and blinked them back, able only to silently mouth the final words, *with liberty and justice for all.*

The pastor stood and gave a long invocation, then JD rose and walked to the microphone in silence. In a clear, rich baritone voice he sang a simple, unadorned, *a capella* rendition of the National Anthem, more beautiful and moving than any she'd ever heard. Velma and the choir joined him in beautiful harmonies and accompaniment on verses 2 and 3 and then invited the audience to sing along on verse 4 from the text printed in their programs. And those less-familiar words brought the tears back to her eyes. *Oh, thus be it ever that free men shall stand between their loved homes and the war's desolation. Blessed with victory and peace may this Heaven-rescued land praise the power that has made and preserved us a nation. Then conquer we must, when our cause it is just, and this be our motto: in God is our trust.*

And the star-spangled banner forever will wave o'er the land of the free and the home of the brave.

The audience applauded vigorously and took their seats, then an elderly gentleman in a sharply pressed uniform was helped in a walker to the microphone to recount an amazing story. In a voice surprising clear for his age, he gave an account of the uncommon courage and valor he had witnessed and been a part of in a naval battle, called the Battle of the Komandorski, against the Japanese in WWII.

Their ship, the heavy cruiser USS Salt Lake City, on its way to the Aleutian Islands, was hit amidships by Japanese destroyer shells, damaging her rudder and leaving her unable to maneuver. Salt water fouled her fuel lines rendering her engines unable to run. Fires from the hits soon cloaked her in thick, black smoke that mercifully hid the fact that she was dead in the water. An overwhelming Japanese naval force was closing fast, and the US fleet was too far away to help them. Their second in command, Worthington 'Worthy' Bitler, assembled the men and told them they were likely done for and to not bother donning life vests when the attack came because the water was below 40 degrees, and they'd likely not live long enough in it to be rescued. He said, and his men unanimously agreed, they would go down fighting before they'd surrender. So, the men kicked into action and moved all guns and ammo to the side of the ship facing the enemy's approach. They'd hit the enemy with everything they had. Their destroyers would make a crazed zigzagging run right at the enemy battleship and hope to get within range to launch their torpedoes. Even the radio operator got into the act, sending out messages in a code known to have been broken by the Japanese, intimating that the American bombers and fighters were moments away. The trickery worked and the Japanese fleet turned and sailed away. And then, by the grace of God, he said, the engineers were able to restart her engines. Their ship sailed more miles, fired more rounds, and lost fewer men than any other of its class, he proudly related. And she made it through the war to finally be purposefully, peacefully scuttled when her days of usefulness were done.

When he was finished and the applause for him died down, the choir sang a beautiful, haunting rendition of *Shenandoah*. And when they'd finished, the mayor rose again and spoke, paying honor to the sacrifices of both the veterans who'd answered the call and their families, and reminding all present that freedom isn't free.

"The cost of the freedoms we enjoy and too often take for granted has been paid for by the blood and sweat and sometimes the lives of the men and women who serve. We owe them an everlasting debt of gratitude," he said at last, "and we thank them all for their service."

Then he asked all veterans present in the audience to stand as their branch of the military was called out and their spirited service anthem sung by the choir. Beside Miz Hendri, Papa rose from his seat and stood proudly at attention when 'Army' was called, and his service anthem was sung. She saw JD stand as well.

Maggie scanned the crowd as here and there veterans of each branch rose and stood in turn—the old and not so old, men, women, black, white, brown—to accept the thanks of this tiny corner of a grateful nation. Then she noticed Waylon's beat up truck parked across the street in front of Molly's Café. He and Rose Ellen sat quietly in the cab, windows down, present but apart.

When the medley ended, the mayor thanked everyone for coming and invited them to enjoy the food and drink, courtesy of the local VFW chapter, set up on the tables on the lawn behind them. The color guard retired the colors, and a pair of buglers played Taps, their plaintive melodies echoing one another on the soft breeze. As the last note faded, Maggie saw Waylon's truck pull away.

Afterward, she stood on the green chatting with Miz Hendri and Papa and drinking tepid coffee from a paper cup. She spotted JD across the green, helping the old veteran who had spoken so eloquently about his service into a car, and excused herself.

"Beautifully done," she said as she came up behind him, touching his shoulder.

He turned around and gifted her with a dimpled smile, so warm and welcoming that it caught her off guard.

"Glad you made it," he said. "And glad you enjoyed it. I don't get the chance to sing much anymore, but this is an occasion that means a lot to me."

"You have a gorgeous voice. In fact, the whole ceremony was beautiful; I'm so happy I came." His eyes scanned her face with an intensity that caused her to look away. "That incredible story of the naval battle...wow!" She shook her head in amazement.

"Yeah, that old guy's a pistol. Lives over at the Veteran's Home now, but apart from needing a little help walking and breathing, he's sharp as a tack."

"Well, he tells an exciting tale. I felt like I was right there on the deck with him."

"Yeah, Jake's still got all his wits about him."

"How old is he?" she asked

"Oh, must be 90 or about that. Not many of those old guys left. About a million and a half now, I think I read somewhere. Something like that. And nearly a quarter million dying every year now. Won't be long before they're all gone and their wealth of experiences with them." He touched her elbow, "Want to grab some food? Singing always makes me hungry," he laughed.

They got at the back of the food line that snaked its way toward the tables and Maggie said, "I just can't get over how wonderful today was. I'm not sure what I expected, but this exceeded it. Who puts it all together?"

"Velma, you know over at the post office? She's ramrodded this Veteran's Day event every year for as long as I can remember. And the one on

Memorial Day, too. She marshals the local scout troops to decorate every veteran's grave with the flag, and she sees to it that we get to hear the old timer's stories straight from the source."

"She's a ball of fire, isn't she?"

"She's a gold star wife, you know."

"Yeah. She mentioned -"

"Somebody get the doc!" The shout came from the gazebo stage. Maggie saw a gaggle of people crowded around someone lying on the stage floor. She took off at a run, with JD right behind her.

When they got there, she scaled the six stairs up to the stage level in two jumps and the crowd parted to let her in. Velma Bradford lay on the boards.

"What happened?" she said, kneeling beside Velma and feeling for the pulse at her wrist, finding it very fast and her skin pale and sweaty, though the day was cool.

"I don't know for sure. I was helping her load up her music, and she just went down. Didn't say a word. Just slumped to the floor," Eldon Medlock, who was squatting beside Velma said.

"Velma? Velma? Can you hear me?" Maggie said, lightly slapping the back of Velma's hand, but getting no response.

"Did she hit her head?" Maggie asked, feeling Velma's skull and neck gingerly. *No lumps, nothing bleeding.*

"No, I was right by her, and I caught her before she hit," Eldon said. "She's diabetic, I know that."

"Where's her purse? Or bag?" Maggie said urgently. "If she's diabetic, she probably has a glucose monitor with her. Does she take insulin?"

"Here it is," a woman handed the shoulder bag to Maggie, who opened it and immediately found a black zip case with the glucose monitor, test strips, lancets, syringes, alcohol swabs, and vial of insulin. *That answers that question.*

Maggie activated the monitor, opened and inserted a new strip, swabbed and pricked Velma's finger, and touched the strip to the bead of blood that formed. The monitor beeped: 68. She needed glucose. Sugar tablets. *Where are they? She's bound to have some with her.* Maggie dug into the purse again and came up with a roll of Sweet Tarts candy. Perfect if you're conscious, but she'd need to chew those and right now she was out.

"Can somebody get me a container of orange juice or some packets of sugar from the coffee table, please?" Maggie said. "And a bottle of water." Moments later, JD returned to tell her there wasn't any juice left and handed her the sugar and a small bottle of water and a straw. She emptied three packets of sugar into the bottle and shook to dissolve it, inserting the straw.

"Eldon, can you help me raise her up?" Together they brought her to a sitting position and Eldon supported her back.

"Velma?" Maggie gave her cheeks some gentle slaps. "Velma? Can you hear me?" This time her question elicited a muffled response. "Velma, your blood sugar is very low. I need you to drink this." Maggie put the straw to Velma's lips, and she drank a little sip. Then drank again. And again. And began to slowly come around.

In a few minutes, Maggie rechecked her blood sugar and was gratified to see it had risen to 72, and they were able to get her into a chair, where she continued to take a few sips of her sugar water.

"Oh, lordie, what happened?" Velma whispered, looking at the concerned faces surrounding her.

"Your blood sugar crashed," Maggie said. "Did you eat breakfast this morning?"

"I did, I think," Velma said, still a bit groggy. "I remember I ... no now I think on it, I don't believe I did. I took my breakfast insulin, I know that. And I beat up a couple of eggs and put them into the microwave. I was plannin' on them and a bowl of yogurt and berries."

"So, you injected enough regular insulin to cover that meal, or you took a long-acting dose?" Maggie asked.

"Just regular, 5 units. And then the phone rang and there was a problem with the PA system. So, I came right on down here and figured I'd get something to eat once I got here…" she trailed off and took another small sip of the water. "I guess I never did. It just ain't like me to do something that stupid," she said at last.

"Mama!" Deputy Ben Bradford, breathless, clambered up onto the stage and hunkered down like a grasshopper beside his mother. "I got here quick as I could. They told me you fell. What happened?"

"I'm OK, Benji," Velma reassured him. He looked from her to Maggie for confirmation. Maggie nodded. And only now did the connection click that Deputy Ben was Velma's little Benji.

"She's going to be fine, Ben. She missed breakfast and let her sugar get too low."

"I knew I shoulda waited and driven you down," he said to his mother.

"I'm OK, honey. Honest." Velma caressed his smooth cheek with her hand.

"Let me check her sugar one more time, and then if all's well, you can take her home," Maggie said. "And tomorrow, Velma's going to come see me at the clinic first thing, and we'll check everything out." She pinned Velma with a pointed look. "OK?"

"Yes'm," Ben answered for her. "I'll have her up there at nine sharp."

Maggie and JD helped Ben get Velma to her car, despite all her protestations that she didn't want all this fuss being made, and Ben drove her home.

"Thanks for your help," Maggie said to JD as they walked back across the green together.

"Glad to help. But mostly I'm glad you're here," he said, then corrected himself "were here, I mean, to help Velma."

"Me, too. And I really enjoyed hearing you sing today."

"Thanks," he said simply. "Need a lift back to Miz Hendri's?"

"No, I think I'll just walk over. It's such a beautiful afternoon."

"That it is," he agreed.

He hesitated, and Maggie felt like he had something more he wanted to tell her, but a moment later he touched her elbow and slid his hand down to her fingertips, holding them just an instant longer than he needed to and said, "Well I guess I'll see you around." He walked backward a few steps, a hint of a smile playing across his lips, before he turned and left her standing on the green. She watched until he disappeared around the corner, oddly still feeling the energy of the touch of his fingertips in her own. She shook her hand out and headed across the green in the opposite direction toward Miz Hendri's. She was reaching into her bag to pull out her cell phone when it buzzed. It was Charlotte.

"Hey! Are you reading my mind again? I was just about to call you," Maggie said, crossing Main Street.

"I felt a disruption in the force," she teased. "What's up?"

"Nothing much. Just had a double helping of small-town Americana that filled me to the rim with patriotism and family feeling. And made me want to reach out to my one and only sista from anotha motha."

"Always here for you, my sista," Charlotte said. "What was it that swelled your heart with all this patriotic pride?"

"Veteran's Day Tribute. All red, white, and blue, with music and heroic stories. The green grass, the blue sky, the flags snapping, the birds tweeting. I swear it was like something out of a movie."

"Sounds delightful."

"It really was. This is just such a nice little town; I can't wait for you to see it when you visit. And my friend JD, you know the one I told you helped me with my flat tire when -"

"The one with the eyes you couldn't stop staring at?" she interrupted.

"Yeah. That one," Maggie said. "He sang the most gorgeous rendition of the national anthem I think I've ever heard."

"Better than Whitney Houston at the Super Bowl?"

"Apples and oranges," Maggie said. "Simple and unaccompanied. Just his voice, which is so rich and mellow. Like a cup of Angelina's hot chocolate would sound if it was music. It just flowed all around you and seeped into all your pores and filled you up with… I don't even know what. Comfort, maybe."

"Sounds like you're interested in him," Charlotte teased in a sing song.

"No. Well… I don't know," Maggie said. "He's been a good friend. He's nice and very easy to look at. But I'm still trying to figure out the whole Jeff thing, and I just seem to go in circles with it."

"That 'thing' is a big thing, Maggie May. Take your time with it."

"Yeah, I am."

"But in the meantime, maybe Smoky Eyes could cheer you up."

Maggie ignored her. "You called me. What's up?" Maggie pushed open the front door of Miz Hendri's and went inside.

"Ainsley has a weird rash that just showed up last night in the bath. He feels fine, he says, and he doesn't have fever or anything. And before you ask, yes, I actually took his temp with the ear thingy. I wondered if I took a picture of it and sent it to you if you could take a look?"

"You know you don't have to ask. Were his cheeks bright red, too?"

"They were a couple of days ago! How did you know?"

"Sounds like it could be Fifth Disease. Just a little virus; totally nothing to worry about. Listen, I just got back to the house, and Miz Hendri's got Sunday supper on the table. Send the photo, and I'll take a look and get back to you. And don't worry; it's probably nothing big."

"Great! Go enjoy your lunch or supper or whatever it's called this time of day. Love ya, bye."

"Love ya, back!"

CHAPTER 16
Swinging Bridge

Monday morning at just after nine, Maggie picked the chart off the door and took a quick look: 52 y/o WF w/ DM1 FBS 89. She opened the door to find Velma sitting on the end of the exam table, swinging her feet like a kid.

"Good morning, Doc," Velma greeted her.

"Good morning yourself. How are you feeling today?"

"Oh, I'm fine. I'm just sorry about yesterday. I caused such a fuss."

"Don't be," Maggie said, putting a gentle hand on Velma's shoulder. "So, about your diabetes. How long have you been on insulin?"

"Forever, or darn near," she joked. "Since I was a teenager."

"How much insulin are you taking now?"

"Little as I can get away with," Velma said with a little laugh. "I'm always real careful about what I eat: no bread, potatoes, sweets, no nothin' like that. And I promise I don't usually flub up and forget to eat like I did yesterday."

"Well, your blood sugar this morning looks good. It's 89. Is that about usual in the morning fasting?"

"Yes'm. Bit lower usually. Long as I stick to eatin' what I ought to *when* I ought to, my sugar stays pretty well in line, and it takes less insulin. That stuff's so expensive anymore, even with insurance, I do everything I can to keep it down."

"Velma, you are a woman ahead of your time," Maggie said putting the stethoscope earpieces into her ears. "Let me listen to you and look you over, and then Therma Faye can draw your blood, and we can get you a cup of coffee or tea and something to eat."

"That'd be great, Doc. But I'm meeting Benji at Molly's for breakfast when I get finished here, so just a little coffee would be nice. All I've had is some water."

"You know I didn't realize when I met him before that Deputy Bradford was your son. Guess I should have matched the names. I know you must be so proud of him."

"I am that," Velma said. "It's always just been him and me. He was so little when his daddy died. Now, he's all grown up and thinks he's gotta take care of his mama and be sure she eats right."

"I'm sure he worries about you. You know you're really lucky to have each other." Seeing their strong, loving bond made her feel the loss of her own family—and the collapse of what she had believed had been a solid, loving, committed relationship with Jeff—all the more acutely. She brushed the sadness aside and focused on the work at hand. "OK, let's get everything checked out and lay his worries to rest."

The remainder of the morning's patient load had been remarkably light for a Monday, and they'd dealt with all the appointments by 1 o'clock. Since it was a beautiful autumn day, Maggie sent Therma Faye and Donna home early, made herself a Nespresso, and settled down at her desk with a little James Taylor and her coffee to get caught up on charting and correspondence.

She typed in her password to open the screen on the big new iMac desktop computer that had finally arrived and logged onto the clinic network.

Outside the window of Maggie's office, JD stood quietly watching her at work, her earphones on, totally absorbed. He carefully lifted the screen from its hangers and set it aside, then slowly, noiselessly eased the window open.

"Way too pretty a day to be cooped up inside," he said loudly once it was raised.

Maggie turned, startled, pulling the earphones out of her ears. "Jesus, I was a million miles off. I didn't even hear you come up." She patted her chest. "That'll get your heart rate up."

"I sometimes have that effect on women," he joked. "Hey, I brought you something."

He placed a perfect Scarlet Maple bonsai on the windowsill. "Peace offering. Can we talk?"

"Oh, my goodness. It's gorgeous," she said, going over to the window to pick it up and admire it. "Come on in the back," she motioned with her head. "It's unlocked."

When he came into the office, she said, "Where do you think? Here," she put the tree on the corner of her desk. "Or this corner," she moved it to the other side. "Or maybe on the bookshelf?"

"None of them for long," he said. "Bonsai won't make it permanently cooped up inside. They need to feel the sun on their leaves and the wind in their branches." He closed and locked the open window, took the bonsai from her, and placed it back on the wide sill in the sun.

"But I think you and I need to straighten out a thing or two about the other day."

"Such as?"

"Such as what I was doing at Prescott's house. I saw the look on your face."

"Go ahead," Maggie said, leaning against the desk and folding her arms across her chest. "I'm all ears."

"Not here. I don't do so well cooped up inside either." He extended his hand to her. "Let's go for a walk; I'll tell you all about it." She didn't move from her spot.

"Is that why you like bonsai? They're like you?"

"No, not really," he said. "I like their philosophy. A bonsai represents the whole of the universe – rocks, hills, trees, water, sky – all the elements of nature brought together in one tiny perfect space. Cultivating a bonsai is creating a world you can hold in the palm of your hand."

"So where do I put my little universe then?"

"For now, it's fine there. We'll find the right place. Meantime, let's go feel the wind in our branches."

When she still didn't budge, JD pointed to the backpack he carried. "C'mon. I even packed a lunch."

Maggie looked at her desk, at the backlog of work she ought to be doing, at the rays of the glorious Indian Summer sun slanting through the window, at JD's kind, hopeful eyes, and smiled. "Let me change my shoes."

They took a sun-dappled path that meandered through the woods, the leaves rustling softly overhead and the fallen carpet of them crunching under their feet. Where the trees thinned, she could see the Caddo flowing lazily along below them. They strolled leisurely side by side, JD talking, Maggie listening.

"So that's pretty much it," he said at last.

"Mineral rights," she said. "You were just offering to buy Waylon's mineral rights?"

"Or buy his land. He needs the money."

"What's in it for you?" she asked, skeptical.

"Protect my own mineral rights."

"I don't get it. How does buying his mineral rights protect yours?"

"My land backs up to the old Morrison farm – now Prescott's land. He sells his rights to some less-than-scrupulous gas exploration yahoos, and they could lateral drill and drain my field."

"I see. I think."

"Plus, we go back," he said. "He was the person most influential in my decision to join the Army."

"Waylon?" she asked, incredulous. "How so?" At her confused expression, he went on.

"I was kind of lost after my dad died. Wasn't sure I even wanted to go to school or how to pay for it if I did. The Army gave me the structure I think I needed. I wound up in Ranger school and served my time and was lucky enough to come back whole. Lotta guys didn't. I've got Waylon to thank for that. He was in the Army then, and he encouraged me to join up after high school and let Uncle pay for my college once I got out. Good advice, as it turned out, and I feel like I owe him something. Waylon wasn't always the way he is now. And it's clear he's struggling."

JD stopped and picked a handful of wild blackberries from a bramble beside the trail, holding them out for her to try, chuckling at her hesitance.

"Go on, try one. They're delicious," he said, tossing one into his mouth. "Look they won't hurt you."

She took a particularly plump one and cautiously bit the tip of it. "Mmmmm," she popped the rest of it into her mouth. "So sweet." She snagged a second one from his purple stained palm.

"Told ya," he smiled. "They grow wild in the woods and all up and down the fence rows; you can gather up a big bucketful of them in no time."

"That sounds like fun," she said.

"Word of advice, city mouse: if you do decide to hit a berry patch, wear long sleeves, plenty of bug juice, and a good, stout pair of high boots. And watch your step. Snakes love 'em, too."

"Ah. I'll just grab a quart at the store, then," she said.

"Fair enough," he laughed.

They came to a fork in the path and took the steeply descending trail that wound its way down to the rocky riverbank. The sound of the river was louder on the water's edge as it burbled over little cataracts and around the smooth larger boulders dotting the riverbed. And the river smell was so fresh, clean, and alive, it made Maggie almost dizzy.

JD showed her how to select the perfect small flat river rock for skipping. He'd release an easy sidearm throw and the rock would bounce eight, ten, sometimes a dozen or more times across the water's surface. Her first several attempts just went *kerplunk*, but she finally got the hang of it well enough to get three or four skips and felt an odd sense of accomplishment.

They walked a bit down the bank to where the river was narrower, and a handful of well-placed flat-topped boulders made it possible to hop across.

"If I fall in, you're coming in to get me," Maggie put him on notice.

"Absolutely. On my honor as a gentleman. But you're going to be fine; just follow me." JD led the way, helping her from perch to rocky perch until they reached the other side, safe and dry. Then they clambered up the bank and back across its ridge to the rickety, old, swinging cable bridge that spanned the river upstream.

Maggie started across the bridge, got about halfway, and turned to see JD still hanging back. She spread her arms wide. "Come on, wind-in-your-branches guy!"

JD took a deep breath and tentatively stepped onto the bridge. As he cautiously neared the center, a mischievous look crossed Maggie's face, and she grabbed the cables and began to shift her weight from side to side to make the bridge swing.

"Whoa!" JD grabbed both cables, but that just encouraged Maggie to make the bridge swing higher.

"You sure it's just mineral rights you're after?" she teased.

JD held on tighter. "Couldn't be more sure."

"What about the mounds?" she taunted a bit more.

"They're safe as long as nobody's drilling, and if you'll quit swingin' this damn bridge, we'll be safe, too." JD released his grip and covered the space between them in two bounds, covering her hands with his own, removing them from the cables, and pulling them together between their chests. Their faces now inches apart, he whispered, "Stop."

One look at those soft gray eyes and his earnest face made Maggie instantly regret having teased him.

JD released her wrists and took her face in his hands, tipping it up toward him. She couldn't take her eyes from his, and she leaned toward him, inviting his kiss. He covered her lips gently with his own, and she found herself happily giving in to delicate flicks of his tongue, gently probing her parted lips. She laced her fingers around his neck and pulled him closer to her for a kiss that was deeply sensual and hungrier.

He pulled back, took a ragged breath, and released a deep sigh. "Can we please get off this bridge?" Easing her arms from around his neck he tugged her by the hand, back toward the comfort of the far bank.

As the late afternoon sun dipped closer to the tree line, the air took on a decided chill. She and JD gathered a pile of leaves, twigs, and some larger sticks, and he started a small fire in a circle of smooth, round rocks at the edge of the river. He spread a blanket from his picnic pack next to a large boulder that could serve as a comfortable backrest for them, and they sat, side by side, with legs out and backs up against it, enjoying the warmth it retained from the afternoon sun, welcome in the gathering coolness.

He took a bottle of wine, chunk of cheese, and a couple of apples from his pack, along with a pair of small, plastic, collapsible, souvenir drinking cups that he twisted open with a flourish, revealing the imprinted slogan "Enjoy Mt. Valley Water". He opened the wine and poured each of them a cup.

"Thanks," Maggie said. "Interesting barware."

"Oh, nothing but my very finest for you, ma'am." He cut off slivers of cheese and slices of apple with a pocketknife and passed them alternately between them.

Maggie eyed him curiously in the flicker of the fire. "Who is JD Langston?"

"Huh? What do you mean?" He levered an apple slice off the knife blade and into his mouth, then cut another and offered it to her.

"Well, so far, I know about a road-side Samaritan, a physicist, a singer, a bonsai enthusiast, an Army Ranger, a Southern gentleman. And a person who does *not* like swinging bridges," she smiled apologetically.

"It's not every swinging bridge. That one's older than me, barely hanging together with spit and a promise. And I don't want to swim in the Caddo tonight."

She nodded. "Velma says you've lived all over the world."

"Velma doesn't know everything," he said, looking upriver. "I've been here and there."

"But what is it that you do? Not just tinker with bonsai all day." She accepted a sliver of cheese and took a bite and another sip of wine.

JD poked up the fire. "Right now, I'm having a pretty good time watching you in the fire shadows."

"You know what I mean," Maggie persisted. "Did you live in Japan?"

"Yeah, I did for a while. Had a couple of ideas worked out pretty well. Japanese company bought the patents."

"Sounds exciting."

"I did all right," he said. "Speaking of excitement, Miss Velma said you had a some yourself down at the river the other morning."

"You mean Roy Owens? I think he'll be okay. He's still in coronary care at the hospital in Hot Springs. I checked in with his cardiologist yesterday, and it looks like he's doing well and probably going home soon."

"Glad to hear it. But what I meant was about you. Velma said something about—I believe her exact words were—Roy deputized her and made her a junior coroner."

Maggie almost spewed wine out her nose suppressing a laugh. "Oh, that," she dabbed her nose and lips daintily with a napkin. "Well sort of. He did appoint me to be the official charged with dealing with the bones they found, which so far seems to mean locking them up for safe keeping and signing off when they get picked up."

"Which will be when?" He poured more wine into her outstretched cup.

"I'm hoping this coming week. They're going to the State Crime Lab in Little Rock, but they're waiting on a forensic specialist to get there. Both Roy and Dub seemed to think they were from the mound – ergo, Native bones – but until they examine them officially in Little Rock, we have to treat it as if it might not be a relic." She wrapped her arms around herself and rubbed them briskly.

"You cold?" JD said, putting an arm around her and pulling her closer to him.

"Yeah, a little," she said, turning her head to look at him directly. "We probably ought to head back soon."

"But not just yet," he said, touching her lips with a kiss so tender it made her weak. Then a clattering, creaking noise broke the silence, interrupting the moment.

"What was that?" Maggie said, pulling away, startled, peering into the darkness.

JD got up and took a few steps in the direction of the noise. "Sounded like somebody or something just ran across the bridge. Probably a raccoon or a possum."

Maggie suppressed a shudder. She didn't like the idea of being out here in the dark with some wild something-or-other running around. And, if she was honest, she wasn't entirely sure she was ready yet for whatever seemed to have suddenly changed in this friendship with JD, unmoored as she was from the trauma with Jeff. She stood and picked up the blanket and shook it out. "We should get back."

"Yes ma'am," he said, taking the blanket from her, rolling it up, and stuffing it into the pack. He filled the empty wine bottle with water from the river and doused the fire. "If you're ready, let's head up."

***

The black-clad figure that crept along the back wall of the darkened clinic building was scarcely visible against the deep, tall shrubbery plantings that grew against it. The moon had set early, and the night sky was lit only by stars without enough brightness to really illuminate the parking lot behind the clinic or the two vehicles still parked there. The figure stopped and laid down a large bag by the back door of the clinic, snapping on a red headband light. He—or was it she? Impossible to say in the dark—quickly crossed the parking lot and felt the hoods of each of the cars. The condensate that had collected on their windshields said they'd been there a while.

Returning to the back door, gloved hands worked at picking the lock, then stopped when muffled voices and the sounds of laughter drifted up from the trail beyond. Snapping the headlamp off, the figure snatched up the bag and ducked into the leafy space between the thick row of tall red-tips and the building's back wall, crouching there, silent, and quietly breathing through opened lips. The voices grew louder, distinctly two voices, male and female. The gravel crunched beneath their feet.

"Thank you for this afternoon," Maggie said. Her car *chirped,* and the headlamps flashed as the doors unlocked.

"My pleasure," JD said, opening the door for her. "I'd love to cook dinner for you, sometime."

"My God, do I have to add chef to your eclectic resumé, too?" she teased, laughing lightly.

"Not hardly," he demurred, "but a guy who lives on his own either eats out a lot or learns to cook." He paused, then went on. "And I'd like to show you the bonsai forest."

"Yeah, I'd like that," she said, starting the car.

"Well, it's a date then?"

"Sure," she replied, closing the door, starting the engine, and pulling away.

In short order the other engine rumbled to life and the gravel crunched as JD's truck pulled out, leaving the parking lot silent and empty.

From the cover of the bushes the figure re-emerged with the bag and in an eerie red halo of light resumed with the lock pick until the door opened.

Inside the darkened hallway a single night light glowed. The figure located the door marked STORAGE, sat down the large bag, and made short work of the flimsier interior lock.

On the floor inside the storeroom, between shelves lined with cleaning products and office supplies, lay the orange bag. The evidence tag, attached to a D-ring through the zipper pull with a standard gray zip tie, read: Office of the Montgomery County Coroner, EVIDENCE, the number, date, time, and a couple of sets of initials. The figure snipped the zip tie that held the tag and removed it, then reaching into a pocket, removed a handful of ties—white, black, gray, clear—selecting a gray one close to the original and using it to attach the tag to the zipper of the other large orange bag. Removing the first bag, the figure closed and locked the storeroom, then went out, pulling the clinic door closed.

CHAPTER 17
Token of Trust

The morning sun streamed into the window, filling Maggie's office with a welcoming warmth that she appreciated on this chilly fall morning. She hung her coat and purse on the rack and noticed the little maple tree sitting on the bookshelf, on the shelf below the flop-eared stuffed bunny, whose long legs dangled down. *Quite a collection of gifts I'm amassing*, she thought.

"How about some wind in the old branches," she said to the tree, then immediately felt a rush of stupid. *Now I'm talking to a tree like it's a pet.*

As she leaned up to retrieve it, one of the bunny's long legs brushed her arm, and she involuntarily jerked, bumping the effigy pot Rose Ellen had given her on the shelf beside the bonsai, sending it toppling from the shelf and Maggie scrambling to catch it with both hands just inches before it would have met an untimely, smashing end on her floor.

"Dr. Mac, Sheriff Perkins is... whoa, close one." Therma Faye said from the doorway as Maggie juggled the pot, then carefully replaced it, and lifted the bonsai down.

"Oooooh, is that one of those little what-cha-ma-call-its?"

"A bonsai?" Maggie said.

"Yeah. I hadn't ever seen one like this," Therma Faye said, coming in closer to touch its delicate red leaves. "They're usually gnarly little cedary-looking trees, aren't they?"

"Can be almost any kind of tree, I think. JD Langston gave it to me. He called it a universe you can hold in the palm of your hand." She smiled. "I like that."

"Hmm. Never figured JD for a romantic." Therma Faye twitched her eyebrows up and down. "Must be sweet on you." She gave the brows another twitch and turned to leave, then stopped and immediately turned back and palmed her forehead. "Oh, almost forgot what I came in for. Must be losin' what's left of my mind," she chuckled. "Sheriff's here. Needs you to sign some papers about that thing they're picking up."

"Ah, OK. Tell him I'll be right out." Maggie said, setting the bonsai on the windowsill in the sun. She cracked the window slightly. "Enjoy the breeze, little buddy," she whispered, plucking the brown paper bag with the ring off her desk on the way by.

In the hallway, Sheriff Perkins and Deputy Bradford stood sipping coffee and chatting with Donna outside the storage room door. More the Sheriff chatting and sipping, and Ben and Donna flirting, Maggie noticed, and not for the first time. There was clear attraction between those two.

"Good morning, Sheriff, Ben," Maggie greeted them.

"Mornin', Doc," Sheriff Perkins gave a half salute with his coffee cup. "We've come to get that Indian off your hands."

Maggie handed him the sack.

"What's this?" he said.

"It's something I found that morning at the river, near where you pulled the bones out."

The Sheriff opened the sack and pulled out the zip bag, holding it up to the light. "Huh," he said. "Some kinda metal washer or something?"

"I don't know. I just wasn't sure if it was important, so I kept it safe."

"Probably not. Don't think, so anyway." He dropped it back into the sack and handed it back to her. "Too small for prints. Couldn't be a weapon. Probably just junk the river brought through."

Maggie stuck the sack under her arm, unlocked the door, and opened it, so Ben could step inside and retrieve the body bag. He bent to check the tag number on the Chain of Evidence forms on his clipboard against the tag on the bag, then jotted down the tag number, compared the two again, and handed the clipboard to the Sheriff, who initialed it, then he handed it to Maggie to verify and sign.

"Put your John Hancock there. Or I guess it would be a Jane Hancock, wouldn't it?" the Sheriff, said, elbowing Maggie jovially and chuckling at his humor. Maggie glanced up at him and gave an anemic smile but said nothing, and his grin soon wilted. "Anyway, put it right there," he indicated the X on the appropriate line.

Maggie signed the forms, and Ben picked up the heavy bag, heading for the front door.

Therma Faye blocked his path, hands on her hips. "Don't wag that thing out through the front. You'll scare off the patients," she admonished him.

"Don't nobody know what's in it, Therma Faye," Ben said.

"Anybody's ever seen CSI on tv knows a body bag when they see it," Therma Faye said. "You parade that thing out there, and they'll think we screwed up or something. Y'all go out the back."

Ben set the body bag down and went to bring the patrol wagon around to the back lot. The Sheriff hefted the bag and took it out through the back door. Therma Faye waved them off and closed the door behind them.

"Shooo," Therma Faye said with a shiver. "I'm glad that thing's out of here. Gave me the creeps just knowing it was there," she said.

"Well, there are plenty of live ones sitting out there to keep us busy," Maggie said with a glance to the waiting room. "Let's get it going, ladies."

***

A few days later, Maggie was sitting at her desk, enjoying a little break, and trying to eat her lunch when Donna buzzed on the intercom. "Doc, that guy from the State Lab's on the line for you."

"Thanks, Donna," Maggie said, picking up the receiver. "This is Dr. McKinley."

"Hey there, Doctor," the caller said. "Wilbur Aaronson again. I've got a prelim on your bones. Full report isn't in yet, but forensics says they're real old. Just be an educated guess at this point of how old. We're sending them on up to the University and their folks'll do all the definitive aging tests and such. At this point all we can say with certainty is it's a young adult male who met his end a long time ago."

Maggie suddenly sat up and focused intently, drawing her brows together. "I see. And they're sure." She grabbed a pen from her labcoat pocket and jotted something down on her pad. "Could you email me the final report as soon as you have it, please?"

"All right if we fax it?"

"Sure, that's fine. Either way, email or fax. And thank you for the call. I appreciate the early update." She hung up the phone and was still sitting, pen in hand, when Therma Faye stuck her head in and announced that the rooms were loaded up and ready for her.

"She's not first, Dr. Mac, but could you maybe step in to see Lyla. Her blood pressure is a little high, and she's complaining of a bad headache."

Lyla Green was only 18 years old, somewhat overweight, and now just over 8 months pregnant with her first baby. When Maggie had picked up her pre-natal/OB care when she'd first come to town a few months back, Lyla had expressed her strong desire to have the baby here in Caddo Bend and not have to go over to Mt. Ida or all the way to Hot Springs. So, she'd transferred her care from the OB there to Maggie. The plan was for a home birth, and so far, things had been on track, although there had been a trace of protein in her urine on her last visit. The blood pressure elevation was new. And worrisome.

Maggie pulled the chart from the door, and she and Therma Faye stepped inside. The room was dark. "Lyla?" she said softly, turning on the gooseneck exam lamp and directing it down and away from the girl. "What's going on?

"I'm sorry, Doc. The overhead light was really making my headache worse, so I turned it off," she said. She was lying down on the exam table.

"No, no. That's fine. When did the headache start?" Maggie said, taking the ophthalmoscope from the charging unit on the counter.

"A day or two ago, but it really got bad this morning."

"OK. Therma Faye's going to help you sit up, so I can take a look in your eyes."

"Here we go, girl," Therma Faye said taking her arm and supporting her from behind, "On three. One, two, three and up," she said, pulling the young woman to a sitting position.

Maggie said, "This is going to be bright, and I'm sorry. Try to keep both your eyes open; I'll be as quick as I can." She put the scope up to her own eye, focusing the bright light into the pupil of first one eye and then the other. Even without drops to dilate the pupil, she was able to see the optic nerve heads were swollen. Not a good sign; it meant that the pressure inside Lyla's head was high. *Papilledema. Pre-eclampsia?*

She snapped off the light of the scope. "OK, Lyla. Your pressure is high, and we need to get it down," Maggie said with a calm she didn't feel. This condition was quite serious, fatal even, if untreated. "And the quickest way will be for us to give you some medicine into your vein. Is that OK?"

"Whatever you say, Doc. I just want to feel better."

"Therma Faye, I'd like to give Lyla a 4-gram bolus of mag sulfate IV. Then flush the line and give a 6 mg bolus of dexamethasone. Pull a red top and a purple top before you give any meds, OK?"

"Got it," she said, leaving to gather the needed supplies.

Maggie stayed in the room with the patient. "Lyla, did your husband bring you in today, or did you drive yourself?"

"Kenny's out there. He took off work and brought me."

"Is it OK if I speak to him about how you're doing?"

"Yes, ma'am," she said, "I'd appreciate it. He's a little freaked out."

When Therma Faye returned to start the IV and administer the meds, Maggie stepped out to the waiting room and brought Kenny Green back to her office.

"How is she, Doc?" he said, the worried expression on his face telling her volumes.

"She's OK, but her pressure is up a bit higher than we'd like, and at this stage of her pregnancy, it could be dangerous, both to her and the baby, if we don't get it under control quickly. We're giving her some medicines now that will help bring it down and will protect the baby, but I think she's going to need more than just that. I haven't told her this yet, but we're going to need to transport her over to Hot Springs to the hospital, where they can keep close watch on her for the next several days and continue the medicine." She paused a moment to let him process what she'd said. "And they may have to take the baby early."

"Wha…it's not time." His eyes went wide, and he looked terrified.

"I know. And I know she didn't want to deliver in the hospital, but sometimes circumstances have the upper hand. At the end of the day, we want a healthy baby and a healthy mother."

Kenny slumped into the chair beside Maggie's desk, rubbing his face with his hands.

"It's going to be OK. Just hang in there," she said with a gentle hand on his shoulder. "I'll ask Donna to phone for the EMTs to take her over, if that's OK with you both."

He nodded, looking a little lost. He wasn't much past 18 himself.

"Would you like to come in with me while we tell her? Then you can sit with her while we wait for the ambulance to get here."

***

184

It had been a full, long day at the clinic and dusk had long ago deepened to dark when Maggie finally pulled into the lot behind the boarding house. Nick was sitting alone at the kitchen table, drinking coffee, and reading. Maggie came in through the back door, laid her purse on the counter, and pulled Rose Ellen's pot from it.

"Evening, Princess," Nick said without looking up from his book. "Miz Hendri left a plate for you in the oven. Told me to be sure you ate it all."

Maggie put the pot on the table in front of him, drawing his attention immediately. He reached for it, whistling softly.

"Nice piece. Where'd you get it?"

"First tell me what it is," Maggie said.

"For starters, it's a helluva nice effigy pot." He turned it around in his hands, examining it from all sides. "Superb quality. Handy engraved. Unusual form. An armadillo, it looks like."

Maggie got the pitcher of tea from the refrigerator and poured a taste to be sure it wasn't sweet. Satisfied, she poured herself a glass, setting it down on the table, then retrieved the plate from the oven and sat down to eat.

"Probably Caddoan," Nick went on. "Looks real. Worth a load of money if it is." He sat the pot down between them. "And so, I ask you again, where'd you get it?"

"I'm pretty sure Rose Ellen Prescott left it on my windowsill at the clinic."

"Prescott's kid?" He picked up the pot again. "Huh. Maybe old Waylon is pilfering that big mound for real. She say anything?"

Maggie laid down her fork and fixed him with an incredulous stare. "Of course not," she said, a little irritated at the insensitive remark. "I didn't see her put it there, but she was waiting outside. And when she saw I'd found it, she ran off." She took a few bites of her dinner. "Will I run afoul of the repatriation laws by keeping it if it's real?"

"Oh, I suspect it's real enough," he said. "I'd have to take it over to Little Rock to the University's lab and do some testing to be sure. Let me hang onto it for a few days. As far as keeping it, if it came from one of the mounds at Prescott's place, technically speaking, she can legally give it to whoever she wants. But I doubt it would please Waylon much for her to give it away."

Maggie stood up and moved the pot back over beside her purse on the counter. "Ultimately I do want you to test the pot."

"But?"

She sat back down at her plate. "But not yet. It's a token of trust, and I'd like to find out what that means first. She's reaching out; I don't want to screw that up."

Nick nodded. "I'm here to serve, ma'am." He turned his attention back to his book. "It's a fabulous artifact if it's real. But play it your way and see where it goes."

The phone rang in the hall and kept ringing. "Miz Hendri must be buttoned up in her room already with her hearing aids off," Nick said. Maggie started to get up, but Nick put a hand on her shoulder. "Sit and eat your dinner. I'll get it." He disappeared into the hall for a bit then came back to the kitchen.

"For you," he said.

Maggie looked up, puzzled. "A patient?"

Nick shook his head. "Long distance, I think."

Maggie's heart gave a tiny flip, and her breath caught. *Jeff?* She dabbed her mouth with her napkin, tried to look unfazed, and went to the phone, completely unsure if she was ready to speak to him.

When the muffled tones of Maggie's conversation floated in from the hall, Nick eased over to quietly take his field pack off the hook by the door. He reached into it, removed a Polaroid instant camera, and tiptoed over to the counter to snap a picture of the pot. He laid the instant photo down on the counter and took a few more snaps with his phone camera as well. He peeled the print apart, waving it in the air and blowing on it as it developed, then swabbed it with the fixative pad. He carefully replaced the pot just as it had been sitting beside her purse, put the camera and photo into his pack, and sat down just as Maggie pushed through the hallway door.

"Medical?" Nick asked.

"Personal," she sat and resumed picking at her plate.

"Wanna talk about it?"

"Nope," she replied.

"Dinner still warm?" he asked after a bit.

"Warm enough," she said, taking a bite or two more in silence. "Cold food goes with the medical territory. You get used to interrupted meals," she said and sliced off another piece of her now-not-so-warm meatloaf.

"One of the glamorous parts of a career in medicine that they don't tell you about in the brochure, huh?" he teased gently.

"Yeah," she nodded. "There are others," she finally smiled a little, appreciating his efforts to smooth over an awkward situation; she was sure he knew who was on the phone and was just relieved he'd let it go. She didn't want to talk about it, especially not with him.

"You could warm it up in the microwave," he suggested helpfully, "if Miz Hendri had a microwave."

***

The next afternoon Maggie put in a call to Lyla Green's OB in Hot Springs and was relieved to learn she was doing well and that the baby was in no imminent danger. They'd gotten her pressure down and, so far, it was staying down, but they were keeping her in the hospital for a few more days out of caution. And best of all, they were cautiously optimistic she'd be able to go to term. *Good news.*

Since all the scheduled patients had been seen, she decided to leave the clinic a little early; JD was cooking his promised dinner for her tonight, but she wanted to make a stop on the way out to his house. She pulled into an empty space in front of a row of Main Street shops, climbing out just as the streetlamps on the square flicked on and began to brighten. She went into The Jewel Box, a tiny hole in the wall tucked between the local bank branch and Medlock's General Store.

The proprietor, Max Rosenthal, sat at the rear of the shop at a small desk strewn with watch parts, expertly plucking first one tiny piece and then another from a bowl of cleaning solution, dabbing them on a towel, and setting each one carefully into place in a watch case. When the bell over the door jingled, he put down his tools, removed the loupe from his head, and put on his glasses.

"Good evening, Dr. McKinley," he greeted her as he came around behind the display counter. She couldn't quite get used to people she hadn't ever actually met, knowing her on sight by name. "What can I do for you?"

She pulled the zip bag out of her pocket and removed the ring. "I was hoping you could tell me something about this," she said, placing it on the suede pad on the counter between them.

He picked it up and slipped it onto a conical ring sizer. "Size 6 looks like."

"So, you think it is a piece of jewelry, then?"

He put a jeweler's loupe to his eye and examined it more closely. "Possibly, in the broadest sense. No inscription or markings I can see. It's definitely not silver or platinum. Probably just polished steel," he said. "If it's jewelry, it's homemade." He set the ring down on the pad again. "Not of any value, I'm afraid."

Maggie picked the ring up and put it back into the zip bag. "OK, thank you," she said.

"I do have some very delicate bands in gold and platinum, if you're in the market."

"Oh, no, no." She waved the idea away. "I was just curious about this one," she said, smiling at him. "But I'll keep that in mind. And thanks again," she said, taking and glancing at the name on the business card he offered her, "Mr. Rosenthal."

CHAPTER 18
The Forest

At JD's house, Maggie settled comfortably against the soft pillows on an overstuffed sofa, pulled up before a crackling fire in the great room, sipping a most welcome glass of lightly chilled Sauvignon Blanc. The room was one of those rustic open plan affairs, where the kitchen was fully part of a large space designed for lounging, conversation, and casual dining. Generous and intimate at the same time. The river rock fireplace that dominated one wall soared all the way to the vaulted beams overhead and threw beautiful light and comfortable warmth into the whole room. The vibe was distinctly masculine, lots of polished wood, stone, and sparkling glass. And a huge number of books that filled floor to ceiling built-in shelves that bracketed the fireplace. A framed Navajo blanket and a few other pieces of interesting art hung on the walls. Comfortable furnishings, good quality, nothing fussy – everything was neat and orderly and well-tended.

She took her glass of wine over for a closer look at his library and found the titles spoke to an eclectic taste in reading, ranging from *Beowulf* to *Cold Fusion* to *Cold Mountain* and everything in between, it seemed. On a stack of books, she was drawn to a framed studio portrait of a beautiful woman. From the vintage look, she guessed it was his mother. Then another photo caught her eye: a man running a ferocious-looking rapid in a kayak.

"Is this you braving the rapids?" she said, holding up the framed picture.

"Yeah," he nodded. "Middle fork of the Salmon. Good while back, though."

She replaced it on the shelf and picked up the one next to it of him and another man, both clad in hiking gear, at an overlook somewhere.

The sign next to them said Haleakala Peak, elevation 10,023'. *Hmmm. Quite the adventurer.* Then her attention was drawn to something in the bookcase she hadn't seen in years: a sound system with a turn table for playing vinyl and a collection of albums, neatly shelved beside the impressive multi-component system. She was interested to see they spanned a wide array of musical genres—classical, rock, jazz, even country—as eclectic as his literary taste.

She noticed, too, that the collection ran heavily to vocals. Her parents had been huge fans of vocal jazz, especially her dad, and this music had been the soundtrack of her younger years. She was pleased to find all the blues and jazz greats there: Ella, Dinah, Lady Day, Sassy Sarah, Frank, Duke, Nat, Coltrane, Satchmo. But she recognized more recent voices among them, as well, such as Nat's daughter, Natalie, Diana Krall, and Norah Jones, who was currently beckoning in that enchanting, breathless way she had for them to Come Away from speakers Maggie couldn't quite locate. The soft sound seemed to be coming from everywhere.

"Amazing collection of vinyl," she said, joining him at the polished stone island, where he was chopping greens and veggies for their salad. "Everything from Gregorian Chant to great choral masses to Billie Holiday to Eagles and CSN."

He gave a little half smile and a shrug. "Yeah. Great vocals. Great harmonies. My mama had a beautiful voice. That's maybe the thing I remember about her most. Absolutely loved to sing. She sang while she cooked, sang in the shower, with the radio in the car, and every Sunday in the church choir."

"And you sing."

"Not much anymore. But I love listening. Reminds me of her. She used to say the human voice was God's first, most perfect instrument. Everything else is just trying to imitate it."

"That's beautiful," Maggie murmured. She poured a little more wine from the bottle sitting open in the chill sleeve on the island and nodded toward the cutting board. "Can I help?"

"Thanks, but I got it. My treat, remember?" he replied, playfully pointing the tip of the chef's knife in her direction. He popped the skin on a clove of garlic and minced, releasing its sharp aroma into the kitchen. Then added some coarse salt to the pile and with the flat of his chef's blade worked it into a paste that he scraped off the board into a large wooden salad bowl. He splashed in some vinegar, added a dollop of mustard, a pinch of dried herbs, a drizzle of honey, and ground in some black pepper. Then he began whisking in a stream of olive oil she could smell from across the counter. Verdant and fresh.

Maggie admired his hands as he worked; she'd noticed them when he changed her tire and then again when she'd removed the splinter. They were tanned and strong, beautifully shaped, and he used them with such dexterous grace. She had a thing for hands. Hands and smooth chests. And eyes. The trifecta.

"You do that so well," she said, shaking off the image that insisted on forming in her mind of what his chest might look like without that soft chambray shirt.

"Like I said: live alone, like to eat." He picked up his wine glass. "You might have noticed there's not a glut of fine dining options here in Caddo Bend. Some good Southern home cooking spots, though." He came around the island. "We're all good here for a minute; let's sit," he said, putting a hand lightly to her waist and directing her toward the sofa.

She sank into the soft pillows again and for a few minutes they just sat, saying nothing, sipping their wine, listening to the music, and watching the flickering fire. It seemed oddly natural to sit together quietly like this; she felt none of the need to force conversation that she'd felt early on in other relationships. She caught herself: *Was this a relationship?* Norah

Jones ended her set, and JD got up to change the music, carefully dusting the album with a special tool before stowing Norah back in her sleeve and queuing up the next selection. Soon the room filled with the sultry sounds of Sarah Vaughan.

"Misty," she said quietly. "One of my parents' favorite songs. I can't count the number of times I've heard her sing this."

"Your folks jazz fans, too?" he said, sitting down again close beside her.

"They were," she said, the sadness evident on her face.

JD put his arm around her shoulders. "I didn't mean to…"

"It's OK," she said. "They've been gone a long time now."

He pulled her a little closer to him but said nothing, just kept a gentle arm around her and waited quietly for her to go on, if she wanted to.

"They were killed in a car wreck," she said finally. "I was thirteen. One day it was the three of us. The next, it was just me."

"I'm so sorry." After a moment, he said, "My father's been gone a long while, too. Just after I graduated high school; I think I told you that already."

"Yeah," she said. "What caused it?"

"Heart attack," he replied. "Then it was just me and Mama until she died a couple of years ago."

She bit on her lower lip and nodded then shook off the somber mood. "You know my father was a total jazz snob. He'd have been quite envious of your collection, I think."

"He'd have loved this recording, then. It's a live performance, recorded in Sweden in 1964."

"Yes, he would have approved of your taste in music," she said. *Actually, of more than just your taste in music,* she thought. "I do, too."

He got up and brought the bottle of wine over to refill their glasses and settled back beside her.

"On a totally different subject," she said, "I wanted to ask your opinion about a couple of things. If you don't mind."

"Shoot," he said.

She went to retrieve her purse and pulled out the ring in its zip bag. "I got a call today from the State Crime Lab about the bones."

"And?"

"Forensics says they're old. Most likely Native American. An adult male." A questioning look knitted her brows.

"And your face tells me you doubt that assessment," he said.

Maggie nodded. "I saw the skeleton *in situ*. And while I'm admittedly no serious forensics expert, half of my undergrad dual track was Anthropology. I grew up with it; my dad was a paleoanthropologist. I do know a little about bones."

"So?"

"So based on the size, width of the pelvis, and brow ridge, my impression at the time was it was a female. I didn't do anything remotely like a careful examination, so I could have been mistaken," she said and unzipped the plastic zip bag, pouring the ring into her hand and holding it out. "And I found this with the bones. Well," she corrected herself, "near the bones."

JD put down his wine glass, took the ring from her palm, and held it up to examine it in the light. Then he surprised her by taking her left hand and slipping the ring onto her finger. She looked up at him, hoping the blush that sprang to her cheeks wasn't visible in the firelight. He held her gaze until she looked away.

"Not a Caddoan artifact, for sure," he said at last.

She reached into her purse and removed the effigy pot.

"But that is," he said, taking the pot from her hands. He turned it in his own, looking at it from all angles in the flickering firelight and shook his head.

"Is what?"

"Caddoan. Where'd you get it?"

"It showed up on my windowsill a little while back. I think Rose Ellen Prescott put it there, though I didn't see her do it."

Outside, the wind whistled, and rain began to spatter on the metal roof of the house. Suddenly the front door banged open, and JD jumped up, pot in hand, to close it.

"Sorry about that. Blowing pretty good out there," he said, settling back beside her. "Nick seen this?"

"Yeah, I showed it to him. He thought it was Caddoan, too. Said it's a good piece and probably valuable. If it's real," she said.

"And if that's true, whoever it belongs to won't be pleased to have lost it." He handed the pot back to her. "Be careful. The snakes who traffic in black market relics aren't the harmless kind. Who all knows you have it?"

"Just Nick and Therma Faye. And Rose Ellen, of course. And now you," she casually slipped the ring from her finger and put it and the pot back into her purse. "Are you saying you think I'm in danger?"

JD got up and poked the fire. "I'm just saying there are folks in this world who'd stick a knife in you for twenty bucks, let alone what that pot might be worth." He stared into the fire then turned his face to her, his gray eyes serious. "And you might be surprised who they are." He replaced the poker, turned back to her, and with a disarming smile, put out his hand. "How about that tour of the bonsai forest I promised you? Before we eat."

"In the driving rain?"

"Afraid you'll melt? Come on, sugar; I won't let you drown."

JD grabbed an umbrella for their quick dash from the kitchen door to the greenhouse in back, and true to his prediction, Maggie did not melt. They were giggling and shouting like a couple of teenagers by the time they ducked inside, and JD secured the door behind them. The smell of warm, loamy soil enveloped her immediately. He flipped the switch beside the door and the soft lighting illuminated an amazing space. Architecturally, its simplicity was stunning, intricately interlocking beams of polished, oiled teak, framing the translucent panes that made up the walls and peak-ed roof. An impeccably clean oiled teak workbench sat in the center, and wooden shelves extended along each side of the structure, each holding dozens of bonsai specimens.

"My word," Maggie said, looking around. "They're incredible."

"Let me introduce you," JD said, taking her elbow and leading her to what looked like a tiny copse of trees in a flat ceramic pot. "This is Benjamin."

"You have names for them?"

He chuckled. "Some of them. This one's actually a *Ficus benjamina*. Weeping fig. I've had him the longest." He moved past a few more typical spruce and cedar specimens, some deciduous varieties leafed out in autumn colors, like her Scarlet Maple, and stopped at one that was simply breath-taking – a thick, twisted, knobby, gray trunk under a crowning perfusion of delicate, pale pink blossoms. "This is my pride and joy. An Autumn Cherry. She blooms both in the spring and the fall. I call her Cio-Cio-San.

"Isn't that the name of the geisha in *Madama Butterfly*?" she asked.

"Hunh," he said narrowing his eyes with curious appreciation, "yeah. Opera fan?"

"Somewhat. My..." she paused, "I have a friend in New York who has a box at the Met, and we used to go, when our schedules would allow. I really loved some of them. That one in particular. Why is this tree your favorite?"

He thought for a moment. "She's beautiful and delicate," he said. He was standing so closely to her now that, given the difference in their heights, she had to tip her head backward to look into his face as he spoke. He caught an escaping tendril of her hair between his fingers and gently hooked it behind her ear. "But incredibly strong, and a stickler for being treated well."

Maggie was certain the pulse pounding at her throat was visible. She felt herself leaning ever so slightly toward him, drawn almost as if she were a magnet and he steel, and all she could think of was that she wanted him to kiss her. No, if she were honest with herself, it was more than that. She wanted him to make love to her, right here, right now. She felt the warmth of his breath on her face and then his lips on hers. Softly, tenderly.

"What about dinner?" she pulled back a little and whispered.

"It'll keep," he said as he wrapped his arms around her and pulled her closer. "And right now, dinner's not what I'm hungry for. Not since the instant I first saw you."

She threaded her arms around his neck and pressed her body tightly to his, feeling the heat of his desire and answering it with her own, kissing him deeply and working open the buttons of that soft chambray shirt. *Yes, dinner can wait.*

Maggie felt the morning sun on her cheek before she opened her eyes. She kept them closed and reveled in a warmth she hadn't known in a long time, a warmth that was more than just the coziness of soft sheets and down duvet, and she wanted to soak in it for a while before she got up. It was Sunday morning, after all, and she didn't have anywhere to be.

Last night had been amazing, beyond anything in her wildest imaginings, and she let herself luxuriate in the recollections. The passion that had ignited in the greenhouse had surprised them both. Her sweater and camisole lay discarded with his shirt on the floor amid the bonsai. She'd clung to him when he'd scooped her up and carried her through the rain from the greenhouse to his bedroom. There, they'd urgently stripped off their remaining rain-soaked clothing and he'd lowered her, tenderly, onto his bed. Her skin tingled again at the thought of the hundreds of gentle kisses he had showered all over her body, tracing a line from her damp hair down her neck to her chest to her belly and all the way down to her inner thighs – and of that moment when his strong hands cupped her hips and first drew them up to meet his. And then again and over again. She felt a warm rush just thinking of it.

As if he'd read her thoughts, JD stirred beside her, and when her lids fluttered open at last, she found those sexy, smoky eyes gazing into hers.

"Morning, gorgeous," he whispered, smoothing the hair away from her face.

"Morning," she smiled almost shyly.

"Sorry about dinner," he gave a sheepish grin. "Guess I still owe you one. But I will freely admit," he leaned in and kissed the tip of her nose, "I wouldn't trade last night for every seared sous vide scallop on the planet." He tipped her chin up to brush her lips with a kiss. "But if you're starved, I do a mean truffled egg scramble."

"That sounds wonderful," she smiled up at him, a hunger of a different sort clear in her eyes, "but maybe not just yet," she said, snuggling closer to him and guiding his muscular, naked body over hers once again.

CHAPTER 19
Rolling River

When Maggie walked into Miz Hendri's kitchen on Monday morning, Nick was already there, pouring himself a cup of coffee.

"Morning," she said.

"Has broken, like the first morning," he sang the familiar 70s melody. "Coffee?"

"Please."

"Late night? I didn't hear you come in." He handed her a steaming cup.

"Yeah. I told Miz Hendri I wouldn't be at Sunday dinner." She stirred in some cream and took a sip, then before he could pursue why she'd not been there, she changed the subject. "Looks like another drippy day. I am so sick of rain."

"I hear you. I've either been rained out or it's been too muddy to work at the site for days. The digging season's almost over, and I haven't been able to excavate so much as a bird point in a week. May be all done for the year if it doesn't stop."

"It does quit, eventually. Right?" she asked, taking a sip.

"Usually." He rinsed his mug and put it on the counter by the pot. "I'm gonna run over to Little Rock today to see my advisor, Jonas York, at the University. Want me to take your pot? See what he thinks?"

"It's not here," she said, opening the refrigerator and taking out a cup of yogurt.

"What do you mean it's not here? Where is it?"

She peeled the foil from the container and around a spoonful said, "No great mystery. It's at the clinic."

"I'll swing by and pick it up on my way," he said.

"No rush."

"Might be my last trip to Little Rock for a while. Once this rain stops, I'll be in a hole at the dig from sunup to sundown 'til we close up for the season."

Maggie tossed the empty yogurt container in the trash and rinsed her own coffee cup.

"I'm just not ready to let go of it yet."

Nick raised his palms in surrender. "Your call."

Maggie reached for an umbrella from the peg by the door, but it was hooked around the strap of Nick's field pack. She gave it an impatient tug, and it and the pack both came off the peg, spilling his notebook, some loose papers, and a polaroid photograph to the floor.

"Oh, I'm so sorry," she said as they both stooped to pick up the scattered contents. Nick reached for the photo, but Maggie's hand found it first.

"What's this?" She said, turning the photo around to get a better look.

"A photo of a pot," he said, reaching out to take it.

Maggie pulled it away from him. "Not *a* pot, *my* pot. And that's not the question. Where did you get this?"

"You asked me to find out about it," he said with a casual shrug. "I took a snap of it the other day when you first showed it to me."

Maggie gave him a questioning look, then handed the photo back to him, picked up the umbrella, and left for the clinic without another word.

Late afternoon found Maggie and the clinic staff gathered in the front office. The rain that had persisted more or less all day now pounded loudly on the roof. The skies were so dark that the streetlights had come on in the parking lot.

"That's the last of 'em," Therma Faye said nodding in the direction of the front door, "and good thing, too. With the weather so awful the poor things'll drown before they get home."

Maggie checked her watch. "It's 3:30. Why don't you and Donna go on before it gets any worse? If that's even possible."

"Don't ever say that. From the looks of it, it probably will. Radio said severe thunderstorm watch all night tonight," Therma Faye said.

"Didn't it say flash flood, too?" Donna added, gathering their purses and rain jackets and handing Therma Faye's to her.

"Uh-huh. And I don't doubt it for a second," Therma Faye added.

"You two get out of here," Maggie shooed them, "I'll finish up. I don't have far to go to Miz Hendri's."

Therma Faye shrugged into her jacket. "Don't you stay too late," she admonished Maggie. "And keep the radio on and listen for the sirens. Around here it can be thunderstorm watch one minute and tornado warning the next."

"Yes, mother," Maggie teased.

"And if it comes a tornado…"

Maggie gently pushed Therma Faye toward the door. "I'll get in the storeroom."

"Where that thing was?" Donna asked, incredulous.

"It's not there now. Scoot."

The pair pulled up their rain hoods and ducked out the door, leaving Maggie alone in the waiting room, looking out at the rain.

In the gravel parking lot next to the clinic, the school bus pulled up and stopped, lights flashing, as children poured out, scattering to waiting cars. Wearing a cheap neon yellow poncho and carrying a ragged book satchel, Rose Ellen stepped off the bus into the rain. She crossed to the clinic lot and passed beside Therma Faye, who was scurrying to her car.

"Rose Ellen, do you need a ride honey?" Therma Faye shouted to her over the wind and rain. The girl shook her head.

"Is your daddy meeting you on the far side of the bridge?" Rose Ellen bobbed her head.

"OK, sweetie," Therma Faye said, unlocking her door. "You hurry up now and be careful."

Rose Ellen walked quickly on in the downpour, around the side of the clinic, and down the short, wooded path toward the swinging cable bridge. She started across the bridge, and the wind caught her poncho, causing her to slip and stumble a little on the wet boards. She regained her balance and picked up the pace, almost running. As she neared the end of the bridge, a pair of black-clad arms reached out from the bushes that flanked the bridge's moorings. One hand clamped over her mouth and a strong arm wrapped around her torso, sweeping her toward the underbrush.

"Think you're a pretty clever girl, don't you? Stealing that pot," the harsh deep voice rasped.

Wide eyed, Rose Ellen struggled against the arm that held her, kicking, and twisting her head and torso back and forth, until the hand covering her mouth slipped, losing its purchase for a brief instant. Rose Ellen opened her mouth wide and bit down hard on the hand, drawing blood. Her assailant let out a hoarse scream and grabbed the injured hand.

Suddenly free, she scrambled up out of the wet brush and ran back onto the bridge in the direction she had come, toward the clinic. Her attacker pursued her but was pulled up short when the sleeve of his rainsuit caught on the jagged end of a bridge cable, slowing his pursuit briefly and giving her a few steps lead as she dashed across the slippery, swaying bridge. But, before she could reach the middle of the span, he was on her again.

On the road that ran beside the river, on the far side of the bridge, Waylon had pulled up in his truck to wait for Rose Ellen as she came off the bus. He killed the engine and drained the rest of a long neck beer, rolling down the window to toss out the empty bottle. The windshield had fogged up considerably as he waited, so he turned on the wipers and cranked the heater up to defog the window. In the gradually clearing glass, between arcs of the wipers, the bridge came into view, and on it two people struggling in the middle of the span, a larger figure dressed all in black and a smaller one in a tattered yellow poncho. The bridge pitched violently in the wind, and the roiling waters of the Caddo rushed and tumbled below it.

"Oh, sweet Jesus," he whispered aloud, "Rosie." Waylon threw open the door of the truck and set off at a run toward the bridge, shouting over the storm, "Rosie! Rosie!"

On the bridge, the struggle continued, and Waylon watched, helpless, as the attacker backhanded Rose Ellen, knocking her down on the wet boards. She was quickly up and scrambling to get away, but he was on her again. She twisted and kicked, pushing to get free, when all at once, the side netting tore loose from the cable, and she tumbled over the side into the roiling river.

Waylon saw her fall and immediately changed directions, heading for the river itself. Slipping and sliding down the wet riverbank, he leaped into the water, struggling toward mid river. Just upstream, he could see Rose Ellen in the yellow poncho tumbling along in the white water. He stroked harder to intercept her, but the current took her past him, until, in a stroke of good luck, her poncho caught on a jagged limb. Waylon fought his way to her. She was submerged and still. He grabbed her head and shoulders and pulled her above water, struggling against the current to free her entangled clothing, finally succeeding.

He clutched the limp child to him, wrapped one arm across her body, and desperately side-stroked across the current, letting the water take them downstream, angling toward the far bank. Gasping for air, he got a secure hand hold on a gnarled tree root and, with monumental effort, was able to pull them both up the slippery, vine-choked incline to the muddy bank above. Waylon turned her onto her side and firmly struck the center of her back with his cupped palm several times, calling her name. Rose Ellen coughed and belched out river water. Her dark lashes fluttered briefly open, then closed again. He brushed the sodden strands of hair from her pale face. "Rosie. Hang on, baby. Please hang on."

Maggie clicked off the waiting room lights and checked to be sure the front door was bolted. She stopped to marvel at the deluge through the front office windows. *Will it ever stop raining?* In the cone of light thrown by a streetlamp in the parking lot, Maggie saw Waylon running through the driving rain toward the clinic, a limp child dangling in his arms.

Maggie unbolted and threw open the front door, and he dashed in, wet and panting. Rose Ellen, drenched and unconscious, lay in his arms. "Help! Help her!" he pleaded.

"My God," Maggie grabbed her wrist to feel for a pulse. "Bring her this way," she said, leading him to the treatment room. "Put her there," she said, pointing to the treatment table.

Waylon laid her gently on the table and backed away to give Maggie room.

"What happened?" Maggie asked, as she pulled her stethoscope from her pocket.

"She fell off the swinging bridge into the river," Waylon said.

"How long was she in the water?" Maggie asked, removing the poncho and sodden sweater beneath it. She opened Rose Ellen's thin blouse and her heart clenched when she saw a deflated exam glove suspended on a length of twine around her neck like an amulet, the remains of the chicken balloon she'd left behind the screen door for her. Maggie reached up to touch her own crystal pendant.

"A minute or two, I guess. I saw her go in and went right after her," he said.

Maggie clipped a pulse oximeter to Rose Ellen's finger and put the stethoscope to her chest, listening for several seconds. The pulse ox beeped, and Maggie looked at the display. It read 70. *Very low.* A look of worry clouded her face. She listened again to both sides, then without warning, hit the center of the child's small chest and felt for pulses at her neck.

"Call 9-1-1," she said to Waylon as she began rescue breathing and compressions.

Waylon hesitated. "She gonna be all right?"

"9-1-1," she said between breaths. "Now!"

Maggie continued to perform CPR, while Waylon stumbled to the office and picked up the receiver of the desk phone and dialed 9-1-1.

"9-1-1, what is your emergency?" the operator said.

"We need an ambulance," he blurted out. "My daughter-" and the line went dead. "Hello? Hello?" he kept shouting. "Are you there? We need the ambulance here!" Waylon tapped the hook switch several times, then slammed the receiver back into the cradle, as the lights flickered on and off. He tried to dial again. Again he slammed down the receiver.

Waylon returned to the treatment room, where he found Rose Ellen with an IV line and blood pressure cuff on her tiny arm, oxygen tubing in her nostrils, and Maggie listening to her chest and trying to palpate a blood pressure.

"Line went dead before I could tell them where we are," he said. "Storm musta knocked it out."

Maggie tossed him the cell phone from her pocket. "Try this."

He keyed in 9-1-1 and waited. The call didn't connect.

"No. Nothing," he said. Waylon stood beside the table and took his child's small hand in his. "Oh, sweet Jesus," he said, "is she gonna be all right?"

"I've got a heartbeat and a very weak pulse. She's breathing on her own."

Rose Ellen stirred and whimpered softly. Waylon gently rubbed her arm. "Please let her be OK," he whispered. "You gonna be OK, baby. You gonna be OK."

"She's still a long way from OK. We need to get her to the hospital. Try the land line again."

Waylon seemed unwilling to leave her.

"I've got her. Go call," Maggie reassured him.

He dashed quickly away but returned just moments later. "Still dead," he told her. "What are we gonna do? What am I gonna do? This is all my fault... all my fault."

"She fell. You can't blame yourself for an accident," Maggie said.

"Wasn't any accident. That sumbitch hit her and knocked her down. Just like he'd done to Ruth." The fury in his eyes was palpable

"What are you saying?"

"He said he didn't mean to, and besides wouldn't anybody believe me if I told," the words came tumbling out in a spate.

CHAPTER 20
Unmasked

Nick appeared at the doorway to the treatment room, a shotgun in his hands.

"No, Waylon, what I said was 'who'd believe your drunk, sorry ass.' Or were you too wasted to remember it right?"

Maggie's head jerked up, and she removed the stethoscope from her ears. "Nick, what are you doing here?"

As if he hadn't heard her, he went on, "And as for your whiney wife, she thought she'd stop me, and we know how that worked out, don't we? And then your bratty kid stuck her nose in."

Maggie edged toward him. "Nick, put down the gun."

"And you, Princess," he said, pointing the barrels in her direction. "You just wouldn't let go of it, would you? And I really hate that because I thought we could have been a thing. But hey, that's the breaks, right?"

Waylon stepped a little closer to him.

"Uh-uh-unh," Nick raised a brow and gestured for him to get back with the barrels of the gun. "Get back on the other side of that table." Waylon joined Maggie behind the table and Nick went on, "Really, it would have been so much simpler if all of you had just minded your own business. Nobody would have gotten hurt."

"Don't do this," Maggie pleaded with him.

"Do what? I'm not going to *do* anything. Well, nothing you haven't forced me to. Sometimes accidents just happen. Like with poor little Rose here." He walked over closer to the child who lay semi-conscious on the table. "I have to admit—though I hadn't planned it this way—it's very convenient for me that you're all here together." He swiftly jerked the IV line from Rose Ellen's arm, sending an arc of bloody fluid into the air.

"What are you doing?" Maggie cried in disbelief.

Waylon lunged around the table at Nick. "You lousy sumbitch. I'm gonna kill you."

The shotgun blast roared in the small room, and Waylon fell, blood soaking his lower abdomen and groin.

"Daddy!" The scream tore involuntarily from Rose Ellen's throat, but her eyelashes fluttered open only briefly and closed again.

Maggie rushed to Waylon's side and knelt beside him.

"Rosie," he panted, reaching out, trying to rise.

Maggie put a restraining hand on him as she fumbled for a towel from the exam table drawer and applied pressure to his wound. He was woozy, but alive. "Nick why are you doing this?" she said, trying to keep any trace of panic from her voice.

"Some of us don't have settlements and trust funds. Folks have to make it however they can," Nick said. "If a few innocents get caught in the crossfire, well, that's just the breaks. Collateral damage. Just ask Captain America, there. I'll bet he knows all about that," he said with a tilt of his head in Waylon's direction.

Maggie looked up, anger burning in her eyes. "Who are you? I don't know you at all."

"No," he shook his head, "you don't. And now you won't because this party's over. Get the kid and the drunk to your chariot."

"We can't. Rose Ellen is in critical shape, and Waylon's lost too much blood already. They need a hospital."

Nick's laugh was almost comical, but the wildness in his eyes suggested otherwise. "You just don't get it, do you?"

The questioning look on Maggie's face answered him, so he went on to explain.

"You're all going to meet with a terrible accident, on your *way* to the hospital," he said. "It's perfect. I couldn't have planned it better."

Maggie fixed him with an icy stare and turned her attention back to Waylon, feeling for pulse at neck and wrist. "Waylon? Can you hear me?"

Waylon moved his head to nod slightly and whispered hoarsely, "I hear ya."

"Can you roll a little if I help you?"

"Maybe," he said, so softly she almost couldn't hear it.

"I need to get some pressure on your wound." Maggie said quietly, taking a large roll of self-adhering bandage from the exam table drawer and wrapping it securely around his thigh. "Waylon, I'm going to pull you toward me, then push the other way. Just work with me as best you can," she said, "and it's going to hurt." He groaned each time she pulled his hips toward her and rolled the bandage under him, then gently pushed him the other way to free the roll and wrap it around over the towel on his pelvis and thigh again. Then repeating again and again until she had it secure. She crabbed over and pulled the crash cart closer, opening the bottom drawer and removing a large clear bundle from it.

"Hey, what do you think you're doing?" Nick barked.

"I need to be able to keep some pressure on this bandage," she said over her shoulder. Then turning her face to him, "If you want this *accident* to look authentic, I mean." Maggie opened the packet, removing the pair of medical anti-shock trousers, she laid them out beside Waylon, immediately worried she wouldn't be able to apply them by herself. Or inflate them properly. Where was Jeff when she needed him? She'd never actually put a pair of MAST on a patient herself, but she'd seen it done on video, and as they say in med school: see one, do one, teach one.

"What the hell is that contraption?" Nick asked. "Just wrap a towel around his leg and get him up."

"They're compression trousers. Honestly, do you think anybody would believe that I'd throw a patient into the car with a fresh and actively bleeding gunshot wound with just a towel thrown over it and let him bleed out on the way to the hospital?"

"Hmm. Clever," he gave her a nod. "Just don't try to get too clever."

She wanted to keep him talking. The longer she could keep them here, the better. Maybe Waylon's aborted call got through. Maybe someone, somewhere knew.

"Or what?" she said to Nick. "You'll kill me a little sooner? You'll shoot me instead of incinerating me or whatever it is you've got planned?" She hooked the tubing of the trousers to the foot pump from the packet.

"Don't be cute," Nick said. "Just hurry up and get those things on Prescott."

Maggie bunched up the legs of the trousers at each of Waylon's feet and then worked each one up to his knees, then to about mid-thigh. She was going to need his help to lift his hips, and she wasn't remotely convinced he could do it. Had the blast shattered pelvic bones? She couldn't possibly know, but they had little choice at this point.

She leaned close to Waylon's ear. "Waylon? You with me?" She got a slight double head nod for answer. "I am going to put a pair of compression trousers on you."

"MAST," he managed to whisper. "We used … in the war."

"Yes, and I'm going to need you to lift up your hips and pull them up over your lower body. Like pulling on a pair of jeans, OK? I'll help as much as I can. Here" she grabbed both his hands and put them on the waist of the trousers at his thighs.

He nodded again and opened his eyes, looking directly into hers.

"Ready?" Another nod. "On my count," she said. "One, two, three."

Waylon groaned aloud, a guttural roar, as he pushed up his hips and pulled on the trousers. Maggie gave a strong, quick tug on the back side of them as his hips cleared the floor. He collapsed immediately, moaning pitifully.

Maggie secured the fastenings on the trousers and opened the stop cock on the tubing, then stood up and began stomping hard and steadily on the foot pump to inflate the air sacs on each leg and the abdomen. To her everlasting relief, the bladders puffed up and appeared to hold. She closed the stop cocks and disconnected the foot pump.

"Get the kid unhooked from the rest of that stuff," Nick ordered.

Waylon tried, weakly, to raise up. "Leave her be," he rasped.

"She's just a baby," Maggie implored Nick. "She can't hurt you. I'll go with you, but leave her here."

"Can't hurt me?" Nick snorted a laugh. "Where do you think she got that pretty little pot she gave you? Hmmm?" His brows raised in question. When he got no response, he continued, "Had it in my hands two years ago. Little thief must have been there and snatched it the night her mother… got in my way."

Maggie pulled a band-aid from the crash cart drawer and peeled it open slowly, stalling, taking her time, and covered Rose Ellen's IV site. "You can't possibly think you will get away with this."

"No?" he smirked. "I'm in Little Rock, remember? All checked in at the University Suites. Got an early breakfast scheduled tomorrow with Jonas York. I'm rock solid."

"You're insane," she said.

"No, not entirely. But I am running out of patience. Get that oxygen thing off the kid and get her to the car. And give me your keys."

Maggie turned the valve of the oxygen cylinder and gently removed the loops of the cannula from around Rose Ellen's ears and the tips out of her nostrils. She took her keys from the pocket of her lab coat and tossed them onto the floor at Nick's feet. They clattered sharply in the still room. In the momentary distraction, as Nick bent to retrieve them,

Maggie picked up the heavy oxygen cylinder, hoisting it up over her head. But Nick was too quick and jumped back.

"I wouldn't," he said, standing up and training the gun on her. She set the cylinder down, and he dropped the keys into his pocket. "Get the kid," his tone now was more menacing as he motioned with the gun barrels. "Now!"

Maggie pulled a thin blanket from the exam drawer and wrapped it around the child, lifting her up into her arms.

"Now, give her to me. Easy and slow," he said.

Maggie laid Rose Ellen high against his chest, and he wrapped his free arm around her, shifting her torso up over his shoulder.

"Now, drag the hayseed over to the back door."

Waylon was a big man, and while Maggie was small, she was strong. She squatted at his head, wrapped a hand and forearm under each of his shoulders, and pushed up through her hips. *Just think of it as a deadlift. And pray it isn't.* Once she felt secure, she began backing up step by step down the back hall. The slick fabric of the MAST pants actually helped to slide him a little.

At the back door of the clinic, she left Waylon against the wall by the door, eliciting another weak moan.

"Take the keys," Nick said, "and back your ride up here. And don't try anything heroic." He laid the limp child across Waylon's body and trained the barrels on Rose Ellen's ribs. "Rest assured I can get them both with one shot. And I will not be afraid to pull the trigger."

The rain pounded on the awning overhead, and the wind whistled. Lightening streaked, illuminating the dark parking lot for an instant, but the thunderclap behind it was delayed by several seconds, not sounding until Maggie had reached the SUV. The engine rumbled, and Maggie pulled around and backed onto the walk leading up to the doorway.

Nick opened the hatch and hollered over the cacophony of wind and rain, "Come get the girl."

Maggie, already soaked from the dash to get the car, climbed out and walked slowly to the back of the vehicle, opening the back passenger door as she did.

"Light a fire under it, Princess," he stepped back to let her in the door. "We don't have all night."

She gathered up Rose Ellen and wrapped the blanket more securely around her, taking the opportunity to feel her pulse. It was more robust than she'd even dared hope. *A good sign.* Trying to shield her from the weather, she stepped quickly to the back car door and levered it fully open with her foot. She laid Rose Ellen gently across the back seat, murmuring softly to her, "It's OK, sweetie. It's OK."

"Get Prescott," he said.

"That, I can't possibly do alone. If you want him in the car, you're going to have to help me," she stood, dripping, hands on her hips, staring him down. "You get under one arm, and I'll get under the other, and we'll pull him right behind the cargo gate, and then we can lift together and pull him to standing. That won't last long, so we've got to be ready to let him fall back into the cargo area."

"OK," Nick said, stooping beside Waylon's still form, but keeping the gun across his body, so it still pointed at the man's chest.

"One, two, three," Maggie counted, and they moved in unison to drag Waylon closer to the back of the car. "Again. One, two, three," as they lifted him to a standing position.

Waylon gave a miserable groan, and his head lolled to one side. Then, with a reserve that came out of God knows where, he pushed both his hands into Nick's chest, shoving him hard and knocking him off balance.

Nick quickly recovered and in one swift, vicious arc drove the butt of the shotgun into the top of Waylon's head. The injured man fell backward, unconscious, into the cargo space.

Maggie stood in the rain, facing Nick. "You are a sad, miserable waste of human protoplasm."

"I'll consider that high praise," he said. "Get his legs up in there," he barked at Maggie. "And then get in the driver's seat."

The MAST pants made getting Waylon into the cargo area more difficult, but she didn't dare deflate them now. Maggie had to squat crawl into the space to pull him in by his torso, wedging his head and shoulders up onto the back of the back seat and letting his legs and abdomen stretch out diagonally. Even then it was a tight fit getting the hatch door closed.

She got into the driver's seat, and Nick crawled into the backseat behind her; she felt the cold metal of the shotgun on her neck as she cranked the engine. She turned on the wipers and began to nose the SUV out of the parking lot, when a truck came down the road. She flipped the brights on and off, hoping to maybe get the driver's attention, then fumbled around with the controls, finally turning the wipers to high speed.

"Hey, what the hell do you think you're doing?" The shotgun's nose pressed harder into the flesh of her neck.

"Sorry. I just flipped the wrong lever."

The truck slowed slightly, but her heart sank when it turned away from them and moved on down the opposite way, the taillights becoming a distant red blur in the rain. Maggie pulled slowly out of the lot.

"Turn left here," Nick said.

Maggie turned onto the desolate road that she knew led to the river. Soon, the houses and buildings gave way to empty, dark fields. In places, the branches of trees growing beside the road overhung them and underbrush encroached along both sides. Only the *slap, slap, slap* of the windshield wipers and the incessant drumbeat of the rain on the roof broke the tense silence as they crept along. Lightning flashed, brightly illuminating the interior of the car for an instant.

Maggie looked at Nick in the rearview mirror. "How did you manage it?"

"What?" he asked.

"Switching the bones," she replied, watching his face in the fading flash. Then the car was dark again. "That skeleton we pulled out of the riverbank, I thought it was a female. The State lab read it out as male. Native American. We were both right, weren't we?"

Nick stared back at her face reflected in the mirror, illuminated only by the blue dash lights, but didn't respond.

"Weren't we?" she repeated more forcefully. The skeleton the crime lab examined was a Native American relic, wasn't it? You put it there."

"And your point?"

"The river skeleton was Ruth Prescott's, wasn't it? And that cosmic compost was her wedding ring."

"Looks like you've got it all figured out," he said. "Too bad it's too late to do any good. But hey, there's some consolation in being right."

"I don't care about being right," she said. "What I can't figure out is why. What possible benefit could you gain that would be worth killing an innocent woman?"

"It doesn't really matter now, does it?" He chuckled. "You'll all be seeing Ruth soon enough. Maybe you can ask her about it."

Maggie slowed the SUV and came to a full stop. She turned around in her seat to look directly at him, unable to fathom his callousness. Unable to reconcile the person she now believed him to be with the light-hearted, funny companion she'd thought she knew.

Nick put the barrels of the shotgun very close to her face. "Don't try anything, Princess. Just drive."

"And what? Nobody will get hurt?"

"Just drive and cut the conversation."

Maggie stared at him a few long seconds more, the slapping of the wipers beating accompaniment to the pounding of her heart, the drumming of the rain echoing the roar of her blood in her ears. *How could she have been so completely taken in by him?*

CHAPTER 21
Maelstrom

The SUV started again down the way, splashing through water already flowing across low spots, bouncing over downed branches and debris on the road. They finally came to a sudden stop on the steep decline that led down to the bridge, causing Waylon to moan pitifully. In the light of the headlamps, the Caddo River boiled below with white water. The low water bridge was totally submerged. Large limbs and debris tumbled along in the roiling rapids.

"Looks like this is quite literally the end of the road," Nick said. He opened the door and climbed out, coming to stand beside the driver's door.

Maggie grabbed the door handle and set her shoulder to the door, abruptly shoving it open, hoping to catch him off guard. But she wasn't fast enough. Nick anticipated and stepped beyond the arc of the door, then aimed the shotgun at her face.

"Now that wasn't nice," he said. "Close the door."

Maggie complied, closing the door. Nick tapped the driver's side glass with the tip of the barrels and motioned for her to roll down the window. Again, she complied, rolling the window part way down. Nick rested the gun barrel on the glass, inches from her face.

"Now let me brief you on how this will go," he said. "You are going to drive this nice sport utility vehicle right onto the bridge." He looked toward the river and back to her. "Or where you think the bridge might be."

Maggie stared over the hood at the churning white water in the headlamp beams.

"My guess," he said, "is that it's right where the road disappears into the water. That's just a helpful hint from me to you."

Maggie looked at him with disgust but said nothing.

"When you hit the bridge – assuming you do – gun the engine and keep going. There's just the slightest chance that you can make it across."

"You know we can't. The engine will stall out in water this deep."

"Bingo!" He chuckled, again. "And you'll be stuck. Until the river crests and washes you and your buddies downstream." He illustrated their upcoming tumbling path down the river by rolling his left hand over and over and over. "An ideal scenario from my point of view."

Maggie laid on the horn, but its sound was engulfed by the raging of the wind and rain and the roaring of the river.

Nick laughed out loud at her. "Good try!" He backed away a few steps and said, "Oh, and don't try climbing out. I'll be standing right here with this shotgun and a pocket full of shells, and I will not hesitate to blow your pretty head right off."

"Won't look much like an accident then," she said.

"True. And quite honestly, I would prefer it look like a bona fide tragedy, but a guy's gotta do what a guy's gotta do. Besides, this is Prescott's gun, and I'm in Little Rock."

"Go to hell," Maggie said coldly. "No, don't bother. You're already there."

Nick motioned her forward with the gun barrel. "Sink or swim, Princess."

Maggie slowly inched the car toward the water, and Nick walked beside the vehicle, keeping the gun trained on her window until the front tires rolled into the water. He then stepped to the rear of the car and watched.

Inside the car, Maggie, her mind racing for some way out, gripped the wheel with both hands, focused and controlled, fighting down panic, as the car entered the water. Bitter memories of her parents' deaths in a river sprang to her mind, and she forced the thoughts away. *Stay focused on the present.* The force of the river rocked the vehicle and jostled the passengers, eliciting another groan from Waylon.

"Waylon? Can you hear me?"

Waylon moaned again but didn't answer.

"Rose Ellen? Sweetie? Can you hear me."

Lightening flashed again and in the pulsating light, Maggie chanced a backward glance at the girl. As she did, the vehicle lurched sharply, bringing her focus back to what lay ahead. The water rushed loudly around them as the SUV was now fully in the river. She pressed down slowly and steadily on the accelerator, trying to gain some gradual momentum, but the engine coughed and sputtered. And died.

Maggie cranked the starter, *rrrrr rrrrr rrrrr,* but the engine refused to turn over. She waited a bit, forcing herself to count a slow twenty before trying again. She depressed the gas pedal and released it, then cranked again. *Rrrrr. Rrrrr. Rrrrr.*"

"Shit!" She hissed aloud, then taking a deep breath, counted again to twenty and cranked once more and got only *click, click, click.* She pounded the steering wheel in fury and frustration. "Shit, shit, SHIT!"

Water splashed into the partly open driver's side window; she'd neglected to close it. *Damn it!* She reached for the toggle switch to raise the glass. *Dead.* Water had begun to seep in around the door, filling the floorboards. Maggie put the car in Park and set the emergency break.

"Jesus, Mary, Joseph, God Almighty and anybody else listening out there," she whispered aloud. "Hold these tires to this bridge while I figure out what to do." She unfastened her seat belt, turned around and knelt between the seats to peer through the rear window. A bolt of lightening silhouetted Nick, still standing in the middle of the road, shotgun across his chest, watching their plight with apparent calm.

Maggie looked at Rose Ellen, so small and vulnerable, bundled in the seat. "What are we going to do?" she said softly to her. Rose Ellen opened her eyes and stared back at Maggie, which, despite their tough circumstances, thrilled her no end. "Hey, sweetie. Hey," she said, reaching out to lay a hand on her.

Rose Ellen smiled weakly, and Maggie leaned between the front seats to tuck the blanket snugly around the girl, smoothing the damp tendrils of hair away from her face.

"Looks like we're in a little bit of a tight spot, right now. But we're going to be fine. I don't know exactly how, yet, but it's going to be okay," she spoke reassuring words she didn't fully feel to soothe the child.

As she leaned over, Maggie's quartz pendant swung out of the neck of her blouse, and Rose Ellen reached up to touch it. "Are you warm enough?"

The child nodded and murmured, "Mm hmm." Her eyes fluttered and closed again.

Maggie sat back into her seat and put her fingers to her temples, massaging them as she thought. *OK. Daddy would have said "Stay calm, sugar. Figure it out. Work it like an algorithm." What do I know? Power is out. Engine stalled. Can I get the door open? Probably not on this side, the pressure of the water will be too much. Maybe the passenger side? If not, can I break out a window so we can get out?*

She opened the center console and glove box and rummaged through them, finding a plethora of useless items tossing them one by one into the floorboard: breath mints, owner's manual, insurance and registration papers, a map. A compass. *That might prove useful.* She stuck it into her pocket. A little penlight. She tucked that into her pocket as well. And, finally, the ice scraper. She wrapped her fist around its sturdy handle and back fisted a couple of test strikes against the glass.

Could it work? Maybe. But then what? Even if I could get us all out, what? Nick picks us off as we climb out the window? Or we get swept out into the flood? Shit! What's Plan B?

Nick continued to watch the car from the road as the rising, raging current buffeted the SUV, causing it to shift precariously in the swift current. "Bon voyage, Prin..." his retort was cut short, his knees buckled, and he slumped to the road.

JD stood behind him, a tire iron in his hand, two coils of thick rope, slung bandolier-style across his chest. He squatted beside Nick's unconscious form and expertly trussed his wrists and ankles with zip ties, then stood over him. "Bon voyage, yourself, asshole."

JD hurried to the edge of the river and cupped his hands around his mouth, shouting over the howl of the wind and the roar of the river, "Maggie! Maggie!" He took his keys from his jacket pocket and shined a tiny blue laser in the direction of the car, blinking it on, off, on, off.

Maggie saw the flashes of blue light. *Was that lightening?* She turned again to kneel in the seat and stared intently out the rear window. The light flashed again.

"God, please, let it be," she whispered a prayer and grabbed the penlight from her pocket, holding it out the open window and giving three slow, distinct flashes. She received, in return, three blue flashes. *Somebody besides Nick is out there. But who?*

Lightening streaked across the sky, and in the blue-white flash, she could clearly see it was JD standing on the road above the swollen river, hands cupping his mouth. She put her ear as close as possible to the opening of her window, straining to hear, and thought she could discern JD's voice above the roar.

"Hang on... stay put... coming," she thought she understood.

"It's JD," she whispered. Then louder to Rose Ellen, "It's JD, sweetie. Thank God."

JD stood on the road beside the Caddo, already swollen beyond its banks, the water reaching high into the thick underbrush. Moonlight and flashes of lightning glinted off the white foam that collected in pockets against roots and debris as the river raged along. He took his cell phone from his pocket and texted a message to Sheriff Perkins detailing where they were and what had happened. Asking for reinforcements. Texts require less tower strength than calls, so maybe this one would get through. Then he removed the coils of rope and shucked out of his insulated jacket, folding it and placing it on the roadside beside the unconscious lump that was Nick.

Clad now only in his t-shirt, light neoprene tights, and river shoes, he picked up the coils, flung them back across his chest, and began the struggle through the thick undergrowth of the bank upriver from the SUV. He stopped periodically whenever the brush thinned and turned back to check on the SUV. So far, it held fast.

He stopped upstream at a large cottonwood that grew on the bank, its solid trunk at least yard or more across. Removing the coils of rope, he laid one beside the tree, then tied the end of the other rope with multiple knots to the trunk, leaning back with all his weight to check its security. This would be his primary contact rope, the one he would secure to the SUV to hold it in place and make getting back to it easier.

Satisfied, he took another look at the SUV and secured the second rope, the pendulum rope, to the big tree. He made a loose loop of the end of that rope and put it over his head and around his chest. Lightning crashed so close to him that the flash was almost simultaneous with a ferocious clap of thunder that shook the trees around him. Finally, he made a release knot in the loose end of the contact rope, attaching it to the loop around his chest.

After one last check of the security of all the knots and a moment to satisfy himself there were no snags near the coils to catch as their length played out, JD took a few deep breaths and jumped out into the maelstrom, swimming like hell straight across the river. His cross-stream path coupled with the downstream rush of the current carried him in an arc that intercepted the stranded vehicle.

He thudded against the rear fender of the SUV and grabbed a hand hold on the wheel well. Readjusting his grip, he eased himself around to the eddy side of the vehicle. Even on the still side, away from the churning white water, he had to fight the current to find a place to secure the contact line to the SUV. He released the knot from his chest loop and pulled the contact rope as taut as he could, tying it off with a secure bowline to the rear hatch spare tire mount.

JD made his way to the passenger window and cupped his hands around his eyes to peer inside. Maggie pressed her palm to the inside of the window, and JD placed his palm over hers through the glass. Then she moved closer to the glass so he would be able to see her face.

"You OK?" He shouted to her through the window.

To her ears it was the most beautiful sound she'd ever heard. "Yes... now." She blew out her breath in a long stream. She hadn't realized she been holding it. "Where's Nick?"

"Sleeping it off," he said. "Let me get you out of here."

"It's not just me," she said, "Waylon and Rose Ellen are here, too. Waylon's been shot, and he's in pretty bad shape. Rose Ellen's half drowned, but conscious."

"How high is the water in there?"

"Almost to the seats, she said, her feet pulled up under her on the seat.

"We gotta get y'all out and fast. The river's going higher before it crests."

An image of the roiling wall of white water she'd watched flash down the river behind Nick's car the night of the fair entered her mind and made her shudder.

She forced herself again to focus on the present. On JD outside the window. "What do you want me to do?"

"Will this door open?" he said, indicating the back passenger door.

"I don't know. I think so. I don't think it's locked," she said.

"OK. I think I can open it from out here." He thought for a moment, then said, "When I give you the go sign, I want you to gather Rosie to your chest. I'll ease the door open, and we'll let the water level equalize and –"

She interrupted him. "I need to make sure Waylon's at least conscious and that his head is going to be above the water level, before we flood the car."

"Can you move him by yourself?"

"I hope so," she said, crawling between the front seats; she crouched in the rear floorboard and leaned over the back seat to shake Waylon's shoulder. "Waylon? Waylon?" She shook harder. "You with us?"

Waylon roused. "Yeah," he said in a hoarse whisper.

"JD Langston is here. He's going to help us get out. But it's going to mean letting some water in. I need you to help me sit you up higher."

Waylon nodded.

Maggie knelt in the back seat, beside Rose Ellen, and reach again under Waylon's arms and around his chest, clasping one wrist with her opposite hand. "On three. One…two…three." She pulled him toward her with all her strength, and he was able to push with his arms and against the back hatch with his uninjured leg, though the effort cost him, and he groaned and grimaced in pain.

"OK, he's up," she shouted to JD. "Now what?"

"Take the blanket from around Rosie and hug her to you," he said. "When we open the door, the water's gonna rise fast. Soon as the door's out of the way, I want you to pass her to me. Can she hang on at all?

"She's weak, JD," Maggie said, shaking her head. "I don't know."

"It's OK," he reassured her. "I can hold her safe. You ready?"

"Hang on a second." Maggie cupped Rose Ellen's small face in her hands and put her own face very close, until their noses were almost touching. "Sweetie, listen to me." Maggie pulled the blanket from the girl's body and tossed it in the floor. "In just a second, we're going to open the door and the water's going to come in. It's going to be really cold, but you'll be

OK. It won't be for too long. JD's going to take you through the river to the shore. If you can hang on to him, you hang on, as tight as you can. OK?"

"My daddy?" she whimpered in a tiny, frightened voice.

"He'll be fine, honey. JD's promised to come back for both of us. We're all going to be just fine." *I hope to God.*

Rose Ellen nodded and whispered, "OK." Maggie kissed her on the forehead and gave the OK sign to JD as she gathered the girl tightly to her chest.

The door swung open and icy water rushed in around them, swirling and filling the car to the bottom of the windows, causing Maggie to gasp. She passed Rose Ellen to JD, who slipped his chest loop over them both and clutched her to him with one arm, hanging onto the pendulum rope with the other.

"Hang on, honey," he said to the girl. Then looking back at Maggie, said, "You, too." He pushed off the SUV and swung out into the swiftly moving water with Rose Ellen clinging to his chest. The white water boiled around them, buffeting them and driving them down the river, until the arc of the rope pulled taut and swung them into the bank.

JD struggled to get a purchase on the slippery bank, a tough go with the sucking current, Rose Ellen's added weight, and just one arm to grab a hand hold. He lost his footing twice, sending them back into the water, before he was able to finally get good traction and lever them out, scrambling up to higher ground and finally onto the roadway, where he put her down. He retrieved his thermal waterproof jacket, shook the water from its surface, and wrapped Rose Ellen in it.

"You stay right here, darlin. Don't move. I'll be back before you know it," he promised, giving both shoulders a squeeze and leaving her on the road. Nick was trussed up nearby, and JD stooped to check that the zip ties were secure. He gave the skin on Nick's side a good hard pinch, and it elicited little more than a soft grunt.

The rain had slacked off and now almost stopped, just a light drizzle persisted, but the risk of flash flooding from upstream rain was not gone. Time, in fact, was decidedly not on their side. He dropped the loop of the pendulum rope into the river and trudged back upstream.

When he reached the big cottonwood, where the two lines were secured, he gathered the pendulum rope hand over hand, slipped the loop over his head again, and tied the trailing end in a release knot around the taut contact line – the one now attached to the SUV. Then with a last check of the security of all the knots, he leapt back into the water, this time, riding the whitewater current down the contact line straight to the vehicle.

Some sort of debris in the churning water slammed into his side when he thumped against the vehicle. It knocked the wind from him for a moment, and he held onto the rope, trying to recover his breath. He shook his head and inhaled a ragged, painful breath as he made his way around the back hatch to the eddy side to the open door.

"Ready to ride?" he asked Maggie.

"JD, you've got to take Waylon first. He's bad; it may take us both to get him out and into the water."

"Can he help at all?"

"Not much," she said. "One thigh is shot. I don't know how much damage in his abdomen or about the stability of his pelvis. One leg is OK, but he's weak. Let me fold the seat back down on the near side. I think the air bladders of the MAST pants will let us float him out to you."

"Whoa. He's in anti-shock trousers?"

"Yes," she said.

JD released the lever to drop the seatback nearest him, laying it flat, but the inflated MAST pants held Waylon's legs straight out and made it impossible to maneuver him to the opening, even with Maggie's help. She looked at the ashy color of his face and knew he had little reserve left in him. They needed to get him out, now. Another chunk of tumbling debris thunked hard into the side door, causing the SUV to rock. *Hell, we all need to get out of here now.*

"Waylon, I'm going to drop the other seatback," Maggie said, "and JD and I are going to try to pull you out. If you can get any leverage to help us with your good leg, do it." Then, using one hand to support his head, she released the lock of the other seatback. When both seatbacks were flat, with JD and Maggie pulling and Waylon pushing as best he could with his arms and uninjured leg, they finally managed to float him out of the door.

JD wrapped one arm under Waylon's arms and around his chest to pull him close, then removed the pendulum loop and slipped it over them both and put the pendulum line into Waylon's hands. "Hold on to the line for all you're worth," JD said. "When we push off, try to keep your head above water and your face to the shore."

"I always knew you'd make a good soldier," Waylon rasped. "Let 'er rip."

JD took a last look at Maggie, gave her a nod and a wink, and pushed them off. The rope played out normally for a moment, then hung up on something, leaving them twisting in midstream. Maggie watched helplessly as the white water churned heavily around them, and JD struggled blindly and futilely to free the rope.

She followed the line of the rope with her eyes back from the men to where it disappeared into the water at the back of the vehicle itself. *Maybe it's hooked on the bumper or something under the car.* She eased herself into the chilly water on the eddy side of the car, and, gripping anything that offered a hand hold, felt her way down the side of the SUV to where the rope disappeared. Hanging onto the spare mount, she felt below her with her feet. There was the rope; she could feel it, and she eased her foot along its taut length. It went under the bumper and was hooked on something farther below. She stood on the rope and tried to bounce up and down with both feet, hoping to dislodge it, but it didn't budge, and her bouncing rocked the car, which she was pretty sure wasn't a good thing. *Now what?*

Maggie hooked her elbow around the bend of the tire mount and with one hand unbuckled her belt and worked it free. She then looped it and buckled it around the base of the mount to lengthen her reach. Slipping her foot through the loop of belt, she took a couple of deep breaths, unhooked her elbow, and dove under the surface. She opened her eyes, but visibility in the roiling murky water was next to nothing.

She reached out to feel the taut pendulum rope and followed it down to where the rope ended. She felt all around and discerned what she thought was a branch. If she opened her eyes and strained, she could almost make out how the rope had hung up on it. But figuring it out had taken her longer than she'd hoped, and her lungs burned ferociously; she came up for some air, breaking the surface, sputtering and gasping. After a few sweet gulps, she dove again, this time able to go straight to the snag. She pushed hard on the branch trying to snap it and free the rope, but she didn't have enough arm strength under the water. So, she broke the surface again and gulped in more air.

She needed more length than the looped belt allowed, so she removed her foot from the loop and unbuckled the belt. Then she wrapped the belt around the contact rope well above the knot and fed the end of the belt through the buckle, cinching it tightly around the rope. That would give her almost double the previous length to descend deeper in the water without letting go.

She wrapped the end of the belt around her wrist and grabbed it with her hand, then took another deep breath and used her free hand to push herself down the side of the car to the level of the bridge, to where the branch trapped the rope. She positioned both feet on the branch and with her back to the tire of the SUV she gave a powerful push with both legs. She felt the branch crack slightly, and encouraged, did it again and once again, finally breaking the branch, but the rope was still caught around the broken stub. Her lungs were screaming, and she surfaced again for air.

She realized she would need both her hands to free the remaining snag and that meant she'd have to let go of her one point of contact with the car. She took a breath and dived again, stretching as far as she could toward the snag, then let go of the end of the belt. She grabbed onto the pendulum rope just above the snag and tugged it with both hands with all her strength. It broke free at last, but once loose, the slack played out quickly, taking Maggie with it.

All was chaos and white water for a few moments, and it was all she could do to hold on. After what seemed like endless minutes, but couldn't have been more than a few terrifying seconds, she popped to the surface, gasping for air, and clinging to the rope like her life depended on it, which, she quickly realized, was the case. The current swung the rope in its pendulum arc into the bank, but the force of the water slammed Maggie's head and shoulder hard into a gnarled root of a tree on the bank, sending a stinger of electricity through her arm to her fingertips and dotting her vision with stars. She grabbed onto the slippery, mossy root with the other hand and shook her head to clear the cobwebs. She was alive. And for that she was thankful. *But where are JD and Waylon? Where is Rose Ellen?*

Maggie was still trying to get her bearings and muster the strength to climb out of the water and up onto the steep bank when there was a deafening *crash* and *snap* behind her. She craned her neck and looked around just in time to see something slam into the side of the SUV. It rocked precariously, the contact rope frayed and snapped, and the car tumbled downstream, swept along by the current.

"Maggie!" JD's voice barely carried above the cacophony and sounded very far away to her, but she was sure she'd heard it and the anguish in it.

He's alive! Maggie peered into the darkness downriver. "JD," she yelled above the roar of the river. "JD! Can you hear me? Are you OK?" Some of the feeling was returning to her right arm, and she opened and closed her hand to check its function. It seemed to be working, but she didn't know how strong her grip would be. And her shoulder throbbed fiercely. Could she climb out? She had to try.

Then, from somewhere above her, she heard his voice again. At first, she thought she was imagining it, but when she looked up, she saw his hand and his face.

"Grab hold," he said, stretching a hand down to her as he held onto a sturdy limb, higher on the bank with his other hand.

Her immediate thought was that she might never have seen a more beautiful sight. She reached up and grabbed his outstretched arm with her own hand. His fingers closed around her wrist, and he pulled her strongly up and out of the river to safety.

Maggie and JD sank down, exhausted, onto the muddy bank above the river, and JD wrapped his arms around her shoulders.

"Ungh," she winced.

JD pulled away from her and looked down, seeing the ripped shoulder of her blouse and the bruised and bloody scrape there. "What happened here?"

"Slammed into a root. It's OK, I think. Just banged up," she reassured him.

"Can you move it?"

She gingerly lifted her elbow out until it was level with her shoulder, then brought it forward and pushed it back. "Yeah. It hurts some, but it works now."

He wrapped his arms around her again, cradling her ever so gently and stroking her wet hair. "You sure you're okay, babe?"

"Mmm-hmm," she murmured. "Now I am. You?"

"Never better," he said, kissing her wet forehead. "Never better."

"Where's Rose Ellen?"

"She's safe on the road over there. Not far," he reassured her.

"And Waylon?"

"Downriver a little way. He's in bad shape, but he's alive," he said. "You gonna be okay to help me get him out of the water? We all need to be on higher ground before the river crests."

"I'll do my best," she said, rolling her shoulders backward and forward several times to loosen them up. "Let's go."

He stood first and helped her up. She held tightly to his hand, unwilling to let it go as they made their way down the slippery riverbank to where Waylon lay motionless, barely out of the water. The terrain there was quite a bit steeper than where she'd thumped into the bank, and JD had managed to pull only Waylon's head and shoulders up onto a tangle of roots and vines; his legs in the inflated MAST were still in the water.

"At least the MAST held," Maggie said as she crabbed down the bank. Once beside him, she felt for pulses at his wrist and neck. They weren't bounding, for sure, but they were there. "Waylon," she said, shaking his shoulders and taking hold of his hand, slapping the back of it sharply. "Waylon."

He moaned and squeezed her hand weakly in return.

"JD and I are going to try to get you up the bank to higher ground," she said, receiving a barely perceptible nod for answer.

JD hunkered down at Waylon's head and hooked his forearms under Waylon's arms and around his chest. Maggie straddled JD from behind and wrapped her arms around his chest, interlocking her wrists.

"One step at a time, back up right-left, on three," JD said to her. "One…two…three!" Together they backpedaled in unison, *right foot-left foot …rest… right foot-left foot…rest,* dragging him step by laborious step up the bank until they reach the flatter ground of the rough trail well above the water. Panting, they put him down on the trail.

"OK, now I'll take his shoulders, and you just keep his feet up off the ground for me," JD said when he'd recovered his breath enough to move on. "We don't have far to go to get him to the road from here, and we can rest as often as you need to."

"How did you know?" Maggie asked as they slowly moved Waylon along the trail toward the road.

JD didn't immediately understand, then her meaning dawned. "I called your cell, and it went straight to voicemail. I knew you should have been home already, so I called Miz Hendri, and she said you hadn't come in. So, I drove by the clinic, and I saw your car in back with the lights on."

"Let's rest a second," she said, puffing a bit. "My shoulder is aching."

She laid Waylon's feet on the trail and bent over, resting her hands on her knees, gulping the night air. "Go on," she panted.

"Well, I slowed down to see if you needed help and that's when I saw you flash your brights, but the lightning flashed right then, and I thought I saw somebody in the back seat. Something just didn't look right, so I turned slowly off so I could watch in the rearview. Then you pulled out and turned left. Isn't but one place that road leads to and no reason for you to be taking it on a night like this, so I came back around and followed at a distance. Glad I did."

"Me, too." She smiled at him and held his eyes then took a deep breath in and blew it out. "OK. Let's go," she said, squatting and picking up Waylon's feet. Together they slowly moved him the rest of the way down the trail to where it crossed the road and laid him gently down beside his daughter. Nick, still out and trussed securely, lay a few yards away.

"JD," Maggie said. "There's one more thing you should know. The body in the mound. It was Ruth Prescott."

"Damn," he said. "Are you sure?"

"Yes. Pretty sure. Nick admitted to me he killed her when she tried to stop him pilfering the mound."

"That bastard."

"For sure. But there's another worse shoe that will drop." He looked at her with concern and question in his eyes, and she went on. "Waylon knew and helped hide it."

"Oh, God. Does Rosie know?"

"I don't know how much she heard. She was in and out."

JD and Maggie squatted down beside Rose Ellen, and Maggie touched the small, pale face gently, then felt her neck, finding the pulse.

"JD, her pulse is fast and thready and her skin is icy cold," she said, concern evident in her eyes. "We've got to get her to the hospital or at least back up to the clinic."

"OK. My truck's not far. Y'all stay here; I'll bring it right back."

Maggie stayed at Rose Ellen's side, speaking gentle reassurances to her and stroking her cheek. JD hadn't jogged more than fifty feet down the dark road when headlights and blue lights appeared around a curve in the distance, silhouetting him against their harsh glare.

Beside Maggie, Waylon stirred and lifted his head, murmuring so softly she almost didn't hear him, "My baby gonna be okay, doc?"

Maggie found his hand and gave it a squeeze. "We've all got a better shot than we did a little while ago. Don't worry; she's hanging in there. She's a fighter. You lie back, now. Save your strength."

JD walked backward toward the others and stood in the middle of the road, waving his arms over head. As the big patrol vehicle pulled up to a stop, Dub leaped out.

"What the hell happened here?" he barked.

"Long story. Upshot is Rose Ellen Prescott's half drowned, and we need to get her to the hospital. And her daddy's pretty bad shot," he said. Then he walked over and kicked Nick's boot, "And there's your shooter." At the jolt, Nick roused and opened his eyes to glare silently at JD.

"Freeman did it?" Dub asked.

"Looks like," JD answered. "There's the gun," he said pointing to the shotgun lying a safe distance away from Nick. "And that's not even the whole of it. The bones in the mound."

"Yeah," Dub said.

"He may have killed Ruth Prescott, too."

"Aw, hell."

"I don't know all of it; the Doc and Waylon can tell you more. But Freeman's not going anywhere. We need to take care of these other folks first."

"Chopper's already on the way from Hot Springs. We called soon as we got the 9-1-1 from the clinic; they got up once the rain quit. Should be at the doc's place any minute. Then we got the text from you with your 20." He yelled toward the patrol car, "Bradford. Bring some blankets from the back for these folks and come get this one," he said, pointing down at Nick.

Deputy Bradford joined them, handing a couple of blankets to Maggie and a couple to JD. Then he pulled a folding knife from the pocket of his pants and bent down to Nick. Putting a boot on his legs, he cut the bindings at Nick's ankles and hauled him to his feet by the elbow to stand in front of Dub.

"Nicholas Freeman, you are under arrest for the crimes of murder and attempted murder," Dub said. "Read him his rights, Bradford."

"You have the right to remain silent," Bradford read the words from the card he kept in his shirt pocket. "Anything you say can and will be used against you in a court of law. You have the right to have an attorney present at…" the litany trailed off as they moved away toward the patrol wagon.

"Wasn't that your truck down the road there a little ways?" Dub asked JD.

"Yep."

"If you can get the Doc and the little girl in your truck, Bradford and I can put Prescott in the back of mine and get 'em to the clinic quicker. Sheriff is there now, waiting on the MedFlight. And then we're gonna need to get statements from you two."

"Can do," JD said. He bent down to Maggie. "Here. Take this other blanket for Rosie. Stay here and keep her as warm as you can. I'll be right back." He left at a brisk run to retrieve his truck.

When JD's truck pulled into the front lot of the clinic, Maggie said, "Can you take her. There's something I want to get inside."

JD lifted Rose Ellen from Maggie's arms and carried her to where the sheriff waited in his patrol vehicle with Waylon, all of them watching as the MedFlight helicopter hovered and settled down on the road. The paramedic team disgorged rapidly from the craft with equipment and a pair of stretchers. JD laid Rose Ellen gently on one and backed away so the team could do their work, connecting her to oxygen, inserting intravenous lines, and placing cardiac leads. Maggie sprinted from the door of the clinic to where the team was working on Rose Ellen and Waylon, the flop-eared rabbit and a chicken balloon in tow.

Maggie held out the rabbit to the lead paramedic. "Can she take this with her? She's going to need some comfort." The paramedic nodded and smiled, taking the rabbit and laying it gently across Rose Ellen's thin chest, securing them together on the stretcher with the safety belt. Maggie knelt beside the stretcher and took Rose Ellen's hand in hers, slipping the tied-off end of the chicken balloon into it. Rose Ellen smiled.

"Sweetie," she said, stroking the girl's cheek. "It's all going to be OK. They're going to take good care of you and your father, and I will be right there with you soon. I promise you."

"We need to get going, ma'am," the paramedic said. Maggie squeezed Rose Ellen's hand and stepped back into the circle of JD's arms and watched until the helicopter lifted off.

Maggie and JD sat side-by-side, on the end of her desk in the office, still wrapped in the grey woolen blankets. The blue and red lights from the patrol car outside washed the walls of her office, illuminating their faces in flashes. Maggie leaned across him to plug in her iPhone, which she'd picked up from the hall floor as they'd come in. She assumed it must have been dragged out along with Waylon.

"Fat lot of good this did when I needed it," she said. "That's twice this spotty service has let me down in a pinch. And come to think of it, you've been in the mix both times."

"Don't blame it on me," he laughed. "The tower's probably down from the storm."

"What do you think will happen to Waylon?" she asked.

"I don't know," he shook his head and shrugged. "I reckon if he gives the State enough to put Freeman away, he can plea bargain. Maybe won't do much time."

"What about Rose Ellen? She'll be without both parents now. At least for a while. I've lived that story, and it's pretty awful."

"That, I don't know. Maybe there's some family somewhere. Or I guess Child Protective Services will step in and find a temporary foster situation until things are sorted out with Waylon."

"I want to go over to Hot Springs tomorrow to the hospital. Make sure she's OK."

"Well, your car is somewhere downstream, headed for Lake DeGray," JD said. "I can drive you over."

"She shouldn't be with a bunch of strangers after what she's been through, no matter how well intentioned they are. Maybe there's a family here in Caddo Bend willing to foster her. Maybe even…"

Her cell phone rang.

"Now it works!" she said, answering it.

"Hello?" Startled, she looked at JD. "Oh. Jeff."

JD got up and walked slightly away, giving Maggie some space as she took the call; she spoke in quiet tones every so often.

Finally, she spoke somewhat louder, "No, I won't be there for New Year's Eve." She stood and walked over to stand behind JD and took his hand. "I'll be staying home for the holidays." She paused a moment listening, then clarified, "No, not *coming* home. *Staying* home."

JD turned to her with a smile and took the phone from her hand, disconnecting the call and laying the phone on her desk. He wrapped his blanket around them both, enfolding her in his embrace and kissing her, long and sweet. Then he pulled away and scanned her face with those smoky gray eyes.

"Welcome home," he said.

About the Author

Mary Dan Eades is a native Arkansan and a retired medical doctor, who trained at the University of Arkansas, and who, with her husband, developed and operated a chain of urgent care family medicine clinics for many years. She is a *New York Times* best-selling author, having written or co-authored 14 non-fiction books on nutrition, health, and fitness, including the best-seller *Protein Power* (Bantam 1996) as well as multiple books on low-carb and sous vide cooking.

She is married to the physician, author, and blogger Michael Eades. The couple have three sons (all married to strong, smart women) and seven grandchildren. The Drs. Eades divide their time between Montecito, California and Dallas, Texas. Find out more about them at proteinpower.com.

Caddo Bend is the first fiction work for Dr. Eades and is the first of a planned series of books that follows the life, loves, and medical adventures of Dr. Maggie McKinley in the small rural Arkansas town. An early draft of the novel, written in 1997, became a registered screenplay in 2003; the novel appeared for the first time in print in its current form in 2022.

If you enjoyed meeting Maggie, Jeff, JD, and all the characters who populate Caddo Bend, you'll want to look for Caddo Bend Book 2 expected to be released in Spring 2023.

Visit caddobend.com for publication updates and more.

www.ingramcontent.com/pod-product-compliance
Lightning Source LLC
Chambersburg PA
CBHW031217260626
47169CB00007B/2090